Shattered

Book Two in the Crushed Series

Book Two in the Crushed Series

JENNIFER K. THOMAS

ISBN 978-1-7323987-3-3 (Print)
ISBN 978-1-7323987-4-0 (ePub)
ISBN 978-1-7323987-5-7 (Kindle)

Library of Congress Control Number 2019938362

Cover design by Fiona Jayde/Fiona Jayde Media
Interior formatting by Tamara Cribley/The Deliberate Page
Edited by Nikki Groom/The Indie Hub

Printed in the United States of America.

Published by On The Verge Publishing
P.O. Box 891633, Temecula, CA 92589
Visit www.authorjenniferkthomas.com

To Mom and Dad
Thank you for showing me what love
and commitment really look like.
I miss you both every day.

Chapter 1

I flinch when I realize how fast we're passing the other cars on the freeway. One glance at Luke confirms how focused he is. He's staring straight ahead, my concern not registering with him, so I look away and let him focus on getting us to our destination in silence. The quiet is preferred over either of us uttering our horrible suspicions aloud.

I stare out the window at the dark stores and nearly deserted streets. Under different circumstances I might describe the scene as peaceful, but the gravity of the situation at hand doesn't leave room for that word. Desolate seems more fitting.

Luke only begins to slow as we enter the off ramp and the tires audibly protest when he still takes the right turn too sharply. I grab the overhead handle and continue to hold it as we pull into the parking lot.

Luke swings violently into an open spot and jumps out. He's at my door before I've finished removing the seatbelt and I glance up at him as he reaches for me. His eyes are a brilliant shade of blue, their beauty a stark contrast to the panic swirling in them. I don't need his assistance out of the car, but I allow him to take my arm anyway.

After we've entered the large sterile room, I take a look around us. A mother holds a pale, sweaty toddler in her lap. A man winces every time he moves, in case the woman he's with has forgotten how much pain he's in. An elderly woman quietly reads her book, I can't tell if she's here for a loved one or if she's waiting her turn to be seen. Women tend to do that, hide our pain beneath smiles and politeness. Would the doctor suddenly become more capable, a miracle worker, if I came in crying and carrying-on? No, he wouldn't, so better to not make anyone else uncomfortable.

I take a seat on one of the vinyl covered chairs in the corner, as far away from the other people as possible. I pick up a magazine from the table next to me and turn to a random page. The letters all blend together and I can't seem to make any sense of the words.

"Jess." Luke's voice startles me. I look up at him, but don't say anything. "I need your insurance card and your driver's license."

I reach into my purse that's stuffed between my hip and the arm of the chair, find the cards and hand them to him. He bends down and kisses the top of my head and my heart clenches. I love Luke even more when he shows his softer side, something I hope he does more often as we settle into our second attempt at a relationship and prepare to be married.

When he returns from the check-in desk a few minutes later, I'm back to pretending to read the same page. Luke sits next to me and places his hand on my thigh.

"I'm sure everything's fine, but better to get you checked out." He's trying to reassure himself as much as he is me.

I remain silent, paralyzed by fear and my desire to not make the situation more upsetting than it already is. Besides, no need to kill his hopes yet, the doctor will do that shortly. It's not my intention to be negative. I wish I still had the luxury of optimism, but sometimes a woman simply knows things, can feel them. Even though it wasn't a large amount of blood on my pajama bottoms tonight, I know that it was life changing...life ending.

"Jessica Rogers," a nurse calls while holding open one of the swinging doors with her back.

I set down the magazine and Luke and I stand at the same time, walking over toward the woman studying the clipboard in her hands. I steal a glance at Luke and note the look of determination contorting his handsome features into their less friendly versions. I would bet money he's running over everything in his head, trying to decide his next course of action. Luke is used to taking charge and making things happen.

"Follow me," the nurse says as she leads us to a room and motions for us to sit. She proceeds to ask all the basic questions: When did the bleeding start? What was I doing when it started? Am I having any cramping? She takes my temperature, pulse and blood pressure before leaving us to wait for the doctor.

"Do you want me to call your mom?" Luke asks, trying to keep his brain busy.

"Not yet. It's late, I'll call her in the morning." I mutter.

Before Luke can try to change my mind, we hear footsteps approaching.

A tall, middle aged woman in a white coat walks in the room looking down at a folder she's holding. "I'm Dr. Halloway," her eyes meet mine while shaking my hand. "You're having some bleeding and you're eight weeks pregnant." She turns her eyes down to the papers again.

"Yes," I say softly.

"Have you been to your OB yet for this pregnancy?"

"Yes, about a week ago. Everything seemed fine then." It was a little early for a first prenatal appointment, but Luke was excited, and my doctor was happy to oblige. Despite the youth of the pregnancy, the doctor was able to find the heartbeat and said everything looked great.

"Good. This is your second pregnancy?"

"Yes, my daughter is eight." Thank God Amelia wasn't home tonight. I usually hate that my divorce forces me to split my time with her with my ex-husband, but in this instance, it's worked out for the best.

"Any complications with that pregnancy?"

"No." I shake my head. As I answer, I realize I took my easy pregnancy with Amelia for granted. I felt good throughout most of it, well enough for me to finish out my junior year of college before she was born the subsequent summer.

"Are you the father?" She looks at Luke for the first time.

"Yes." Luke answers anxiously, but the doctor simply looks back at me.

"Well, bleeding isn't uncommon in early pregnancy, but it can be a sign of miscarriage, so I want to get you in for an ultrasound to see what's going on." She briefly returns her attention back to Luke. "You can go with her if you'd like."

"Thank you," Luke says, and the doctor nods. After she leaves, he reaches over and takes my hand. "She said it's not uncommon. Everything's going to be all right. Try to stay positive."

I know he means well, but his comment irritates me. Like my gut feeling that everything is, in fact, not all right is somehow causing this. That I'm somehow to blame because I can't muster enough faith to make the outcome different.

Several minutes later, I've changed into a scratchy hospital gown and I'm being wheeled into the ultrasound room. The technicians make small talk with us as they prepare their equipment. I let Luke answer their questions about how long we've been in the area and the lack of rain we've had so far this season, and focus on breathing instead. Once the first black and white grainy image appears on the screen, they turn the monitor away from us and stop speaking to us. Instead they talk to each other about their weekend plans.

After a few minutes of listening to the details of a weekend trip to Big Bear, it's over. "All right, Jessica. We're all done here. We'll call the nurse to come take you back to your room. The doctor will discuss the results with you."

"Okay," I say, even though I've never felt less okay in my life.

Luke and I don't say anything to each other, but once we're back in my room he takes my hand again. "It's going to be okay."

That word again. "Luke, the techs stopped talking to us during the ultrasound, that isn't a good sign."

"They aren't allowed to discuss the results."

"I understand that, but if they found a heartbeat, they would've shown us the screen."

"Not necessarily," he responds quickly, right before Dr. Halloway walks in. She sits across from us and motions for Luke to have a seat.

She leans in before beginning. "We weren't able to find a heartbeat during the ultrasound," she says in a softer voice than she used earlier.

Even though I'm not surprised, the words cause physical pain in my core. I faintly register that Luke has grabbed my hand.

"Being only eight weeks pregnant, the heartbeat can still be hard to find. There's a chance that we simply couldn't find it tonight." I barely feel present, like I'm in a dream, as she continues to speak. "It's Saturday, so you won't be able to follow up with your doctor until Monday. In the meantime, I'm going to order labs to begin tracking your hCG levels. You'll need to come back to the lab tomorrow and have blood redrawn."

It takes a moment to realize she's done and has stopped talking. I look at Luke, but he doesn't look at me. He's staring at the ground, shoulders slumped.

"Can I go now?" I ask quietly.

"Wait," Luke says, and looks up at the doctor while rubbing the back of his neck. "We were just at the doctor last week and everything was fine."

"Luke…" I say gently.

His eyes meet mine. I've never seen him look so confused. "This doesn't make any sense."

"I'm really sorry." Dr. Halloway attempts to sound sympathetic, but I can tell she's ready to move on to the next patient. My early-term miscarriage is too common for her. Something so regular in occurrence, it won't even make the list of stories she shares with her family and friends. The thought makes me not want to share this moment with her any longer.

"I'll come back to the lab tomorrow and I'll call my doctor Monday," I say, effectively dismissing her.

She nods and leaves us. I stand and so does Luke. Once he wraps his arms around me, I can't hold my emotions in anymore and he rubs my back as my tears soak his T-shirt.

"I need to get out of here," I say into his chest. I need to get home to my own bed and my own clothes. He releases me, and I get dressed while he speaks with the nurse responsible for my discharge.

I quietly cry toward the window the entire drive home. I can't bear to look at Luke again. He doesn't say anything, but keeps his free hand firmly grasping mine the entire time.

It isn't until we're in bed, wrapped up in each other, that we fully accept what's happening. It was only a few weeks ago when I realized my period was late. Luke's return to my life had been filled with a season of ups and downs, but we were finally heading in the right direction. When I told Luke I was pregnant, sooner than either of us planned, I was nervous. Luke's difficult relationship with his own father has tainted his views on life and family, more than I think he even realizes. Nonetheless, I was pleasantly surprised when he was genuinely excited about the baby. The thought only makes the tears come faster.

I turn my face toward Luke's. When I see the tears in his eyes, I know it's an image that will stay with me forever. The sobs tear through my body until I've fully exhausted myself and I fall asleep.

I wake up only a few hours later with a headache and a dry mouth. I experience a brief moment of relief before I remember; it's a terrible, cruel feeling when you realize the bad dream you think you're waking up from is your reality. It seems horribly unfair that the events of the previous night are real and I won't be able to sleep them away.

Luke is snoring lightly. I'm glad he's getting a respite from this nightmare, andI'm also happy to not have to see the disappointment in his eyes right now. He would never blame me for this and logically I know it's not my fault, but I still feel like I've let him down somehow.

I quietly slip out of bed and go downstairs. I get a glass of water and curl my legs underneath me on the couch. I don't have any more tears to give right now. To feel so much pain and still somehow feel numb at the same time is perhaps the most unsettling feeling in the world.

I can't yet wrap my head around the fact that only yesterday I was pregnant and happy. I was sure when Grant cheated on me and I left him, that my chance for a happy family was gone. Then Luke reappeared after a lifetime apart and slowly my hope grew and that dream felt attainable again. I feel almost lied to, like I was made a promise and now it's been taken back.

I retrieve my phone and push the button to call my mom. It's early, but I know she'll already be up enjoying her morning cup of coffee. She answers after the first ring.

"Why are you up so early on a Sunday?" she asks in a serious tone. I rarely call this early and she's automatically suspicious something is wrong.

"Mom…" My throat feels dry.

"What's wrong, Jessica?" The alarm in her voice rises.

"We lost the baby." I manage to say the words before choking back a sob and the grief immediately makes me miss the numbness.

"Oh, Jessica," is all my mom says. She waits as I unleash the emotions threatening to rip me apart. Once I can steal a breath and steady myself a little, I tell her the whole story from the night before. Being a nurse, I imagine she's curious about the details, but she listens with her mom ears and doesn't offer any medical opinions.

"I can be dressed and there in an hour."

"That's okay. Luke's here and we both didn't get much sleep last night. I'll probably nap most of the day. Thank God Amelia is with Grant for the week. How am I going to tell her?" I wonder aloud, the last words punctuated by a fresh round of tears.

"Let's not worry about that right now. How's Luke?"

"He's upset." My voice cracks remembering the look on his face last night while we lay in bed together.

"Of course he is. I want to give you two space, but I want to help, too." As a nurse, she knows what I'm going to go through physically. As my mom, she knows what this will do to me emotionally. "At least let me bring you some dinner later and maybe throw in a load of laundry for you."

"Okay." With anyone else I would insist I can handle everything on my own, but not with her. She's always been the only one I feel safe enough to admit I need help to.

"I'll call you in a little while to see what you want to eat. Call me if you need anything in the meantime."

"I will."

"I love you, Jessica. And tell Luke I love him, too." My mom's voice cracks a little and it causes the tears to well up in my eyes again.

"I love you, too, Mom. Bye," I manage to squeak out.

I hang up and grab the blanket from the edge of the couch. I've just wrapped it around me and laid down when Luke walks in.

"Did you talk to your mom?" he asks, taking a seat and pulling my feet into his lap.

"Yeah."

"What did she say?" His large hands skillfully knead my calves.

"She loves us. She's bringing us dinner later."

"That's nice." Luke's voice sounds hollow, echoing how I feel.

"Yeah."

Luke's quiet. Not knowing what to say is undoubtedly uncomfortable for him. "Let me know when you're ready to go to the lab for the bloodwork."

"Okay."

"And the doctor tomorrow?"

"I'll call them first thing in the morning." With that settled, the silence stretches out between us.

Luke stares straight ahead and continues to rub my legs. "Who knows, maybe they will be able to find a heartbeat today."

I stare at the blanket in my lap. "I don't want you to get your hopes up."

"I'm just trying to stay positive, you should, too." Luke reclines back against the cushions.

"There's nothing positive about this situation." I wipe a fresh tear from my eye.

"Jess…" Luke leans toward me and reaches for my hand, but I lean away.

"I can't change the outcome with good thoughts." I pull my feet from his lap and stand up, his words filling me with sudden defensiveness.

Luke stands quickly and pulls me against his hard chest. He doesn't say anything, just holds me against him. He holds me so tightly, eventually I melt against him and start to cry again.

"I didn't mean it like that. This isn't anyone's fault," he whispers as he places his hand on the back of my head, pulling me in even closer to him.

"I can't believe this is happening." I struggle to catch my breath. "I...I...I already loved this baby."

"Me, too," he whispers as he strokes my hair.

The week after the onset of the miscarriage goes by as a blur. A seemingly never-ending fog of appointments, condolences and sadness. I have some physical pain, but it's nothing compared to the psychological hell I endure. I alternate between feelings of overwhelming sadness and indescribable emptiness. I can't decide which feels worse, feeling too much or too little.

Luke stays with me all week, working in small spurts on his laptop. I've caught him watching me on several occasions. He looks at me like he's afraid he'll never see the Jessica he fell in love with again. He hasn't cried again since that first night. He must be hurting, too, but he won't talk about it. In all fairness, every time I've brought it up, I start crying again and he just ends up consoling me.

Grant returns Amelia after their ski trip to Utah on Saturday afternoon. I give her an extra-long squeeze at the door before Luke takes her inside to get a snack so I can fill my ex-husband in.

"How was it?" I ask, trying to break the ice.

"It was good. Amelia's a natural on skis. I'll have to get her out on the slopes more often." Grant shoves his hands in his pockets. Our post-divorce interactions still carry a twinge of awkwardness, but the anger I felt about his affair has dulled considerably. I'm not sure I'll ever be completely over the betrayal, but I'm determined to get along with him for Amelia's sake.

"I'm sure she'd love that." I offer a small smile.

"Maybe we can work out a schedule for spring break where I can take her for another week. I'd love the time with her and it would give you and Luke some alone time," Grant offers.

Despite Luke proposing so quickly after our divorce was finalized, Grant has been surprisingly accepting of the situation, even after I turned down his attempt at a reconciliation. It reminds me that deep down Grant is a good man. I'm not expecting him and Luke to be best friends, but their mutual civility makes things a lot easier.

"I'm sure we can work something out." I look at the ground, trying to come up with a smooth segue. I can't think of one, so I just blurt out the news. "Hey, Grant. I don't want you to hear it from Amelia…I had a miscarriage."

"Oh, shit." Grant tilts his head at me and grimaces. "Sorry to hear that."

"Thanks. It's been a hard week." I admit. "I'll tell Amelia tonight."

"Thanks for the heads up." Grant looks as uncomfortable as I feel. He doesn't know what to say any more than I do. "Has your mom been helping out?"

"A little bit."

"That's good." Grant nods his head repeatedly.

"Yeah." I roll my neck. We're both quiet, neither knowing what else to say.

Grant finally thinks of something. "Let me know if you need me to take Amelia for some extra time."

"I will, thanks."

Grant nods and I watch him walk back to his car. I open the front door and hear Amelia's giggles coming from the kitchen. I lean against the door jamb and soak it in for a moment longer. It's my favorite sound in the whole world and know once I enter that room, I'm going to end it.

Chapter 2

With the physical pain of the miscarriage behind me, the expectation is that I begin to move on. I return to a workplace full of sympathetic looks and cliché words of encouragement. People don't know what to say and are only trying to be supportive. It's uncomfortable for everyone.

I don't feel like myself, but I have responsibilities, so I fall back on my favorite coping strategy of using work as a distraction. I've worked at Bianchi winery for almost nine years now, first as an accountant and then as the controller. The owner, Mrs. Bianchi, and I have a great relationship and she would completely understand if I asked for additional time off, but I can't sit at home. I reassured her that the week I took was enough.

Luke didn't like the idea of me returning to work so quickly and took it upon himself to call Mrs. Bianchi to ask for some extra time off for me. As an investor in the winery, he may not deal directly with her everyday like I do, but it's clear they have a great amount of respect for each other. When I found out, I was irritated that he wasn't listening to what I wanted to do. Eventually he gave up his argument, but insisted on staying in town instead of returning to his business in San Francisco.

Luke owns an investment firm with his partner, Aaron, which allows him a certain degree of flexibility in his scheduling. So he's adjusted his usually busy travel plans, instead opting for phone calls and video conferencing. This has allowed him to work from Temecula the past two weeks.

I wish I was enjoying the extra time with him, but his constant attention isn't helping at the moment. He hovers, waiting for me to say something, anything to indicate that life can go back to normal. I can muster enough energy to go to work, but all I want to do when I get home is spend time with Amelia, put on some comfy pajamas and go to bed. I'm not sure when, if ever, we'll return to our previous normal.

Amelia was initially upset when I told her she wasn't going to be a big sister quite yet, but she seems to be doing all right. The divorce taught me that kids are resilient and will bounce back from disappointment faster than adults tend to think. I'm sure all the extra attention from everyone has helped, too. On the evenings she's been at home with us, Luke has been playing games with her, helping with her homework, and taking her out for dessert after I've thrown together some type of dinner for us.

Amelia is at her dad's for the weekend, so I arrive home to an empty house. Luke texted earlier to let me know he had some errands to run and he'd be home later. I run a hot bath and slip in. The water is steaming, almost too hot, but I force my body in. I feel achy even though I haven't done anything more strenuous than walk up the stairs to my bedroom.

I unlock the screen on my phone and open the YouTube app. I watch several funny videos of puppies learning how to go downstairs, before a video of puppies with babies pops up in my suggestions. I click on it even though I recognize the potential danger. The video is cute and I make it through without crying, so I watch another and then another. I don't pause long enough to talk myself out of my next search. I watch a video of a young woman talking about how her miscarriage affected her relationship with her husband, followed by a video of a middle-aged woman describing how she endured multiple miscarriages before resigning to the fact that she would not be carrying a baby of her own. Tears stream down my face, mixing with sweat and melting makeup, as I click on the next video in the queue.

"What're you doing?" Luke's voice startles me, and I almost drop my phone in the bath.

"Jesus, Luke. Don't sneak up on me like that." I shut my phone screen and set it on the side of the tub.

"I've been calling for you since I walked in the door." He stands in the doorway, watching me suspiciously.

"I didn't hear you." I grab the shampoo bottle so I can avert my eyes from his judging gaze.

"What are you doing?" he asks again.

"Taking a bath."

As I risk a glance over to him, I see him twist his mouth. Not the answer he was looking for.

"I was watching some videos." I scrub the shampoo into my thick hair.

"What kind of videos?" he presses.

Better to get this over with. "About miscarriages," I admit. For some reason I feel ashamed, as though I've been caught doing something wrong.

He runs a hand through his hair. "Do you think that's a good idea?" He walks out of the bathroom unbuttoning his shirt and I hear him sigh from the closet.

I don't answer his rhetorical question. Yes, the videos were upsetting, but they were strangely comforting, too. Luke wouldn't understand, so I don't bother trying to explain.

He looks tired when he reemerges into the bathroom. "I picked up food. Do you want me to bring you some?"

"I'm not hungry." I press my lips together. I don't want to argue tonight.

"Have you eaten today?" Luke says with a controlled voice and a pointed stare.

"I had tea this morning and a banana for lunch."

He furrows his brow. "You need to eat, Jessica."

"I'll come get some after I get out of the bath." We both know there's a good chance I won't, but thankfully he doesn't push this time. After two weeks of persuading me to have bites of food I didn't want, he's worn down.

Luke goes downstairs and I finish my bath. He comes up a few minutes after I slip into bed and I pretend to be asleep. I don't want to have another conversation with him where he hints that I need to move on. I wish it were as easy for me as it is for him.

"Time to get up." Luke's voice cuts through my wake-up fog.

I pull the comforter over my head. "Go away."

"Some fresh air will do you good."

"I don't need fresh air." I mumble into the blankets. "Besides, I'm not ready to run yet." Luke and I have a history of running through our problems. It started in high school, when we would use the time to sort through our feelings and gain insight into our teenage woes. It's not going to work for this. This is too heavy, and I definitely don't want to dig deeper into my grief.

"We'll walk." He sits on the bed, but doesn't pull the covers back again.

"Later," I say from inside my cocoon.

"It's almost eleven, Jessica." This time, he pulls the blankets back. "You told the doctor you were feeling fine physically. I think getting out of the house would do you some good."

"I'm exhausted, Luke. Besides, I have gotten out of the house. I work, remember?" I snatch the blanket back from him and roll away from him.

"Jessica—"

"I said no," I raise my voice.

"Fine, but you are not staying in bed all day." There is more than a hint of frustration in his voice. I'm relieved when I feel him rise off the bed and leave the room.

The relief is short lived, he returns just as I'm dozing off again. "We're going out with Vivien and Ed tonight. We're meeting them at six for dinner and then a movie. You can stay in bed until then but be ready by five-thirty." He doesn't wait for my response before leaving me alone again.

I throw the blankets over my head and accept this is a battle Luke is not willing to lose.

I'm reading a magazine in bed when Luke returns to the bedroom at little before four.

"Are you taking a shower before we go?"

"I suppose I should." I still don't want to go, but I know he already considers my day spent in bed our compromise. The thought crosses my mind that if I go tonight, he may leave me alone tomorrow.

I shower and dry my hair before pulling on a pair of jeans and a blue sweater. I have zero interest in doing my makeup, so I only put some gloss on my dry lips.

I walk downstairs at exactly five-thirty.

"You look nice." He tilts his head and smiles softly at me.

"I don't need pity compliments, Luke, all I did was shower and throw on some clothes."

"It's not pity. You know I love you in blue. Let's go." He doesn't wait for me to say something else nasty to him. I regret being so difficult, but I can't seem to stop.

On the way to the restaurant, we make small talk about work and the science project Amelia needs to complete next weekend. Luke offers to pick up the supplies she needs tomorrow. By the time we arrive, Vivien and Ed are already at a table with their first round of drinks. They stand up as we approach and we take turns hugging each other.

"Good to see you, guys," Ed says as we slide into the booth.

"Good to see you, too," I say.

Ed and Luke dive into a conversation about last night's basketball game and I begin looking at the menu.

"What are you getting?" Vivien asks after a few minutes. I look up to see her looking at her own menu.

"Tequila shots," I joke.

"I'm down," she says, without looking up at me.

"I was kidding, Viv."

"I'm not. You've had a shitty couple of weeks. No one's judging if you need a distraction. Hell, I need a distraction." She places her menu between her and Ed so he can't see her face. "Ed's mom is talking about buying the house across the street from us," she mouths, and widens her eyes as big as they will go.

I can't help blurting out a laugh. "Tequila shots it is."

Vivien nods and smiles in an exaggerated fashion.

We're still waiting for our food as Vivien and I toss back our second round of shots. We've been laughing about a ridiculous reality show that we both watch, and it hits me that this is the first time I've laughed or felt any sense of relief since the miscarriage.

"Slow down, woman." Ed frowns at Vivien. I've known them long enough to know he's not really irritated with her, he just likes to give her a hard time.

"Get used to it, husband. If your mother moves in across the street there will be mucho tequila in my future."

"You like my mom." Ed shakes his head.

"I like her better when I have to drive an hour to see her. I like her better when I don't have to worry about her coming over to criticize my cooking more than a couple times a year."

"She commented on your cooking one time, Viv." Ed laughs and holds up one finger for emphasis.

"Not true. She told me last time she was over that it's probably a blessing in disguise that I can't cook. That she doesn't have to worry about her baby boy getting chunky from a bunch of home cooking."

Ed laughs loudly. "There is no way she called me her baby boy."

"Maybe not, but it was implied." Vivien winks at me.

"Didn't you start a kitchen fire making toast one time?" Luke chimes in.

"First of all, shame on you, Jessica, for spreading that false story. Second, I did not start a fire, the toaster malfunctioned and burst into flames. Could've happened to anyone."

Laughter continues through dinner. I catch Luke staring at me while I'm listening to Ed tell a story about a guy at his work who everyone suspects has joined a cult. It's the first time he's looked at me without worry or pity in weeks. I smile back at him causing him to lace his fingers through mine.

We're waiting for our waitress to return with receipts to sign, and the conversation has died down some.

"What movie does everyone want to see?" Luke asks picking up his phone. "We should probably look at times before we head over."

"Didn't that new horror movie come out this weekend?" Ed asks. "I heard it's really good."

"Sorry, Ed, Jessica won't do anything scary." Luke shakes his head while continuing to scroll through his phone.

"I know. Let's go see the new Ryan Gosling movie." Vivien is practically salivating as she wags her eyebrows.

"The one where he's crying in the preview?" Ed scrunches up his face. "No way."

"Sorry, Viv, I'm going to side with Ed on this one. That movie looks depressing." I scrunch my face.

Vivien gives me a sympathetic nod. "Of course."

"Hey, guys," Ed looks back and forth between Luke and me. "Maybe I shouldn't be bringing this up, but it feels wrong to not say anything. I hope you know how horrible we feel about what happened."

"Tonight's supposed to be a fun night, can we talk about something else?" Luke says, giving Ed a death stare.

"It's fine, Ed." I interrupt, causing both men to look at me. "We probably need to talk about it more. It's been a really hard couple of weeks." Luke stiffens beside me.

"I can't even imagine." Vivien frowns at me.

"It's been hard, but the doctor said it's very common." Luke says, before taking a drink of his beer. "I was reading that something like twenty-five percent of women will experience a miscarriage in their lives."

I'm not sure when Luke became so versed on miscarriage statistics. I remember him telling me once before that statistics are misleading, that they could be skewed to represent whatever position one was looking to endorse.

"That many? That's downright frightening," Vivien says.

"It is, but most go on to have healthy pregnancies. It wasn't meant to be right now. We'll try again later." Luke states it like a decision has been made, which is news to me. We haven't talked about trying again. I can only assume his comments are meant to reassure me that this doesn't mean we will never have a child together, but his words don't sit right with me.

"Of course." Vivien gives another sympathetic nod.

I sit through a few more minutes of Luke making ridiculous statements related to miscarriage and coming out of this experience stronger. For someone who avoids the topic with me at home, he sure has a lot to say to our friends. The topic is thankfully changed when we get up to leave and have to decide on a movie.

We end up seeing a comedy that is ridiculous in its prem-
ise, but makes us all laugh nonetheless, even me.

"I'm glad we got together tonight," Vivien says as she hugs
me goodbye in front of the theater.

"Me, too," I agree.

"Coffee next week?" she asks as she digs her keys out of
her purse.

"Maybe…probably." I don't want to commit to anything
yet. I'll call her in a couple of days to make plans if I'm up for it.

"Good night," Ed says as he pulls me into a hug.

"Ed, we were talking." Over Ed's shoulder I see Vivien
has placed her hands on her hips.

"Yes, and you'll be talking all night if I don't interrupt
now." Ed winks at me as he pulls back. "I would like to get my
wife home before she's too tired, if you know what I mean."

Vivien slaps him on his arm and he laughs.

"Good night, you two." Luke takes my hand and holds
it as we walk into the parking structure. When we reach our
car, he doesn't unlock the doors. Instead he follows me to the
passenger side door. I turn around and he gently leans into me,
rubbing my arms when I wrap them across the front of me.

"Tonight was good." He stares into my eyes and my earlier
irritation melts further away.

"Vivien and Ed are fun."

"They are, but I was talking about you. I've missed that
smile." He tucks my hair behind my ear and I shiver when his
fingertips graze the top of my lobe.

Luke lowers his gaze for a moment and when it returns, it's
what I've missed. He looks at me with adoration and little bit of
lust. "I love you." His voice is low, soft, and just a hint seductive.

"I love you, too." I reply, and I mean it when I say it. No matter how frustrated I am with him, I'll always love him.

He gently presses his lips to mine. The kiss is slow, tentative. He tastes like the cinnamon gum he often chews as his tongue gently dances around mine. This is his way of telling me he misses me, misses the intimacy we once shared and took for granted. I deepen the kiss to let him know I hear him. Luke and I have a habit of communicating this way when we can't find the right words.

He slides one hand into my hair and places the other on my lower back, pulling me closer. A small moan escapes my throat before I remember.

"Luke," I murmur against his mouth. He pulls back enough so I can speak. "I can't...the doctor said I should wait until after my next period before..."

He leans his head back further and looks at me carefully. "I love kissing you." His mouth finds mine again. This time the kiss is hungrier. His mouth and hands work in unison, trying to hold onto the moment, trying to hold onto me. By the time he pulls away again, we're both panting.

"You're always worth the wait."

I wake up sweating and shaking.

A nightmare. A terrifying, panic-inducing nightmare. I feel like I can't breathe. I stumble out of bed and go downstairs to get some water. I notice my hand shaking as I reach for a glass, so I set it on the counter quickly, afraid I will drop it if I don't. I lower my head and try to focus on breathing as the tears begin to spill over.

"Jessica," Luke's firm, concerned voice startles me.

"Luke," I screech at him. "Don't sneak up on me like that."

"I said your name three times. Here." He reaches around me and grabs my glass to fill it.

My hands are still shaking as I take the water from him.

"Let's sit." He takes the glass from my hands and leads me over to the couch.

"Luke, I feel like I'm having a heart attack." I put a trembling hand up to my chest.

He places a hand on my knee. "I think you're having a panic attack."

Minutes go by as I try to calm down and steady my breathing. When I finally feel like I can pick up my glass without dropping it, I lift it to my lips. The cold water comforts my dry throat and gives me something to focus my attention on instead of the look of concern on Luke's face.

"Try taking a couple more deep breaths with me." Luke holds my hands and breathes with me until I no longer feel like my heart is going to explode out of my chest. "Do you want me to get you a cup of tea or anything?"

"No." I look down at my feet and feel my cheeks flush. "I've never had a panic attack before."

Luke squeezes the hand he's still holding and speaks in a soft voice. "Hey, you don't ever need to feel embarrassed with me." When I continue to stare at the ground he goes on. "My mom used to get them."

"She did?" I raise my eyes to meet his. He doesn't speak about either of his parents often. From what I remember of our high school days, he adored his mom. Losing her to cancer a few years ago must have been hard for him, but he never wants to talk about it, so I never push.

"Yeah. My dad didn't understand, so I became the one to help her through them." I remember Luke's dad as a tough man. He worked a lot, but when he was home, he was in charge. He rode Luke pretty hard, especially when it came to baseball. Looking back, I'm sure he did it with the best of intentions, but it created friction between them as Luke got older. They're barely on speaking terms at the moment.

I see a lot of Luke's dad in him, but he also possesses some qualities his dad was missing. Luke's more affectionate and attentive than his dad ever was. The time he's spent with Amelia and the gentle way he interacts with her has given us both a glimpse into what kind of father he's going to be.

"I don't remember that about her," I say quietly.

"She had them more when I was younger." Luke rubs the back of his neck.

"How much younger?" I decide to take advantage of his willingness to talk about her and press a little.

"I guess I became aware of them when I was around nine, maybe ten." He shrugs.

"You were helping your mom through panic attacks when you were that young?" That's not much older than Amelia. I would hate for her to have to experience what just happened.

"If it makes you feel better, hers were much worse than what I just saw." He laughs dryly and looks away from me.

My heart sinks. "No, that doesn't make me feel better at all."

"It is what it is." Luke dismisses my concern. For someone who worries so much about others, he definitely doesn't like the attention returned to him. "We all have some unpleasant things from our childhood."

I want to ask more about what he went through, but he's already answered more questions than I expected him to, based on how uncomfortable he appears. "I think I'm okay now. You can go back to bed."

"You're not coming?"

"I'll be up shortly. On second thought, I am going to have that cup of tea."

"I'll make it for you," he offers, standing.

"No," I say firmly, but gently. "I need to be alone for a few minutes."

He doesn't move at first. I appreciate what he just did for me, but I know what I need right now and it's not something he can be a part of.

When I don't give any indication of changing my mind, he reluctantly kisses the top of my head and leaves.

I return to the kitchen and pull a mug from the counter. Once the mug is filled and heating up in the microwave I grip the counter and let the grief pour out of me.

Chapter 3

The next morning, neither of us mention the middle of the night events.

Luke brings me tea in bed and I brace for the upcoming battle. Thankfully he makes no attempts to force me out of my protective layers of blankets this morning. He finds excuses to return to the bedroom several more times over the next few hours, each time eyeing me apprehensively. Finally, he lays down on the bed next to me and scrolls through his phone.

I go downstairs at midday to put in a load of laundry, and I come out to find Luke has moved to the couch to watch television. He continues to relocate as I make my way through the house, taking care of some basic chores. I know he's concerned and he's only watching out for me, but his constant attention to my actions and whereabouts feels stifling.

I look at the clock with the realization that Amelia will be home in an hour. I need to have a conversation with Luke while we still have some privacy.

I return from taking out the trash and find Luke sitting on the couch nearby. He watches sports sometimes, but I can't remember ever finding him like this, just watching a sitcom. He doesn't even have his laptop or phone in front of him like he usually does. He's just staring at the screen. It's a visual reminder of the toll this situation is taking on him.

"Hey." I sit next to him.

He presses the off button on the remote and turns his body halfway toward me.

"The last couple of weeks have been hard, for both of us." I look down at my feet, knowing he's not going to like what I'm about to say.

"I know." He places a hand on my knee. "We'll get through it. You need to stop thinking about it so much, maybe a weekend away would help."

I sigh. "This isn't helping."

"What do you mean?" He tilts his head, trying to understand.

"I appreciate what you're trying to do, but…" I pause, not wanting to sound harsh. "I think a little space would be good for both of us."

Luke sighs as he removes his hand from my leg.

"I'm sure you have things to take care of in San Francisco this week." Despite his normally heavy travel schedule, I'm sure his presence in the office is needed, not to mention he still has his apartment and other obligations there to deal with. Staying with me in Temecula for the last few weeks must mean he has a ton of things to catch up on.

"I'm not leaving," Luke asserts with a glare. This is going to be more difficult than I hoped.

"I need for you to hear me. I need some time to grieve. I know you're trying to help, but the best way for you to do that right now is to give me some space."

"If by grieve you mean you want to lay in bed and cry all day, then the answer is no."

I shake my head. "Excuse me?" Even though I imagined this to be how he felt, hearing him actually say the words is startling.

"I said no." Luke folds his arms across his chest.

"I heard you the first time, I was giving you a minute to rethink your response." I narrow my eyes at him. I realize that asking him to give me some space wasn't going to be easy for him to hear, but I'm tired and not in the mood for him to flat out dismiss what I'm telling him.

Luke doesn't say anything, but keeps his eyes focused on mine. His rigid body giving every indication that he's not giving in.

"God, you're stubborn." I release a frustrated sigh. "You're making this worse."

"Staying in bed all day and isolating yourself isn't going to help. It's not healthy and it's not happening. Not on my watch," Luke says firmly, and sets his jaw.

"Then consider yourself relieved of your watch." I tap my foot against the edge of the coffee table.

"It doesn't work that way."

"Really? Tell me how you think it works, Luke." I uncross my legs and lean slightly toward him.

He runs a hand through his hair. "I love you and I'm not going to just walk away and leave you to…"

"To what, Luke? Be sad? Stop trying to fix me." I quickly rise from the couch and walk into the kitchen.

Luke follows me. "That's a shitty thing to say. I'm not trying to fix you."

I spin around to face him. "Yes, you are. You follow me around and tell me what I should or shouldn't be doing. You tell me how I should or shouldn't be feeling."

Luke pinches his lips together. "That's not fair. I'm not trying to control you, but I'm not going to sit back and watch you hide from the world."

"I'm not hiding, I'm trying to keep it together. And since you brought it up, what's not fair are your comments about miscarriage being a common occurrence and that we'll just try again."

"You don't want to try again?" Luke looks surprised and maybe a little hurt.

"I don't know. That's not the point." I shake my head vigorously.

"What is your point, Jessica? That I've been too attentive? Too concerned? I'm sorry, but when I see someone I love hurting, I'm not going to sit back and do nothing."

He didn't hear anything I just said. "You're making me feel like I'm doing something wrong, like I'm disappointing you all the time."

"You're not disappointing me." Luke leans back against the counter and crosses his arms over his chest. He tilts his head up to the ceiling and blows out a huff of air. "This is ridiculous. If you really want me to leave, I'll leave. I have a board meeting for Second Chances this week, anyways." Second Chances is the non-profit center for children Luke has worked with for several years. It's very important to him and is something he plans to continue to be involved with even after he moves down here permanently.

I squeeze my eyes shut. I know him returning to San Francisco is the best thing for us right now, but I feel guilty knowing I'm hurting him. "A little distance will be a good thing, for both of us." When I open my eyes, Luke is glaring at me again.

"Don't twist it. You want me to leave, that's your choice, definitely not mine."

"You're watching reruns of old eighties sitcoms on my couch. Being here isn't healthy for you, either." The frustration causes my voice to pitch.

"I don't care if it's healthy for me, I'm fucking worried about you." Luke raises his voice and I flinch. He takes a deep breath to calm himself. "I don't want to fight with you. I'll leave tomorrow."

"I don't want you to leave mad," I say in the voice I use with Amelia when she gets too worked up. "I don't want you to worry about me."

"Why won't you let me help?" Luke narrows his eyes slightly and gives his head a small shake. "And don't tell me that panic attack last night was nothing. I saw the look on your face, Jessica. You looked terrified."

I look away, embarrassed by the memory. "I've never had one before."

Luke softens his tone even more. "It's not something to be embarrassed about, but I'm glad I was here." He hesitates before continuing. "Maybe you should talk to someone."

"I don't think that's necessary." I shake my head. Another comment that makes me feel like I'm doing something wrong.

"Something has to change." Luke reaches for me, but I take a step back.

"My baby died, I'm allowed to be sad. If that makes you uncomfortable, maybe *you* need to go talk to someone." I realize how childish it sounds as soon as the words escape my mouth.

Luke drops his outstretched arm and studies me for a moment. "It was my baby, too."

I shake my head. He doesn't understand, and this conversation is only going to piss me off more. Luke's more affected by me and my reaction than by the actual miscarriage itself.

He opens his mouth to say something but thinks better of it and closes it. He stands there looking at me as though he doesn't recognize me. "The wedding venue called, said you haven't returned their calls regarding completing the contract."

Luke and I were so excited about getting married that we toured a few local places right after Christmas. We immediately fell in love with one of the outdoor venues and when they had the date available, we decided to put down a deposit for a Saturday in early spring. "I've been busy."

He runs a hand through his hair and leans back against the counter. "I'm trying here, Jess. I'm trying to understand."

"There's nothing to understand, Luke. I just got busy and forgot." The truth is our wedding hasn't been on my mind at all.

"Not that. I'm trying to figure out what to do here." Luke pushes off from the counter. He eyes me carefully. "I think we should tell them to give the date to someone else. We'll pick a new date later…"

"No, I'll call them back. We'll keep the date." I say in a panic.

Luke shakes his head. He doesn't break eye contact as he steps toward me, speaking softly. "Jessica, I love you and I want to be married to you…someday."

His last word sears my already sensitive heart. "Fine, we'll postpone the wedding." I say quickly and turn away so he can't see my tears.

Luke wraps his muscular arms around me from behind. He buries his face in between my neck and shoulder, holding onto me, almost too tightly. "I'm not going anywhere, and I am going to marry you, but not like this. I want our wedding day and everything about it to make you smile."

I squeeze my eyes shut, but a few tears find their way despite my best efforts.

When a tear lands on his flexed forearm he turns me around to face him. He places both hands on either side of my face and offers a small smile. "There's no rush. You and I, we're forever." He punctuates his words with a gentle kiss.

There was a rush before. He's right, now that there's no baby, there isn't a reason to get married right away.

He wraps his arms around me again and holds me close to him for a long time. "I love you and I'll give you whatever space you need," he says when the silence becomes deafening.

The first night without Luke in the house was a relief. Amelia and I watched a movie after dinner. It was a comedy, but I still teared up when the main character announced she was having a baby near the end of the film. After I put Amelia to bed, I spent some time on the computer doing some online shopping and then watched a recorded episode of my favorite reality show. Sleep found me only after I took an over-the-counter medication to help.

By Thursday night, I can honestly say I miss Luke. As I promised him before he left, I have checked in with him all week. He doesn't ask for details, but I make sure to tell him that I have eaten and that I've been productive at work. He's careful not to react too much to my daily reports, but I can tell they help put his mind at ease.

After I put Amelia in bed, I get a text from Luke.

Luke: How was your day?

Me: Good. Linda and I went to out for lunch after we completed the revenue reports you requested.

Luke: That's good. Hey, I have some bad news. I have an unplanned meeting that came up and I need to stay in San Francisco this weekend.

I'm disappointed, but I don't want to make him feel worse than he undoubtedly already does. He wouldn't stay if it wasn't important.

Me: That's OK. I have Amelia this weekend, so I'll take her to do something. I think that new superhero movie she keeps talking about comes out.

Luke: I won't lie, I really hope you get out of the house. Wish I was going to be there. I was looking forward to seeing both of you.

Me: I know, but work is important.

Luke: Yeah.

I'm trying to think of what to say next, when I see that Luke is typing something.

Luke: I love you.

Me: I love you, too.

It's perhaps the shortest text sequence in our recent past. I wait for a minute to see if he's going to type anything else. When he doesn't, I type "Good night", hit send and plug my phone in to charge. I only make it a few minutes into the crime drama I recorded before falling asleep.

I wake up to a pounding heart and drenched pajamas. Another panic attack.

My breathing is shallow and my chest hurts, but this time I know what it is. I decide to try one of the techniques I read about online this week. I sit up in bed and breathe while placing one hand on my chest and one hand on my belly. After several minutes of controlled breathing, I feel calm enough to get out of bed. I change my clothes then climb back under the covers. I debate for several more minutes before picking up my phone.

"Hello?" His sleepy voice makes me instantly regret calling and waking him.

"Luke?" My voice comes out more strained than I intend.

"What's wrong?" He instantly sounds more alert after hearing my voice.

"I'm okay. I'm sorry to wake you. I had another anxiety attack. I told you I would tell you if I did." The truth is, I'm calling as much for him as I am me, hearing his voice is soothing. The space this week has been good, but I admit I wish he was here right now.

"Do you want me to call your mom? Have her come over?"

"No." I pause for several seconds. "I wanted to hear your voice."

"I should be there." I know he's blaming himself for not being here, even though it was me who pushed him away.

"I wasn't trying to make you feel bad."

"I know." Luke pauses a moment. "I'll change my meeting and come there tomorrow."

"That's not necessary. Hearing your voice is enough for now. I miss you."

"That's actually really nice to hear." I can practically hear the smile in his voice.

"I shouldn't have told you to leave. Everything's been… it's all been a lot to process."

"I'll try to be more patient. It's hard for me to sit back and do nothing." He yawns loudly, and I decide any questions I have about his reaction to me and the miscarriage can wait.

"I'm going to let you get some sleep."

"All right, although I sleep better when I'm with you."

"That's ironic, since more often than not you keep me from sleeping when you're in my bed." I smile at the thought.

"Good point. You should definitely rest up before I return." His voice dips lower.

I can't help but laugh a little. "I'm afraid you're going to have to wait a little longer."

"I know, but you might want to start preparing yourself now for all the things I'm going to do to you." His tone slips from flirty to downright provocative.

"Oh yeah, like what?" I lower my voice to match his.

"Do you still have that nurse's outfit from Halloween?" His voice is gravelly. I bought the costume partially as a joke after the idea was brought up during a phone conversation. Between breaking up, getting back together, and finding out I was pregnant, I haven't had the opportunity to wear it for him yet.

"I do." I'm glad he can't see the ridiculous grin I'm wearing.

"Perfect. I think I have some ailments that will need tending to by then. Some swelling that will definitely need to be eased."

"Don't get me wrong, I'm happy to treat your case, but there are also some home remedies you can try in the meantime," I snicker.

"Home remedies are never as effective. I'm willing to wait until I can be seen by a specialist."

I imagine the wicked grin he's undoubtedly wearing. "What did you have in mind?"

"Prepping the area with that pretty mouth of yours would be a great start," he says with no trace of embarrassment, while I blush instantly.

"That could be arranged."

"I think that followed by a therapeutic massage would do the trick."

I can't contain the giggle that escapes. "Therapeutic massage, huh?"

"I'll need you to really work me, though."

"I can handle that. I'll mark your appointment on my calendar." I force my voice to sound serious.

"We may have to block off a whole day for it." I giggle again and Luke sighs. "This was a bad idea. No way I'm falling back asleep now."

"Sorry." I yawn.

"Don't be. I'm never sorry for losing sleep to you, even if it's only thinking about being with you." Luke yawns again. "Do you feel better?"

"I do. I'm going to try to go back to sleep."

"Okay. I love you."

"I love you, too. I'll talk to you tomorrow."

I fall back asleep easily and dream of a nurse costume and a very satisfying massage.

Luke flies in on Saturday night. By the time he gets to my house, Amelia is already in bed, and he looks exhausted. He pulls me into his lap when he sits on the couch and gives me a quick kiss before laying us down in a position comfortable for movie watching. The hero hasn't even met his nemesis before I hear Luke lightly snoring behind me.

I wake Luke up to go to bed and he groggily follows me upstairs. As I try to fall asleep, my mind begins to race with thoughts of work projects I need to complete next week and Amelia's field trip next month. I sit up and take a big drink of cold water. It doesn't help. I slip on my robe and go downstairs, tiptoeing quietly so as not to wake anyone. I feel the panic and tears building as I hold onto the kitchen island.

They are right on the surface when a hand grabs my shoulder making me jump.

"What the?" I yell as I turn around to confront an apologetic looking Luke. My tears bubble over and I struggle to breathe. The rush of panic makes me crumple down to the kitchen floor in a heap. Luke follows me and sits with a thump in front of me.

"Deep breaths." He says the words calmly, but I see his chest moving up and down rapidly. "Name five things you can see."

"What?" I struggle to inhale enough air.

"It'll help. Name five things you see."

"I see the dishwasher. I see the cabinets. I see the towel that fell off the counter." I look past the kitchen into the family room. "I see the couch." I take another deep breath and close my eyes. I open them to see Luke staring at me intently. "I see you."

He smiles at my last answer. "Name four things you feel."

"I feel the cold tile beneath me. I feel the cool air against my arms. I feel my soft pajamas." I look to my hand rubbing the brushed cotton of my sleep bottoms and Luke rests his palm on my thigh. "I feel your warm hand through the material."

This elicits another smile from him. "Name three things you hear."

"I hear the wind through the window I left open to air out the kitchen. I hear the refrigerator buzzing. I hear…" I close my eyes and concentrate. "I hear you breathing."

"Name two things you smell."

"I smell the plug-in air freshener. I smell your cologne."

"Name one thing you taste."

I swallow, but nothing comes to mind. I lean into Luke and he meets me. I place a soft kiss on his lips. "Cinnamon toothpaste."

He smiles at me and gives me another kiss, but pulls back before we get too carried away.

"Thank you. Did you used to do that with your mom?"

He nods, and his expression turns serious. I place my hand on his.

"Do you want to talk about it?" I see glimpses of the emotions he works so hard to conceal.

"Later." Luke stands and extends his hand to me. I grab it and he pulls me up. "Let's go back to bed."

We don't say anything else, we don't need to. He was there when I needed him, and I realize I need him more than I like to admit. Luke falls asleep with his arms wrapped tightly around me. Usually when we fall sleep this way, the act feels more comforting. This time the gesture reminds me of someone holding onto something, afraid to lose it.

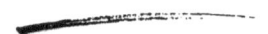

I come downstairs in the morning to find Luke and Amelia eating cereal and watching cartoons.

"Morning, Mom. We let you sleep in." Amelia beams when she sees me.

"I see that, what are you watching?" I grab a mug from the cabinet.

"A Barbie movie. They're Luke's favorite." Amelia giggles and clasps a hand over her mouth.

"You weren't supposed to tell anyone, Amelia," Luke teases her, and she giggles more.

"Amelia and I were thinking we should get out of the house today, head down to the beach and walk around." Luke joins me in the kitchen, rinsing out their bowls and putting them in the dishwasher.

"Come on, Mom, it will be fun." Amelia bounces in behind him.

I don't feel like it, but we have spent a lot of time at home lately, a fact that makes me feel like I'm not being the best mom. "Okay."

"Okay?" Luke raises an eyebrow at me.

"Yeah." I pour myself a cup of coffee. "Give me an hour."

We spend the day walking around and stopping to look in stores. Despite the chilly temperatures, the sun shines brightly and there is something inherently nostalgic about the salty ocean air. Amelia often walks in the middle, holding one of mine and one of Luke's hands. Even though she's getting older, she's still loving and affectionate and I try to soak up every minute of it that I can.

When we stop for lunch, I go with Amelia to use the restroom. There is a young woman changing her infant's diaper. I avert my eyes as much as possible, but they are still damp by the time we rejoin Luke at the table. Amelia gives me a hug once we're back in the booth, but none of us say anything else about it during lunch. I do my best to put on a happy front for everyone's sake, but the knot in my stomach is a reminder of what I lost.

Chapter 4

This is the second weekend in a row that Luke won't be coming back to Temecula. I have no room to complain, though. I miss him when he's not here, but when he is here, I often resent his hovering over me.

We've had some nice moments, mostly revolving around time spent with Amelia, but we're definitely out of sync. I wish we could come out from underneath the dark cloud that seems to be hanging over our relationship. The fact that I've only seen him a handful of days in the past three weeks isn't helping us get back on track any quicker.

"How's the medication working?" Luke asks over the sound of ruffling papers.

I hate to admit it but going to see a doctor was a good idea. After my fourth anxiety attack in two weeks I reluctantly agreed to go. I can take the medication when I feel like I need it and it doesn't make me feel weird, just stops a full-blown attack from happening. "Good, no attacks this week. I even went for a run after work yesterday." This will make Luke happy, a sign that I'm getting back into a normal routine, mentally and physically.

"That's great." He responds as if I'd just told him what I had for lunch. I obviously misjudged how my decision to get some exercise would be received.

"I wish you were coming here this weekend." When I mentioned to Luke I had gotten my period last week he mumbled something about his new client being a moron. I tell myself that he was just too distracted with work and my announcement didn't even register with him. Nonetheless, I was too timid to mention it again and have been waiting for him to bring up something that would serve as an introduction to announcing I'm open for business again. He hasn't.

"Yeah me, too." Luke doesn't sound sincere, he sounds preoccupied. "Can I call you back?"

"Sure."

"I'll call you later. Love you."

"Love you, too." I get the words out right before he hangs up.

I let out a sigh and toss my head back.

"You all right in there?" My assistant, Linda, calls from her desk.

"Luke's not coming again this weekend," I say, walking out of my office. "I don't know. Things feel off. I asked for space, but I didn't expect this much." Linda has been my assistant for over five years now and I've counted her as a friend for nearly as long.

She looks up from her computer to give me her full attention.

"He says he misses me, but he has some stuff in San Francisco he needs to sort out. He's tried to be reassuring and calls often, but I can't shake the feeling that there's something he's not telling me."

"It shouldn't be surprising that he's busy. With the amount of time and energy he puts into this place, not to mention he still has other investments that need his attention, I always assumed Luke was a work seven days a week kind of guy."

"He is, but he's always made time for me and Amelia, too."

"Being here for several weeks at Christmas and then after with the miscarriage, there's bound to be a lot for him to catch up on right now. I'm sure it's temporary." Linda tries to reassure me.

"He doesn't seem himself." I think for a minute before continuing. I'm crossing over into oversharing, but I need to get some of my thoughts out. "It's been six weeks since the miscarriage, physically I'm healed. This weekend was supposed to be kind of a special weekend."

Linda nods, immediately understanding the significance. "And he's not coming…literally."

I laugh. "Stop it. I thought he was looking forward to it as much as I was, but he hasn't mentioned anything about it in weeks."

"Could you go up there?"

"He didn't ask me to. I would have if he'd he asked." Red flags are waving frantically at me and alarms are blaring in my head, but I can't bring myself to say aloud what I'm thinking.

"He's busy and he knows you've been having a hard time. Men don't always think of asking."

"You're probably right." I say the words, but don't really believe them. I hate where my thoughts have drifted to. Luke had a notorious reputation when he was single, but he's never given me any real reason to suspect he'd cheat on me. I fear that because of Grant's affair, I'll always have that worry in the back of my head.

I return to my desk and call Luke's cell. It goes to voicemail, but the automated message indicates his mailbox is full. I think of sending a text, but decide I'd rather talk to him. I dial his work number instead. After several rings, the call is forwarded to his assistant.

"Good afternoon, AL Investments, how can I help you?"

"Hi Ashley, this is Jessica. I'm trying to get ahold of Luke."

"Hi, Jessica. Luke just walked out the door to go to his doctor appointment."

"Doctor appointment?" I attempt to cover my stunned reaction. "Oh, that's right." Luke never mentioned anything about this to me. I rack my brain trying to remember is he's hinted at not feeling well.

"You should try him on his cell." Ashley offers.

"His voicemail is full, but I'll send him a text." I think quickly, trying to extract as much information from this conversation as I can. "I can't remember if he said he was coming back into the office after or if he was going straight home."

"He wasn't sure. He said since it's a follow up appointment it shouldn't take as long as last month. He'll call me when he knows what time he'll be back in. I'll let him know you called."

"No need. I'll get ahold of him. Thanks Ashley."

I try not to jump to any nasty conclusions, but there's obviously something going on. I remember Luke specifically mentioning at the first prenatal appointment we went to that he hated doctor offices and avoided them as much as possible.

We laughed about how he was going to have to get over his aversion when he said he wanted to come to every visit with me.

I can't think of one good reason he'd be going to the doctor multiple times and not telling me about it. Unless he's lying to Ashley about where he's going.

"Hi." I attempt to sound as casual as possible. It's been a week since the mystery doctor appointment and Luke still hasn't brought it up. The distance between us feels amplified by my current suspicions that he's lying every time we talk.

"Hey, I only have a few minutes, work is crazy today."

"No problem. What are you working on?"

Luke ignores my question. "How's your day going?"

"Good, but busy. Mrs. Bianchi asked for a revised operating budget in light of the latest projection adjustments, so I had to put those together."

Luke again doesn't respond to what I've just said. "Any more panic attacks?"

"No. I told you earlier I haven't had any more."

"Sorry. It's been a weird day." Luke's distractedness is still foreign to me even though it shouldn't be any more, our conversations are often like this now. I thought it was work at first, but I've come to realize he's like this when we talk in the evenings, too. "I'm looking forward to seeing you on Sunday."

I fiddle with the hem of my skirt. "Are you?"

"Of course. What makes you ask that?"

"This is the longest stretch we've gone without seeing each other. I thought you were looking forward to your massage appointment." I let the words linger.

I hear Luke curse under his breath. "I was. I mean, I am. I just…I have some things going on here I have to take care of."

"Right, that's what you've said."

"I'll make it up to you."

My chest tightens. "I don't need you to make it up to me."

"Jess, I haven't been there, but I want to be. I hate that I haven't been there for you the way I should." Luke sounds like he may be genuinely remorseful, but I don't know what to believe anymore.

I take a deep breath. "Just tell me what's going on. You were practically ready to move down here and now you're too busy for even a weekend visit."

"I've been preoccupied with things here. I'll do better." His voice is strained.

"I wanted some space. I didn't mean I wanted you to leave completely."

"I know. It's not anything you did." Luke doesn't say any additional words to ease my fears. The fact that he's only offering small, nearly meaningless words of assurance is worrisome.

I wait for a few seconds, concentrating on my heart which is pounding in my chest. I'm afraid of what answers I may hear, but I can't hold it in any longer. "Are we okay?"

"Jess…"

"Don't insult me by saying everything is fine when it's clearly not." My voice breaks. "Are you cheating on me?"

"No. I would never do that to you," he says without hesitation, but I know there's something he's not telling me. "I promise that's not something you ever have to worry about with me."

"Things haven't been great lately. I mean, we called off the wedding…"

"We postponed the wedding, we didn't call it off. The day you become Mrs. Taylor will be the best day of my life." Luke's voice is serious, he's definitely not distracted now.

"Then what is it? What aren't you telling me?" I plead.

Luke is silent. I would think we got disconnected, but I can hear him breathing.

"Hello?" I say into the silence.

"I'm going to rearrange my schedule. I'll be there tomorrow afternoon. We can spend the entire weekend together," he says, before halfway covering the phone to respond to someone else. "I'm sorry, but I have to go, Aaron needs me. I have a dinner with clients tonight which will probably go late, but I'll see you tomorrow and we can talk then."

My chest aches, but I manage to say, "Okay."

"I love you." He tries to sound reassuring, but I hear a sadness in his voice. Instead of being comforted by the words, I find them terrifying. Instinct tells me he has been hiding something, something he wants to confess in person. This isn't good.

"I love you, too."

I wait ten minutes after we hang up before I call his office.

"Good afternoon, AL Investments how can I help you?"

"Hi Ashley, this is Jessica. Luke's voicemail is full again and he's not responding to texts. I was wondering if he left in time to get to his doctor's appointment." I take a guess he's either headed to another appointment or has made up a new fake one.

"Hi, Jessica. Yes, his driver showed up in plenty of time to get him there."

"Great. Thank you."

I was relieved when Luke said he wasn't cheating. I feel bad for even thinking it, but I never thought Grant would, either. Being completely caught off guard with his affair somehow made it feel extra hurtful, like he was internally laughing about how stupid and trusting I was.

But Luke isn't Grant and I have to remember that.

"Oh no." I say aloud as realization dawns that Luke may be hiding something even worse than an affair.

I tossed and turned all last night, but I didn't have a panic attack. I should be tired, but instead I'm amped up on adrenaline.

Somehow, I make it through the work day, but I'm eager to leave by the time I hear Linda packing up for the weekend. Linda is heading up north for the weekend to help her daughter pick out her dress and hire vendors for her summer wedding.

"Bye, Linda. Have fun wedding planning," I yell to her in the other room of our small two-room office.

"Thanks, see you Monday," she calls back.

"See you Monday."

It's my weekend with Amelia, but my mom asked for her to spend the night, so she's picking her up from school today. Luke should already be waiting for me at the house.

The ten-minute drive home provides more than enough time to run a couple of worst case scenarios through my head.

I pull into the garage, next to Luke's car and take a steadying breath. I throw in a prayer that this has nothing to do with his health and go inside.

Luke is standing at the island working on his laptop.

"Hey." He steps up to me and places a simple kiss on my cheek. After not seeing each other for weeks, the gesture feels small and it immediately creates an awkwardness between us.

"Hey." I set my purse on the counter and pull a bottle of wine from the fridge. "How was your flight?"

"It was good."

As a general rule, I hate small talk. I hate it even more when it's stalling more important conversations. I lean back against a counter and wait. I'm not sure what I'm going to find out tonight, but it's time.

Luke rubs the back of his neck when he sees my stance. "Let's sit."

I follow and take a seat next to him on the couch. I place a hand on my stomach, trying to calm the angst bubbling there.

"I want to start out by saying I'm sorry I've caused you to worry. My main goal in all of this has been to avoid causing you any additional stress. I realized on the phone yesterday that my efforts have completely backfired."

Luke's speaking quicker than normal, and he's already raked a hand through his hair twice since I sat down. His uneasiness is making me even more edgy. I decide it's better not to say much and let him do the talking.

"I've been trying to handle something on my own. I have been busy at work, but I've been avoiding coming here, too. I don't like keeping things from you and I knew if I saw you, I'd tell you and it wasn't the right time yet. It's been such an awful couple months and with your panic attacks…I couldn't, not yet."

He looks so conflicted, so pained, I can't help myself. "Luke, I already know."

"You do?" Luke's eyes grow wide, but then he narrows them in confusion.

"I do. Don't be angry with her, but Ashley sort of told me. I called a few times when you were out, and she must've assumed I already knew because she inadvertently told me."

Luke eyes me suspiciously. "What did Ashley tell you?"

"I know you've been leaving work early the last few weeks to go to the doctor."

Luke rubs his palm over his face and looks up at the ceiling.

"The last couple of months have been hard. I know my reaction to the miscarriage upset you, but Luke, whatever you're going through, I can handle it. I want to be here for you. We'll deal with whatever is going on with you together. There are a lot of great doctors down here that you could see." I place my hand on Luke's and he brings his eyes back to mine.

"You heard about doctor's appointments and assumed I'm sick." Luke squeezes his eyes shut, like saying the words hurt. I can tell by his tone I've assumed incorrectly and my stomach sinks.

"You're not sick, are you?" My voice sounds shaky.

"No, I'm not sick." Luke looks away from me.

I remove my hand from his and lean back slightly. "Well, that's good news." I say the words halfheartedly. It is good news that he's not sick, but that means there's another explanation for his dishonesty coming my way.

Luke sighs and sits up straight. "Okay." He looks at me, but then looks away again. "Last fall, after the harvest event, I planned to stay away from you."

"I remember." Luke sent some mixed signals that day and then left. I thought we were going to maintain a strictly professional relationship until he showed up at the winery investor dinner with different ideas.

"I went home to San Francisco and tried to resume my life." Luke takes a deep breath. "I never mentioned it, but when I came out for the crush event, I was dating someone."

"Oh." I'm replaying our interactions from that day in my head. There was definitely some sexual tension between us, but nothing happened. I'm more familiar with Luke's bachelor lifestyle than I'd care to be after overhearing things from other women, but this is the first I've heard of any actual relationship. The thought makes me feel like I'm going to be sick and I swallow hard.

"I returned home, but I couldn't stop thinking about you. I quickly realized I wasn't being fair to anyone, not to her, you, or me. So, I ended things and came here to get you back."

My head is swimming through the mess of information I'm drowning in. I'm missing something. "Luke, what does this have to do with us now?"

"I'm getting there." Luke runs a hand through his hair again. "The woman I dated, Claire, and I hadn't talked since I ended things. She called out of the blue."

My chest constricts, and I feel the blood drain from my face.

"Jessica, I had no idea until she called." Luke's voice falters.

"Luke, why did she call you?" My body tenses and my heart rate speeds up.

He squeezes his eyes shut. "She called to let me know that she's pregnant."

I exhale the breath I was holding in tight. I don't say anything, I can't. What am I supposed to say?

Luke opens his eyes and they search mine, pleading for an indication that we're going to be all right. I can't give him anything right now. He places his hand on mine, a move to feel a little closer. "I know it's a shock."

My mind races, causing the room to spin. "If you were with her last summer, then she would be due..." I try to do the mental math, but my head hurts.

"Beginning of June," Luke says quietly.

"Why did she wait so long to tell you?" I ask one of the million questions overloading my brain.

"She said she had to get used to the idea herself before she decided what to do. Apparently, she was angry with me for ending things so abruptly and didn't want to talk to me again unless she had to. She decided to wait until the first trimester was over, just in case..." Luke trails off when he approaches the topic that pushes the knife deeper into the wound.

I think back over the last week and remember Luke acting odd for a longer period of time. He's been different since he returned to San Francisco only a couple of weeks after the miscarriage.

Everything I'm feeling is all swirled together in a tight knot. "How long have you known?"

Luke swallows hard. "Since the middle of January."

I feel like the wind has been knocked out of me. My old companions hurt and betrayal are the first emotions to step forward and reclaim their residency. "January?" I stare at Luke in disbelief.

"Yeah..."

"Wait." I interrupt him. "You've been keeping this from me for a month?"

Luke's face drops. "I'm sorry. When she called I had just gone back to work. It was only a couple weeks after the miscarriage. You were still dealing with it, or trying to, anyway. I couldn't tell you yet. I couldn't risk it." He says all these words as though they explain how or why he could keep something like this from me for so long.

"And you're only telling me now because I thought you were having an affair or were hiding some awful illness?"

"No." Luke shakes his head. "It wasn't that I didn't want to tell you before, it was complicated. Of course, I was going to tell you."

"When?" I raise my voice and get up from the couch.

Luke rises, too. "I was trying to protect you. And I didn't exactly lie to you."

"Keeping secrets, especially big, life changing secrets, from someone you supposedly love is lying. Plus, I'm sure you haven't been truthful about having work obligations the last several weekends." I storm off to the kitchen, rubbing my temples, and trying to process exactly what this means for me, for us.

"It's not that simple." Luke follows me. "I couldn't tell you, not yet. I didn't enjoy keeping it from you. Every conversation was hard. Every time I talked to you, I wanted to tell you, but every time I heard about your latest anxiety attack I was reminded this wasn't about what I wanted to do, it was about what was best for you."

I spin around and take a step closer to him, my eyes narrowed sharply. "You do not get to lie to me and then tell me it was for my own good."

Luke raises his hands in front of him. "That's not what I meant."

"You know my past, you know my issues and yet you still thought being dishonest was your best option?" Having my dad abandon me and my former husband cheat on me, I admit I have some deep rooted trust issues. Luke, of all people, should know how this would hurt me.

"Yes." Even though Luke sounds apologetic, this was not the answer I was hoping for.

"What?" I blink several times to make sure I understood him correctly.

"You may not like the option I chose, but this was not news to give you back in January. I was watching you fall apart, and I wasn't about to deliver a final blow." Luke crosses his arms across his broad chest, an action that immediately makes my pulse speed up.

"You don't get to decide what information I'm ready for and what I'm not."

"In this case, yes I do."

I'm so angry, I'm shaking. "You're impossible. I'm not doing this with you right now." I push myself off the counter, but Luke grabs me by the wrist. I stop and try to slow my breathing, but I don't look back at him.

"Don't walk away. You said we would deal with whatever was going on together." He's trying to keep his voice calm, but I hear him breathing faster than normal.

I swing around to face him, and he releases my wrist. "That's not fair. I thought you were dying." My words are sharp, and I regret them as soon as I say them, but Luke ignores them.

He grabs my hands again and rubs his thumbs across the tops of my knuckles. "Let's calm down for a minute. I know this was not the plan, but it doesn't change anything between us."

I pull my hands from his, and turn my eyes down to my pink toenails. I close my eyes and remind myself to breath. My mind feels chaotic, like a maze I can't figure out. I can't make sense of what I'm feeling yet, so I say the first thing I think of. "It changes everything, Luke. You're starting a family with someone else. The family we were supposed to have." Saying this out loud makes the whole situation more real somehow, and I gasp for air.

Luke sucks in a sharp breath. "Don't say that." He grabs my hands again and holds them tightly.

I feel his eyes burn in to me, pleading for me to rethink my reaction, to take back my words, but I can't look at him. "I need you to leave."

"Jessica…"

I remove one hand from his, still squeezing my eyes shut. I place my palm gently on his chest and feel his heart is beating erratically underneath my fingertips. "Luke, I'm serious. I need you to leave right now."

"We don't leave, remember?" Luke repeats the words he said when we got back together following my indecision over our relationship. It feels like a promise made between two different people than who we are today.

I shake my head. "That's not fair."

"Maybe not, but it's all I have right now." He brushes my hair back with his free hand. "Will you please look at me?"

I don't say anything, but slowly open my eyes and watch as the first tear slides down my cheek and hits the tiled floor below me. There's nothing he can say to make this all right and he knows it.

"Let go of my hand," I whisper, and he stills. "Let go, Luke."

"I can't," he whispers, so softly I almost don't hear it.

I pull my hand slowly from his grasp and look up at him. "I agreed not to leave, but that was before there were secrets and lies." My voice catches on the last words and more tears spill down my cheeks.

Luke moves to wipe them away, but I lean back out of his reach. He opens his mouth to say something, but the doorbell rings and we freeze. We don't make a sound, hoping the intruder goes away quickly. Suddenly, the front door opens, and I lean to where I can see my mom walking in.

She catches sight of me. "Oh, I'm sorry, hon. I rang the doorbell, but when you didn't answer, I thought I would just sneak in. Amelia forgot her special blanket."

My eyes widen. I can't have Amelia here right now. I can't have her witness this.

My mom looks at my tear stained face and understands. "It's all right. Amelia's still in the car, she wanted to finish reading her book and asked me to run and get her blanket for her."

"Hi, Jill." Luke passes me and walks toward my mom. She watches me from over his shoulder as he hugs her.

"Sorry to interrupt." Her expression is one of concern as she looks back and forth between us. "What's going on here?"

"Luke…" I only get one word out before my sobs choke the rest. Just thinking of saying the words out loud makes my stomach twist.

"Jessica." My mom walks swiftly over to me and wraps her arms around me.

"Luke was just leaving," I mutter as my mom strokes my hair like I'm five-years-old again. As much as I don't like being coddled, I have to admit, in this current moment, it's comforting.

"No, I wasn't." Luke runs a hand through his hair again and shifts his weight from one foot to the other. "Jessica, we need to talk this out. I'm not leaving you like this."

"Please go. I don't want any more of your protecting." I spit my words out like a weapon.

My mom releases me and marches over to Luke. She grabs him firmly by the arm and leads him to the door. I don't follow them, but instead grab an iced tea from the fridge. I place the cold bottle against my head and listen to the bits of their conversation that I can hear from the kitchen.

"What did you do? Did you cheat on her?" My mom is trying to keep her voice low, but the anger present in it is undeniable.

"Come on, Jill, I wouldn't do that to her," Luke says emphatically.

There is a pause and I can't tell if my mom is waiting for him to continue or if she said something I can't hear.

"I fucked up." Luke's voice is barely audible from where I'm standing.

There's a few minutes where I can't make out anything they're saying, so I take a drink of tea and focus on getting my breathing under control.

"Luke." Her disappointment is evident in her tone. A few seconds pass. I assume Luke must be saying something to her. "She asked you to leave. You need to go."

"I promised I wouldn't leave her again. I need to fix this."

My mom sighs. "Not now, she's really upset."

"I know, this is why I didn't tell her. I can't leave her like this. Please don't try to make me."

My mom lowers her voice again, but I can still make out her words. "You staying here right now isn't going to help anything. Go get a room and try to get some rest, maybe she'll talk to you tomorrow."

Luke doesn't say anything. I think maybe he's left, until I hear his low voice. I have to strain to make out the last part of what he says. "I can't lose her again."

Chapter 5

My eyes sting when I open them, a side effect and instant reminder of the night before. After my mom convinced Luke he needed to leave, she put on a movie for Amelia upstairs, promised they would try a sleepover again in two weeks, and stayed with me. She listened as I cried out my disappointment. After I told her good night and put Amelia to bed, I went to my room and shed a few more tears. How did life get so messy in such a short period of time?

I silenced my phone right after Luke left yesterday. I'm not ready to talk to him yet. Amelia is up and watching cartoons in the family room as I make myself a cup of tea and fold the load of laundry I left in the dryer last night. It isn't until we're dressed for the day, that I work up enough nerve to check my phone.

As expected, there are several missed calls and texts from Luke. I'm surprised he's shown enough restraint to avoid coming back over here unannounced. He won't be patient all day, though. Amelia has been invited to spend the night at her best friend Sam's house tonight and they're picking her up at midday to go to the movies first. I send Luke a text letting him know he can stop by after five to talk.

In between chores, Sam's dad arrives to pick up Amelia. Once she is off, I return to cleaning the house. I turn up the volume and allow the pulsating music to fill the house and my head, leaving room for little else. I sing, loudly and slightly off key, as I dust, wipe and scrub. Once surfaces are sparkling and I'm sweating, I run upstairs for a quick shower. I'm wrapping my hair in a towel when I hear the doorbell. I check the clock on my nightstand and am not surprised it's five o'clock on the dot.

The doorbell rings again as I'm walking down the stairs, but I don't pick up my pace, I use the last few seconds of solitude to brace myself to see him again. I open the door and sigh at the man I almost don't recognize. The angles of Luke's face look harsher when they aren't softened by a smile and the huge bags under his eyes cast a haunted look across his entire face.

I step aside and he brushes past me without saying anything. The fleeting contact causes my pulse to quicken as I shut the door and follow him into the family room.

"Thanks for letting me come over," Luke says taking a seat on the couch.

I sit in the chair across from him and place a throw pillow in my lap, nervously fiddling with the fringed edges.

"I don't know where to start." Luke leans forward, his elbows on his knees.

"The truth is usually a good place." I lean back into the chair cushion.

Luke nods before looking directly at me. "I want to clarify that we weren't together when I was with her and I had no idea about the pregnancy."

"Until you did…a month ago." The thought and the words cause my stomach to clench. "You chose to keep it from me for a month, Luke."

"I know you feel lied to."

"Because I was lied to."

He focuses his eyes on mine. "I wasn't trying to get away with anything. I was waiting for the right time or at least a better one. My intentions were good, that has to count for something."

I avoid answering in an effort to control my emotions for as long as possible. Once the tears start again, they'll be hard to reign in.

Luke tilts his head to one side. "Talk to me."

I take a deep breath and try not to cry. "It's scary how quickly and easily you lied to me."

He shakes his head defiantly. "Not true. It wasn't easy. I felt horrible about it every day."

"Maybe you felt bad, but you seem to still think your actions are justified. Be honest, would you do it again?"

Luke leans back against the cushions and appears to be deciding what to say. "I would," he says plainly.

"Unbelievable." I take a deep breath. "So, I can't trust you. I'd have to be an idiot to knowingly be with someone who's admitted they'd lie to me."

"I don't lie out of sport, but sometimes protecting people means making hard decisions."

"I've had enough untrustworthy men in my life." I look down at the pillow in my lap. It's an unfair comparison, but the feelings are there nonetheless.

"I'm not going to abandon you like your dad did, and I'm not going to cheat on you like Grant did." Luke pauses and

I force myself not to look up. "Jessica, when you're hurting, I want to be the person that you turn to, but with everything I do, you push me further away."

"Do you want to know why I needed space from you? Too much pressure. Pressure to move on and get over something I wasn't ready to let go of."

"I wasn't pressuring you to do anything more than try," he says softly.

I raise my eyes to meet his, but the storm of emotions I see there is too intense for me to handle right now, so I cast them down again quickly. "I would love to say let's move past this, but everything's changed now."

I sense him sit up straighter, but can still feel his eyes on me. "I didn't plan this."

"You're going to be a great father." I stare at the pillow in my lap and choke back the sob threatening to rise out of me. "Do you have any idea how painful it is for me that I'm not going to be the one experiencing your baby with you?"

I hear his breath catch, but don't dare look up.

"I feel like I've already lost you." The truth spills out before I can catch it and stuff it back down deep inside of me.

Luke is off the couch and kneeling in front of me in an instant. He lowers his head trying to get my eyes to meet his, but I don't let them. "You're never going to lose me."

After what feels like a long time, I allow my eyes to travel first to his hands that are gently stroking the tops of my thighs and then to his face. "Let's be honest, you love me, but we wouldn't even be together had you known about the baby."

"That's not true." Luke furrows his brow.

"It is. I can see how much being a good father means to you. We both know that you wouldn't have walked away from her had you known. You wouldn't have left her to come back here for me."

"That's not fair. The fact is I didn't know, and I am with you. I love you and I don't want to play the 'what-if' game because I'm exactly where I want to be."

"Having a baby with someone is a big deal. It's going to stir up feelings, on both sides."

"At the risk of sounding like a real asshole, I was never in love with her. Even if you think I would've stayed with her out of obligation, it only proves that it would've been a mistake." Luke waits until I look at him and the grave expression he wears. "I chose you. Not because I had to, but because I wanted to be with you. I *still* want to be with you."

"I know, but this is messy, Luke. Maybe you'll wake up one morning and realize this other life you have is easier and—"

"I don't have another life. My life with you is it, we just have to include my son now, too."

Son. The word and all its implications stab at my already tender heart.

"It's overwhelming right now, but it'll work out. I had to learn to be part of Amelia's life and deal with Grant." Luke was great with Amelia from day one but had to learn to handle his feelings about my ex-husband.

"It's not the same." I shake my head. "I don't think I can do this."

Panic flashes in Luke's eyes and he swallows hard. "Don't doubt yourself or what we have."

"Me? You didn't even think I could handle the news of your…son." The words leave a bitter taste in my mouth and a fresh flash of anger zings through my body. I'm angry at Luke for creating this situation in the first place, angry he hid it from me, angry I can't see a happy ending anywhere in sight. "I don't see how I can be a part of this. She isn't going to want another woman involved with her newborn."

"I'll deal with Claire. I promise it will be okay," Luke says with the utmost confidence.

My stomach churns at yet another promise he shouldn't be making. He has no idea if anything is going to be all right. "Great, so you handle her and then I just have to learn to live with your lies plus a constant, live reminder of what I've lost."

He flinches, at my anger or the truth I'm not sure. "I would've told you if we weren't still recovering from the miscarriage."

I hate that he's using my grief as an excuse for this. "You mean I was still recovering."

"No, I mean we both were. Jessica, watching you since the miscarriage has been nearly unbearable for me. I know you resent my offers to help, but I don't see how I'm expected to sit back and watch the woman I love suffer."

He's nailed it. He's been worried about me, not upset about the baby. "I can't just forget about our baby."

"No one's asking you to forget."

"You are. Every time you rattle off a miscarriage statistic or tell someone we're simply going to try again, you're asking me to forget. Our baby died, Luke…inside of me." My voice is shaky, overloaded with too many emotions at once.

"Jesus, Jessica." He shifts uncomfortably before standing and walking toward the back door.

I'm tired of him avoiding this topic. I feel another rush of anger move like a current through my body.

"Maybe it's easier for you because you have something else to look forward to," I yell at his back.

He freezes and turns to face me with wide eyes. "You can't honestly be suggesting that I've replaced our baby with another one."

"You haven't?" I breathe heavily, still unable to get enough oxygen into my aching chest.

"No, I haven't." Luke's eyes flare. He opens his mouth to speak, but only lets a small sound out before working his jaw and rubbing his neck. "We both need to take a minute and cool down."

My heart and thoughts are racing, but I have enough sense to hold back any additional anger fueled words.

Luke stares out into the backyard. "I'm not losing you over this. Not over the miscarriage and not over my son."

It feels like a punch in the stomach every time he says the word. If I speak again, I'll start crying, so I don't.

I stare at my feet, hoping for an epiphany of what I should do. I love this man, but I'm so disappointed in him, disappointed in what he's done to us. It's disheartening that our relationship doesn't feel strong enough to weather this storm.

He walks back to the couch and sits. "Jessica, I—" He starts, but I can immediately tell he has nothing new to say.

"No more, Luke." I shake my head vigorously and sit in a chair across from him. "No more today."

He closes his mouth and we sit in silence, waiting for the storm to calm. Once my heaving chest has settled, I pierce the uneasy hush of the room. "Are you hungry?" I'm not, but it's the first neutral thing I could think to say.

Luke looks like he's thinking of something to say, but instead answers plainly. "I could eat."

"I'll order Chinese food." Our problems aren't going away over some noodles, but we need to bury them for a moment. I don't know if the break will dull the pain or give it time to mature, but right now it's the only option. The only other alternative would be to say goodbye right now.

We watch a science fiction movie while we eat. I'm not following the plot very well, but don't bother to say anything or ask any questions. All my words for the day are used up.

When the movie is done, I spend a few awkward minutes looking for something else to watch.

"I'd better get back to the hotel." Luke glances at me several times as he puts his shoes back on. "I'll come back tomorrow before my flight?"

I set down the remote and rewrap the blanket around me. The confusion in my mind leaves me in a fog. I can't decide if I want to punch him or hold on to him until things feel right again. "What if I asked you to stay?"

He gives me a small smile. "I'll go check out of the hotel and get my stuff." He kisses me on the top of the head as he leaves.

With Luke gone, I take the breather to throw in a load of laundry and change into something more comfortable. By the time he returns I'm back on the couch in my pajamas with a new movie started. I want to be near him, but I don't want to talk to him anymore tonight.

For most of the evening Luke sits at one end of the couch, while I keep my legs curled up next to me as close as is reasonably comfortable. At some point, I relax and stretch my legs out. He takes the opportunity to rest his hand on my calf and I leave my leg there, letting the warmth of his hand permeate my skin. Speaking to him or even looking at him feels too risky so we stay like this, tethered, but distant, until the end credits roll.

I silently pull my legs away from him, the loss feels more monumental than it should and I regret getting up so quickly. With the television turned off, we head upstairs and quietly slip into bed.

The darkness of the room creates a safe space where I can be near him, but not feel so exposed. I'm desperate for things to feel normal with him. I want him to make me forget about all the other stuff and remember how I feel when it's just him and me.

I roll over so I'm facing him. He's lying on his back, only his silhouette visible in the dark room.

Carefully, I place my hand on his bare chest and he inhales sharply. When he places his hand on top of mine I close my eyes and concentrate on the rise and fall of his rib cage. I nestle my body up next to his and he snakes an arm around me, pulling me even closer.

He smells like cologne, a mix of woods and bergamot. I glide my hand down his chest until I reach the hem of his boxer briefs. Tracing the edge lightly with my fingertips, I listen to the change in his breathing.

"Jessica..." he says my name tentatively.

"I don't want to talk anymore, Luke." I slip my hand underneath the fabric and claim him, his body, as mine. "I need to forget the other stuff and remember us."

He rolls me on my back and positions himself on top of me. Slowly he lowers his face to mine and takes my lips. The kiss is slow and soft, yet somehow feels more desperate than any other time he's kissed me. I slide my tongue past his lips and am rewarded with a taste of cinnamon and a soft moan.

Luke slides a hand down my side and I shiver at the sensation. He grips the bottom of my tank top. When he can't remove it any further due to our connected mouths, he breaks the kiss and yanks the top over my head and off my body.

He looks at me for only a moment before lifting one of my bare breasts with his hand and positioning it to be accessible to his hungry mouth. He grazes the nipple with his tongue before taking it in his mouth, my gasp urging him to suck harder.

"I want you inside me, now." I demand in a whisper.

He pushes his body away from mine and into a kneeling position. My eyes have adjusted to the dark room now and I watch as he slides his underwear off and grabs his wallet off the nightstand. I stare as he opens the condom and slides it down his erection. When he's done, he grips the waistband of my pajama bottoms and removes them in one motion.

At this point, Luke would normally say something that would make me blush, but not tonight. He settles down on top of me. I feel him at my opening, but he doesn't enter yet. I close my eyes and his lips find mine again. He slides his tongue in my mouth the same moment he pushes his shaft slowly into me. I focus on the sensation of being filled by him and imagine it healing all the brokenness inside of me. He groans. He must feel it, too.

Luke continues to glide in and out of me slowly. At one point, he lifts his head and I catch a better look of his face illuminated by the streetlight streaming through the window. His handsome face looks different and I don't like what I see there. Gone is the adoration I've grown used to seeing. I can't even see the lust. It's all been replaced by a veil of worry.

"I love you." His words reach out to me, searching for reassurance. His slow pace tonight is as much for him as it is for me. He's simultaneously trying to convince me we can recover from this and attempting to remember what we used to feel like. I close my eyes, afraid the intensity of this moment is becoming too much.

"Jessica." Luke's voice is pleading. "Please look at me."

I keep them shut. "I can't." Tears build behind my eyelids.

He lowers his mouth and takes my earlobe between his lips. "I'm yours. I will always be yours," he whispers into my ear.

I squeeze my eyes shut tighter as he kisses my neck and smooths my hair away from my face. Images of us flash through my head. Images of our first date, our first kiss, of him showing up at the winery, of the afternoon he proposed to me in the same spot we met as young, idealistic teenagers. It doesn't escape my attention that none of the images are of a future with him. A tear rolls down the side of my temple.

Luke wipes it away with his thumb and stops moving.

I place my hand on his. "Please don't stop."

Luke doesn't say anything as he resumes. I moan and grab him, pulling him deeper inside of me. My encouragement works, and he grunts and picks up the pace.

When he comes he groans loudly. Instead of collapsing on me he continues to move slowly, in and out. I think he's waiting for me to open my eyes, but I never do. I need a few more minutes to live in this moment and not in our reality.

He leans down and brushes his lips against mine. "I will choose you every time," he whispers before pulling out of me, leaving room for the insecurity to flood back in.

I thought Luke's return to San Francisco would give me some time to digest and settle into the knowledge of his son. I hoped it would give me time to accept the situation. I wasn't expecting to be excited about the idea, but I did hope the hollow, hopeless feeling in the pit of my stomach would dissipate. Unfortunately, I only feel myself growing more resentful with each passing day.

Luke never brings up the baby or Claire and he only talks about either one of them in short sentences when I mention them. This makes me feel like I can't bring them up, either. It's hard to feel connected to a situation no one wants to talk about.

It's been a week and a half. Ten days of physical and emotional distance. Luke arrived this morning for the finance meeting we have scheduled with Mrs. Bianchi. He stopped by my office before the meeting but left fifteen minutes later with some excuse of needing to talk to Monica, our marketing manager, about something. The truth is, we couldn't think of anything else to say to each other.

I arrive in the conference room five minutes before the meeting is due to start. Luke and Aaron are already seated at the long table, phones in hand.

"Good afternoon, Jessica." Aaron stands and approaches, arms outstretched. Luke smiles lightly when our eyes meet but he doesn't say anything.

"Hi, Aaron," I say as we hug our hellos. "How are you?"

"I'm good. So, you two excited about your trip?' he asks, releasing me.

"Yeah," I answer with forced enthusiasm. It's a trip Luke and I planned last year, before the miscarriage. We're leaving tomorrow morning to spend a long weekend on Catalina to celebrate Valentine's Day.

Catalina is a small island off the coast. We had originally planned to hole up in our rental most of the time, enjoying each other's company, but after the heaviness of our last sexual encounter, I wish we had planned some outdoor activities. I'm envisioning three long days making awkward small talk about the weather and local cuisine with a man who I was planning on marrying in a few months.

Thankfully, I don't have to think about it too long as Mrs. Bianchi pushes open the conference door and effectively begins the meeting.

I present the financials to the group and listen politely while they discuss some legal issues pertaining to the expansion. The original plans, the ones that Luke and Aaron invested in, have been amended several times due to constraints imposed by the city. It's delayed the project, but that hasn't deterred Luke and Aaron in the slightest. To the contrary, the extra time has allowed them to formulate ideas for an even larger expansion.

I do my best to follow what the others are saying, but I'm having trouble staying focused. Thankfully no one asks me any questions I can't readily answer.

The meeting concludes, and Luke follows me back to my office to get my stuff.

"I have to take this," he announces when his phone rings as I'm gathering my belongings. "I'll meet you at the house?"

"Yeah." My heart sinks knowing this weekend won't be the romantic one we envisioned when we planned it.

I pull into the driveway and see Luke sitting in his car and still talking on the phone. I go ahead inside and pour myself a glass of wine.

A few minutes later I hear the door leading to the garage open and then close.

"Sorry about that." Luke is trying to hide his anger, but I notice his clenched fists.

"What's wrong?"

"Too many things."

I nod. "Wine?" I raise my glass so he can see the burgundy liquid.

"No thanks." Luke tugs roughly at his tie to loosen it. "There's something I need to tell you."

"Something I'm obviously not going to want to hear."

"No, it's not." Luke scrunches his brow.

I take a large mouthful of wine and as if on second thought Luke takes the glass from my hand and takes a drink as well.

"That was Claire." Luke hands the glass back to me.

I change my mind, I don't like when Luke brings her up. "Oh," I say, wishing I could've thought of something better.

"She picked a name for the baby."

I set the wine on the counter. It feels like my stomach has fallen somewhere between my heeled feet. "What is it?"

"Before I tell you, I want to say, I tried to change her mind. She wasn't receptive, but I'll have another conversation with her. I'll get her to change it." Luke tries to sound confident, but I'm not sure even he's buying it.

I squeeze my eyes shut. I can only think of one name that Luke would ask her to change. One name he'd be so nervous to share with me. "She's naming him Jackson?" I punctuate my statement like a question even though I don't need confirmation to know I've guessed correctly.

"Yes," Luke says, a mixture of anger and apprehension apparent, even in his one word answer.

I stand with my eyes closed for seconds that feel like hours.

"Jessica?" Luke asks tentatively.

"What, Luke?" I snap, and my eyelids fly open.

Luke seems to be searching for words he can't find, so he just stares waiting for me to say something else.

"I don't know what you're expecting me to say," I say when I grow tired of his watchful eyes.

"I don't, either." Luke rakes a hand through his hair. "I'll talk to her."

"Of all the boys names, she chose that one." I try to laugh at my horrible misfortune, but it comes out crackly, making me sound deranged.

"It was her father's name." Luke offers an explanation I don't want. I don't want him to be able to justify the name.

77

I pick up the glass and take a drink accepting my defeat. "This is perfect."

"It's only a name." Luke attempts to downplay something he knows is a big deal.

"Only a name?" I narrow my eyes at him.

"I mean, we don't even know if our baby was a boy or a girl."

I shake my head in disbelief. "Are you actually suggesting that I'm overreacting?"

"No." Luke shifts his eyes downward.

"Do you really think that naming your new baby the name we picked out for our baby is fine?" I glare at Luke until he looks at me.

"I didn't pick the name and it's not okay, I know that." He nods and speaks in a soothing tone.

I down the remaining contents of the wine glass and take off toward the stairs.

"Wait." Luke trails after me.

"For what? For you to tell me everything is going to be okay? It's not," I yell over my shoulder.

"I'll talk to her," Luke repeats, as if that's going to solve things.

"It doesn't fucking matter." My cracking voice gives away the emotions I was trying to conceal until I had a moment of privacy.

Luke grabs my elbow and I yank it forward from him. "It does matter. I'll fix this."

I spin around to face him. "The name is important to her, too." I freeze as reality hits me, threatening to knock me off my feet. "There's no way to fix this. There's no way to make this okay."

"I'll make her understand why she can't pick that name."

I shake my head. "You don't get it, it's not just the name Luke. It's everything. I can't be a part of this."

"I will make this work, I promise you." Luke eyes me with such conviction that I almost believe him.

"Don't you see? I'm jealous and angry all the time. This isn't the person I want to be."

"I know—"

"No, you don't," I interrupt him. "I'm not happy for you, not in the slightest. This should be a happy moment for you and it's awful for me. We can't continue to merely coexist like this. I'm not going to be responsible for ruining this for you."

"You're not ruining it." Luke doesn't sound as convincing this time as he stares up at the ceiling.

"I am. This isn't a healthy relationship for either one of us anymore."

Luke's head jerks down and he levels me with stare that causes me to flinch. "What are you saying?"

I pause and try to catch my breath. Knowing what I need to say and actually saying it are two very different things. "I love you, Luke, and I promise I've been trying." I slide the ring off my left hand. "I'm drowning, and I'll take you down with me."

"Stop," Luke says forcefully as he grabs my hand.

"I'm sorry, Luke, but someone has to be the one to call it." My voice catches at the end of my sentence, but I force myself to keep speaking. "You're going to be a great father and you should go and enjoy that."

"Yes, but I'm also going to be a great husband to you. It doesn't have to be one or the other."

"I know you don't see it yet, but this is the right decision."

"So just like that you give up on me?" Luke scowls.

I get the ring off and try to hand it to him, but he takes a step backwards. "Luke, don't make this harder than it already is."

"You don't know how this is going to unfold. You'll feel different once everything settles down. Once the baby is here, we can work through it."

"That baby doesn't deserve to have someone in his life that resents his existence. I can't heal like this and you can't be the father you need to be with me in the picture. You need to go be a dad and I need to figure out where I go from here." I tilt my head down when the anguish in his eyes threaten to obliterate the flimsy resolve driving me forward.

Luke grabs my face and forces me to look at him. "Don't do this," he pleads.

The tears begin to stream in a steady flow down my cheeks. "I have to."

"No, you don't. Why do you think ending things is your only choice?" Luke's voice grows stronger, more defiant.

"Because you won't." I close my eyes. "Let me go, Luke."

"No," he asserts. When I don't open my eyes or respond, he reluctantly drops his hands and paces the hallway. After several minutes he stops in front of me, his eyes flash with anger. "Tell me how I'm supposed to do that. Tell me how I'm supposed to let the woman I love go."

"I don't know." I don't know how either of us are supposed to move on, but I do know what we're doing right now is hurting both of us. "Goodbye, Luke." I hold out the ring to him once again and look down. If I look at him, I'll start crying again. Eventually his fingers brush against mine and he takes it.

I listen as his heavy footsteps trudge down the stairs. I hear the jingling of his keys as he grabs them from the counter. The door is forcefully shut behind him, leaving me alone to suffer through my choice. A choice that feels logical and right in so many ways but causes me to drop to the floor and grieve.

Chapter 6

"Hello, ladies." Emily slides into the booth next to Vivien.

"Hey, Em," we both say at the same time. We don't bother to point out that she's fifteen minutes late, as per usual.

The waitress returns with the nachos we'd already ordered. "What can I get you to drink, ma'am?"

"Ma'am? I have a birthday and get a boyfriend and I'm a ma'am now?" Emily hangs her head in mock shame.

"Ignore her. She'll have a Cadillac margarita," I say, causing Emily to lift her head and smile sweetly at the waitress.

"So, why are you hiding the new boyfriend from us?" Vivien asks. Emily started dating Rob a couple of weeks ago. She's had several boyfriends since we've known her, so at first we didn't think much of it, but she's different with him. The mere fact that she hasn't tried to share any sex stories about him with us speaks to the seriousness of the relationship.

"You'll meet him soon. He's been super busy with some big project at work. I don't know, it all kind of flew over my head when he tried to explain it to me." Emily takes a chip from the plate and pops it in her mouth.

"What kind of engineer is he again?" Emily has told me several times, but I can never remember.

Emily finishes chewing. "Chemical."

"Speaking of chemicals, Ed wanted me to ask you for your pool guy's info. Apparently, he's too busy to take care of it anymore."

"I'll text it to you." I take a sip of my margarita.

"He would have plenty of time if his mother would stop asking him to come do things at her house." Vivien rolls her eyes. Ed's mother moved into the house down the street from them two weeks ago and ever since I've been getting daily texts from Vivien, venting about the effect it's having on their marriage.

"She lives alone, Viv, I'm sure a mother asking her son for help isn't unusual." Emily winks at me. Vivien is usually the calm, responsible one in our trio, but not so when she gets talking about her mother-in-law. Emily doesn't want Vivien totally worked up, but there's a part of her that enjoys seeing a little fire in her.

"I don't mind him helping her, but does she have to cook for him every time?" Vivien's pitch rises.

"Some moms like to cook." Emily shrugs.

"No. She's trying to make me feel bad. She doesn't think I take care of her son properly," Vivien shrieks, and Emily suppresses a smile.

"I'm sure she doesn't mean it like that." I'm not sure if she does or not, though. I do know that she's offered several times to give Vivien some "wife" lessons, as she called them. She told her that girls these days aren't raised with the skills needed to maintain a proper household. Emily and I thought it was hysterical and came up with our own list of "wife" duties that may be included in the tutorial. Vivien was not amused, especially when Emily mentioned "the art of a perfect blow job" as a potential course.

"She sent him home yesterday with a full pan of lasagna and a dozen cookies." Vivien sounds exasperated.

"That's great, you didn't have to cook dinner." I say.

"I've gained ten pounds since she moved in." Vivien looks at me pointedly.

Emily can't hold back anymore. She lets out the laughter she's been trying to suppress. She's always had an infectious laugh. I join in first, and within seconds Vivien has joined in, too.

"It's a real problem. I can't fit in the new jeans I bought a couple months ago." Vivien complains between her giggles.

Our laughter dies down and Emily changes the subject. "How are you doing, Jess?"

It's been a month since Luke left my house with the ring and my future.

"Hanging in there." I shrug. "I haven't had to see him at work yet, so that's helped."

"Have you talked to him?" Vivien asks.

After I refused to answer his personal calls and texts in the days following the breakup, Luke grew angry enough to suspend all work communication as well. All business was initiated by Aaron during that period. Eventually he needed information from me when Aaron was unavailable, so he broke down and sent me a very professional email with his request. We've kept all conversation since then to business matters only. "Only about work stuff."

"Do you regret ending things with him?" Vivien asks seriously.

"It was inevitable," I say quickly. I've been avoiding this conversation as much as possible because every time I have it, I second guess my decision.

"But you miss him?" Emily asks.

"Every day," I admit. "Eventually, I'll have to see him at the winery. I'm not sure how I'm going to handle it."

"That sounds awful." Vivien looks sympathetic. "I can't imagine if something were to happen to Ed and me and then I still had to see him."

"Do you know when he'll be in town next?" Emily leans in slightly.

"He'll be at the Bianchi's anniversary party in a couple of weeks." They're celebrating their fortieth wedding anniversary with a party at the winery. We're both invited and it's not something either of us would feel comfortable skipping.

"Are you taking a date?" Emily asks then jumps sharply as Vivien elbows her. "Ow! I'm not suggesting she run out and find another boyfriend. I'm simply saying that it may be wise to bring a buffer, a friend who can distract from the awkwardness."

I can't help but laugh. "You've met Luke, right? Showing up with a date would definitely make things worse." He doesn't show it all the time, but Luke has a jealous side I don't want to awaken.

"Those are your co-workers, Jessica, he's the one that should be feeling awkward, not you." I can tell Vivien is a little more testy than normal, probably a residual reaction from her prior mother-in-law rant.

"Do you think he'll bring someone?" Emily asks.

"No," I say too quickly. Then I get the chills. "Oh God, I hope not." I have multiple scenarios currently running through my head and none of them end with me having a great time at this party. "What if he brings her?" My stomach lurches and I quickly take a drink of water to try to calm it.

"Who? Claire?" Vivien shakes her head. "He wouldn't do that."

"For all I know he's with her now."

"Jessica, Luke loves you. I can't imagine him wanting to be with anyone else." Emily flags down our waitress. "We're going to need another round, please."

"They're having a baby. It's likely that some of the feelings they had for each other will come back to the surface." I admit one of my deepest fears for the first time out loud to my friends.

"You think he's going to end up with her." Emily looks like she just figured something out.

"Obviously the thought has crossed my mind."

"I can't picture it." Vivien shakes her head. "Not with the way he looks at you."

"Exactly, we've all seen the look," Emily says, and Vivien giggles.

"What look?"

"The look Luke gives you sometimes. The look that says I can't wait to get you home and tear your clothes off." Emily pantomimes ripping open Vivien's shirt and they both laugh.

"He does not." I blush.

"Does he rip them off with his hands or his teeth?" Emily wags her eyebrows at me.

Vivien pretends to fan herself. "If Ed looked at me like that, I'd probably rip my own clothes off." She turns to Emily "Does Rob look at you like that?"

"No, but I do rip his boxers off with my teeth sometimes." Emily winks at her and we all laugh.

The subject is changed to Emily's relationship and I'm thankful to not have to listen any more about how Luke used to look at me.

"Monica, can you send me the guest list for the Bianchi's party?" I ask, twirling the cord around my finger.

"Oh, I'm sorry I didn't realize you needed it."

"Yes, I need to make sure we have enough staff coverage," I lie.

"Isn't that something Andre should be in charge of? You're busy enough, he shouldn't be pawning his job off on you." Monica sounds irritated and I know why. Our special events manager has a reputation for delegating more of his responsibilities than he should.

"He didn't. I just want to make sure everything is accounted for. A second set of eyes so nothing falls through the cracks."

"That's a good idea..." Monica pauses. "Total headcount is two hundred seventy-six right now, but we should leave a buffer on top of that."

I don't really need the headcount, but ever since the thought crossed my mind during dinner the other night, I want to see that list. He's probably not bringing her, but I need to mentally prepare if he is. "Sounds good. Linda needs my help with something, so just go ahead and email it to me. Thanks, Monica." I hang up before she has a chance to ask any more questions.

I tap my pen anxiously against the desktop. I'm already thinking of a new reason I could give as to why I need the actual list, when I see the new email from Monica pop up in my inbox.

I quickly open the spreadsheet and do a search. The cursor moves to the guest in question almost instantaneously. Luke has accepted the invite and there is a plus one added to his name.

My stomach drops.

"You ready to head over to the party?" Ryan, head winemaker for Bianchi winery, pops his head around the corner of my office door.

I look down at my fitted black dress I changed into an hour ago. "Technically."

"What's the problem?" Ryan steps all the way in and I take in his tall frame. I'm used to seeing him in jeans and a polo at work and I mentally note how well he cleans up.

"Ryan, can I ask you to do something for me and not ask any questions?" Ryan's a good friend, someone I can trust. We had some issues last year when, in a misguided effort, he tried to protect me from Luke. He didn't trust him for a while, but once Luke and I were engaged he saw I was happy and went back to being a supportive friend.

"Is it something I could go to jail for?"

I laugh. "No."

"Is it something I could get fired for?"

I shake my head. "Definitely not."

"Okay, what is it?"

"Would you please walk over to the party and come back to tell me who Luke is with?" I cringe in embarrassment. I've been dreading walking in that room and seeing Luke with someone all week, especially if it's who I suspect. I thought about asking Luke, but every time I typed out a text or started to call him, I got too nervous and chickened out. After not talking for a month, I didn't feel in a position to ask.

"Sure thing," Ryan says with a wink, and true to his word doesn't ask any questions.

I finish applying my lipstick and spritz on perfume while I wait for Ryan to return.

Ryan doesn't say anything when he sits in the chair across from me.

"So?" I prompt.

Ryan only hesitates a moment before seemingly remembering our agreement. "He's with a tall blonde woman."

I don't know how tall Claire is, but I do know she's blonde. Emily and I were drinking wine at her house one night and she talked me into letting her find Claire's social media accounts. In that moment I felt like I needed to know what she looked like. I immediately regretted my decision after seeing numerous pictures of a beautiful, happy, blonde woman with an exciting life full of travel and friends.

"Thanks, Ryan." I know I have to go to this party, so I try to shake off the sick feeling in my stomach. "Let's get this over with."

Ryan and I arrive to a spectacularly decorated barrel room. Soft candlelight flickers against the wine barrels and beamed ceilings. Soothing classical music from the string quartet wafts through the air, mixing with the hum of joyful conversation. I don't chance a look at the tables. I would prefer to save the moment I see Luke with her until after I've had a glass of wine.

Ryan stops to talk to Monica, but I merely wave a hello to her and continue toward my destination. I'm standing in line at the bar when I hear my name.

"Jessica!" Andi, Aaron's wife, walks toward me with open arms and pulls me in for a hug when she reaches me. "So good to see you."

"You, too. You look amazing. I love your dress." Andi is stunning in a strappy black dress that accentuates her tiny waist.

"Thank you." She glances back at the rest of their group approaching. "Have you met Aaron and Luke's newest partner Christina?"

"Not officially. Nice to meet you." Relief floods my body as I extend a hand to the tall blonde. We had a brief encounter at Luke's apartment months ago when I mistook her for someone Luke was dating, but we were never formally introduced. I should have thought of her instead of jumping to the conclusion that Luke would bring Claire.

She takes it with a genuine smile on her face. "Hi, Jessica. Nice to finally meet you."

"We want to start getting Christina more involved with this project and figured tonight was a good time for her to meet everyone. Hi, Jess." Aaron gives me a hug.

"Hi, Aaron." I catch a glimpse of Luke over Aaron's shoulder. He's looking around the room. He looks calm and collected while my heart threatens to leap from my chest.

"At this time, we're going to ask everyone to take their seats, so we can get started," the hired emcee announces.

I excuse myself and find Ryan. I asked Monica specifically if she would make sure we were sitting by each other. He's always good company and hanging out with him may be my only shot at salvaging this evening.

We take our seats at one of the circular dining tables. We're sitting with other winery professionals from the valley, probably because Ryan and I know most of them. Mr. and Mrs. Phelps own another winery in town and have been friends with the Bianchis for years. Jeff Sturgeon, the winemaker from Starlight Winery, and his wife are seated to my right. Jeff did some consulting work for the Bianchis years ago, before they hired Ryan, and they've been friends ever since. On the other side of Ryan are the Maxwells. They own a local tour company and have been bringing their groups to the winery since they opened for business.

Some are still finding their seats when I see Leo, the Bianchis oldest son, walk up to the mic. I haven't seen him in years, but his resemblance to his father instantly reminds me who he is.

"Good evening, everyone," he says confidently, causing the stragglers to quickly take their seats.

"First of all, my siblings and I would like to thank you all for coming this evening. I know it means the world to my parents to have you all here to celebrate with them tonight. I think we would all agree that the love they have for each other is carried forward in the love they have for their family and friends."

Everyone claps as waiters begin filling glasses with sparkling wine.

"My family has an expression that most of you have probably heard at one point or another: you can't run a winery without some shattered glasses. This started as something my parents would say to me and my siblings when we were young and helping my parents here on the weekends. It was designed to make us feel better when we would break something or otherwise screw up, but it's become more than that. It's become a lesson on accepting challenges and difficulties as part of life, as part of marriage. My parents will tell you their marriage isn't perfect, but it's their ability to embrace life's messiness that has made their marriage so durable."

At this point, Leo grabs his glass of wine from the table and lifts it toward the room as we all follow suit. "To my mom and dad, Mr. and Mrs. Bianchi. Congratulations on your long and happy marriage. To many more years of cleaning up shattered glasses together. Salute."

"Salute." I clink my glass against those of my tablemates. The message of the speech had nothing to do with me, nonetheless its irony isn't lost on me.

Dinner commences, and Ryan and I engage in small talk with the other guests. We discuss how the expansion is progressing and new projects the other wineries are embarking upon.

After dessert, the music grows louder, and guests begin to infiltrate the dance floor. I excuse myself to step outside for some fresh air.

I exit the large double doors of the barrel room, eyes glued to a text from Vivien. She's had another run in with her mother-in-law and needs to vent. I'm not paying attention when I lean against one of the low walls bordering the courtyard.

"Are you even going to say hello?" Luke's low voice startles me.

I jerk my head up in the direction of his voice. He's standing about ten feet away from me, wearing a scowl.

"I'm sorry, I wasn't paying attention." I try to explain as Luke pushes away from the wall and walks toward the parking lot.

"Have a nice evening," he says sharply as he walks away. I vaguely hear him mutter something else as he leaves. I don't hear the entire sentiment, but I make out the "fucked up" part.

I nearly have to jog to even keep pace with Luke's long, determined strides. If I want to actually catch up to him, I would need to run, not an easy feat in heels.

"Luke," I call ahead of me, but he ignores my call. "Luke," I say his name louder this time.

"Not now, Jessica." He doesn't look back and he doesn't slow down.

I pray I don't twist an ankle and speed up my pace. When I reach him I step in front of him. His eyes threaten to burn holes through me.

"I said not now." He sidesteps me and continues into the parking lot.

"Please talk to me, Luke."

He stops, spins around and takes a few steps back to where I have frozen. "*Now* you want to talk?"

"I know you're angry with me, but I wasn't ignoring you."

"Maybe you were or maybe you weren't ignoring me tonight, but you've made it clear you'd prefer little communication with me." Luke turns his face up to the cloud filled sky and lets out a big breath. "I don't understand how we got here. We were supposed to be planning our wedding and now we can't even have a conversation."

"I don't want to fight with you, Luke." I say softly. "It's just so hard."

He rubs his hand over his clenched jaw. "I almost didn't come tonight. I didn't want to see you upset, but I didn't want to see you too happy, either."

"I get it. I've wanted to talk to you so many times over the past month, but I don't know what to say and I don't want to make it worse."

Luke looks at me for a moment before taking another deep breath and letting his shoulders relax slightly. "I'm sure coming tonight wasn't easy for you, either."

"I've been dreading it all week." I look down at the ground. "I saw that you added a plus one to your name and I jumped to the wrong conclusion. I thought you were bringing her."

"Claire? Jessica, I'm not going to bring her to anything. We don't have that kind of relationship."

In the spirit of the night I want to believe him.

Luke runs a hand through his hair. "There's only one woman I want to be with."

My chest constricts, and I look away. "We better get back to the party."

"Right. I'll be there in a minute," he says with a hoarse voice. "Oh, I thought you should know, I spoke with Claire and explained the situation with the name. We're naming the baby Finn, after her grandfather."

"Oh." I stand frozen for a moment. The news should make me feel better, yet somehow doesn't. "That's a nice name."

Luke nods.

"I'll see you back inside?" I ask quietly.

"Sure."

It feels hard to breathe as I leave him in the parking lot.

When I reach the doors to the tasting room, I look back at him. Luke's standing in the same spot I left him, hands in his pockets, looking down at his feet. I resist the urge to go back to him and push one side of the heavy double doors open.

"Hey, there." I stammer as I narrowly avoid crashing into Ryan.

"You all right?"

"Yeah, just talking with Luke."

"That's what I figured."

I take a deep breath.

Ryan smiles. "Come dance with me."

"Oh, I don't know if that's a good idea." I hesitate. When Ryan was wary of Luke last year, he did some things that rubbed Luke the wrong way. Luke threatened to go straighten Ryan out more than once, but I was always able to contain the situation. Considering the high stress level of our current situation I'm not sure I would be able ease any tension that could arise between the two men. "I'm not sure I'm in a dancing mood."

"Well, lucky for you I'm a great dancer and I know for a fact that it's impossible to dance with me and not have a great time."

I smirk. "Careful, you don't want to oversell yourself, Ryan."

"Come on." He nods his head toward the dance floor.

"One dance," I agree.

One dance turns into many more. We only stop when I excuse myself for a bathroom break. When I return, I scan the floor for Ryan, looking to see if he found a new partner, but I don't see him.

Finally I locate him. He's standing at the bar talking with Luke. Shit.

They don't appear to be engaged in anything too heated, so I return to our table and have a seat. I'm reapplying lipstick when Ryan pulls out the chair next to me.

"How did that go? I hope you didn't antagonize him." I assume Luke had some words of warning for Ryan after seeing us dancing together.

"It was fine. He just said he wanted you to have a good time tonight."

"That can't be all he said."

Ryan laughs. "He said you deserved a night without him fucking it up, so he was going to do his best not to upset you anymore." Ryan tilts his head. "And that I better not, either."

"That sounds more like him." I nod.

"Come on, I love this song." Ryan smiles as he stands, and I follow him back onto the dance floor.

Chapter 7

"*D*id you have fun at the party?" I ask, as Mrs. Bianchi shuffles through the papers on her desk. She and Mr. Bianchi took the week off after the party to spend time with family and this is the first opportunity I've had to ask her about it.

"We did. It was so lovely to have our kids and friends all there to celebrate with us. And Andre did a fabulous job, as always." She smiles warmly while pulling a pen from her desk drawer. Mrs. Bianchi has always had a soft spot for Andre, our events coordinator, and often overlooks the faults we all see in him.

"The room looked amazing. So did you and Mr. Bianchi."

"Thank you. I appreciate you coming. I know it must've been hard for you to be there with Luke."

"I wouldn't have missed it," I answer, avoiding the latter part of her reply.

"Forgive me for prying, but I didn't see you two together. Did you avoid each other all evening?"

"For the most part." I sigh. Later in the evening I had a nice conversation with Aaron and Andi, but I didn't speak to Luke again.

Mrs. Bianchi takes off her glasses and folds her hands on the desk. "I hate to put you in another awkward situation."

"What awkward situation?" I ask cautiously.

"Mr. Bianchi and I were talking, and we'd like to put together a trip to Napa. We'd like to meet everyone in person before we commit to any deals." Ryan has been working with his contacts in the valley to secure sellers for the additional grapes we need to purchase. We need agreements in place before we can finalize our plans for ramped up production in the fall.

"Sounds like a good idea."

"We can use the trip to meet with owners and GMs, but also take some time to tour other facilities and gather ideas. We thought it would be nice to bring some of you along, sort of a working vacation."

I now see where this is going.

"We wanted to bring you of course, and Ryan and Monica. We also wanted to invite Aaron and Luke. As investors, they're certainly not obligated to go, but I thought they may enjoy it and I value their opinions."

I sigh. Since the party things have been better with Luke. We still only discuss work, but our interactions feel somehow a little less strained. "I don't have a problem with it, if he doesn't. I can't promise we'll be hanging out outside of scheduled business meetings, but we're both professionals. I don't anticipate there being any problems representing the winery in front of business associates."

"Great." Mrs. Bianchi smiles widely at me. "I'll tell Monica to move forward arranging everything."

"Hi, Mom." I answer the phone and proceed to shove my wet sheets in the dryer.

"Hey, sweetie. I'm sorry, but I'm going to have to flake on dinner tonight." My mom is usually so full of life, her subdued tone unusual for her.

"That's okay. What's going on?" I stop pushing buttons on the dryer.

"I'm really tired." Her voice also sounds softer than normal.

"Busy week at work?" I push the button on the dryer and it begins to spin. I shut the door to the laundry room and return to the kitchen.

"Not really. I don't know, maybe it was busier than I think it was. Sorry to cancel on you last minute."

"Don't worry about it. Get some rest and feel better." I'm a little concerned about the exhaustion I hear in her voice, but she won't want any fuss made about it, so I'll let it go for now.

"I will. Did you still need me to watch Amelia in a couple of weeks?" I asked my mom if she would watch Amelia the weekend of the work trip to Napa if Grant wasn't able to.

"No. I spoke with Grant and he wants to have her." I grab the cleaner and a new towel and begin to wipe down the counters, including the toast crumbs I neglected this morning.

"It's good they spend more time together. I'm bummed I won't have her all to myself for a few days, though."

"Summer's almost here, let's plan for her to spend some time with you then." To be honest, it will be a huge help for my mom to take Amelia here and there during the summer. As final phases of the expansion are completed, we're moving into the season were securing new vendors is going to be key. I'm already anticipating a busy summer and fall at work.

My mom pauses a moment and I know what she's going to ask next.

"Any developments with Luke?"

"Our work relationship seems to be back on track."

My mother sighs. I suspect she's disappointed we're not together, even though she doesn't come right out and say it.

"I have to tell you something. Luke came to see me last week."

"Why?" I stop wiping the kitchen counter.

"He wanted to check in and see how you were doing."

"Why didn't he ask me, then?"

"He said he's trying to give you some space."

I roll my eyes. "By going to you? Honestly, I don't love that he did that."

"I know. He knew it, too. Said to tell you when you found out that he just wanted to make sure you were okay."

I let out a frustrated sigh even though part of me acknowledges it was a sweet gesture.

"You should talk to him."

"I have to go. I have to take Amelia to get materials for her history report." I feel bad, but I don't want to have this conversation right now. Talking about Luke is always an emotional endeavor and I'm looking forward to spending a simple afternoon with Amelia.

My mom lets out a heavy sigh. "All right."

"I hope you feel better."

"Thanks. I'll talk to you later, honey."

"Bye." I say and press the end button on my phone.

"Mom?" a little voice calls, and I spin around to see Amelia standing at the doorway to the kitchen.

"Hey, girlie. Ready to go get your stuff for your state report?" I set down my phone.

"Yeah." Amelia lets out an exaggerated sigh.

"What's wrong?" I offer a frown.

"Luke said he was going to help me. He said he did a report on Alaska when he was a kid too." She shuffles her feet beneath her.

"Oh." I walk over to her and pull her in for a hug. "I'm sorry. I know you miss him."

"Don't you?" She asks looking up at me.

"I do."

"Then ask him to come back." She doesn't let go of our hug and neither do I.

"It's complicated, Amelia." I stroke her hair and she pulls away.

"You always say that, but I don't think it is. If you love someone you have them around."

I've tried to shield her from the divorce and now from my breakup with Luke as much as possible. Creating a bad example for her has always been a big fear of mine. "Listen, adult relationships can be complicated, but our relationships with the kids never are. I love you, Dad loves you and Luke loves you, which never changes, even when the time you are able to spend with any of us does."

Amelia nods like she at least understands the gist of what I'm trying to say to her. "Will I ever see Luke again?"

It's such a loaded question and she doesn't realize it. I answer thinking only of what I would want for her in this moment. "I hope so."

I'm not dreading this trip as much as I thought I might. I may actually even be looking forward to a long weekend of wine, good food and establishing contracts that will help solidify planning at work.

"Thanks again for picking me up." I lift my suitcase out of the trunk of Ryan's car.

"Here, let me get that." He grabs the bag mid-air. "No problem. No sense in both of us leaving our cars at the airport."

Ryan pulls his suitcase out and pushes a button to close the trunk. "I can't believe Monica scheduled our flight for six o'clock in the morning. She'd better be waiting with coffee."

"I'm not chancing it. A coffee shop is the first thing I'm looking for once we're inside."

"You and I are going to make great travel buddies," Ryan says as he motions for me to walk ahead of him.

Thankfully, check-in goes smoothly and we're already waiting in line for some morning fuel when I hear a familiar voice.

"Good morning." Aaron's voice sounds too cheerful for this early hour. I turn around to see him approach us with Luke beside him. They both look effortlessly stylish in jeans and crisp button-up shirts. I look down at the jeans and hoodie I threw on this morning and feel underdressed.

"Oh no, are you one of those morning people I've read about?" Ryan deadpans.

"Early bird catches the worm, Ryan." Aaron grips Ryan's shoulder as a greeting. "Good morning, Jessica."

"Morning," I grumble.

"Not you, too?" Aaron laughs.

"Jessica is definitely not a morning person." Luke smirks and his eyes drift off like he's remembering a distant memory. Maybe he's remembering one of the many times he woke me up for a run and I hid under the covers. I always knew he would win those battles, but the resistance was part of the fun.

"It's not that I don't like mornings, I just like them better when people aren't talking." I smile at the end so they think I'm kidding.

"I'll have to remember to never call you in the morning, then," Aaron teases.

"Ten o'clock is still morning. I have no problem with ten o'clock." The line finally moves. "What's going on with this line?" I say impatiently.

"Better make yours a double." Aaron raises an eyebrow at me, a hint of a smile on his lips.

"Don't worry, I will." I nod to him.

"What's on the agenda for today again?" Ryan changes the subject. I'm not surprised he asks, he's never been good at keeping his calendar straight. Some of the people we're meeting with are his contacts, some are Aaron's, but either way Monica is the one who finalized all the arrangements.

"We have a tour and tasting at De Luca winery this afternoon and then dinner at Brix," I say as the line moves again.

"That's right. The De Luca's run an established, successful winery and are interested in selling their overproduction to us. Seem like good people based on our phone conversations. Could be a very promising partnership for both sides." Ryan may not be great with time management and certain details, but he's great with people and knows more about wine than any of us.

"Awesome," Aaron responds as we move up to the front of the line. "All right, Jessica, you're next."

"Thank God," I say, and watch the woman in front of me. I want to be ready to order as soon as she's done. I stare at the register, listening to the men discuss today's events behind me. As I eavesdrop, I note that Luke seems to be in good spirits and it instantly puts me in a more relaxed mood.

Once we all have drinks in hand, we walk to our gate to find Mr. and Mrs. Bianchi waiting for us.

"Good morning," Mrs. Bianchi beams, when we're still several feet away.

"It is for some of us," Aaron says, and then looks at me.

Mrs. Bianchi laughs. "Yes, some people don't appreciate mornings as much as others."

"There's something seriously wrong with all of you." I say before taking a mouthful of hot coffee.

Mrs. Bianchi ignores my comment and is waving to someone behind me. "Good morning."

"Good morning." I turn around to see Monica walking toward us with a big smile on her face. Her boyfriend, Chad, looks like he's struggling to keep up with her. He doesn't appear to be a member of the early morning fan club, either.

We exchange various greetings, but I notice Chad's eyes darting around frantically.

"Caffeine?" I guess.

"Yes," he groans.

"Right back there." I point back to where he just came from.

"Thanks, you're a lifesaver. Monica, do you want coffee?"

"No, I'm good." Monica shakes her head and continues an animated conversation with Mr. Bianchi.

"It's unnatural to be that awake at this hour. I don't think we should trust any of them." I joke.

Chad looks at me and shrugs his shoulders. "I don't get it, either, but I suppose people like us need people like them otherwise nothing in the world would ever get done before noon."

After a flight delay for mechanical reasons and a second hold up due to our baggage carousel being changed, it's late morning by the time we're in the shuttle bus on the way to our hotel. At this point I'm awake and properly caffeinated, so I'm not as annoyed by Monica's perkiness. She passes out folders with our itineraries, bios of the people we're going to meet with and other pertinent information for the weekend.

The bus pulls in the circular driveway of the large stone building. A young man who looks to barely be of drinking age, greets us as we file off the bus and hands us flutes of sparkling wine. A woman with unnaturally red hair, and dressed in a navy suit appears within minutes and hands out room keys and property maps. Besides the crack of dawn flight, Monica appears to have planned out this trip well.

"All right, everyone. We have a few hours before the shuttle will take us to De Luca winery. Feel free to settle in, get cleaned up, whatever you want to do. We'll meet back here in the lobby at three o'clock." Monica says making sure to look everyone in the eye. She pauses when she gets to Ryan. "Three o'clock."

"Got it." He winks at her and she nods.

"You guys want to grab a drink at the bar?" Aaron asks, looking at Luke and Ryan.

"Sure, I need to answer a few emails, but nothing too urgent. What about you, Ryan?" Luke says.

Ryan looks surprised at first but shakes it off. "Sure, why not."

Aaron glances around, but the two couples have already taken off to their rooms. "How about you, Jessica?"

"Yeah, join us, Jessica." Ryan's eyes beg me to stay.

"Thanks for the offer, but I think I'll go lie down for a bit. Enjoy your male bonding." Ryan makes a face as I wave goodbye. I grab the handle of my suitcase and walk to the elevator. Part of me feels bad bailing on Ryan, but maybe this is a good opportunity for Luke and Ryan to get to know each other a little better.

I exit the elevator to the lobby at a quarter to three. I feel refreshed after a room service lunch and a quick nap. I even had time to squeeze in a shower and some proper grooming. As painful as that early flight was, getting here early in the day had its advantages.

I'm about to sit on one of the couches in the lobby to wait for the others when I hear familiar laughter coming from the hotel bar.

When I round the corner and enter the lounge I see Luke, Aaron and Ryan sitting at the bar. All three of them are laughing and trying to catch their breath. They look like they've been having a great time, maybe a little too great.

"Hey, Jess." Ryan spots me first and waves me over.

I give a simple wave back as I walk over. "Have you guys been down here all afternoon?" I ask with a raised eyebrow.

Ryan looks at his watch. "Shit, it's almost three."

"It is?" Aaron isn't caught off guard easily and something about the sight of him realizing he's lost track of time makes me smile.

"Plenty of time." Luke stands and waves the bartender over. He removes his wallet from his pocket and throws a couple of bills on the bar. "Thanks for putting up with us," he says to the waiter, before patting Ryan on the back. "You'll need to come back up sometime and hang out with Aaron and me in San Francisco."

"I will." Ryan stands, too. "I got drinks next time."

Luke nods at Ryan. "I'm going to go hop in the shower." He turns toward the exit and walks toward me. He smiles warmly when our eyes meet. It catches me off-guard and I hold my breath. I haven't been on the receiving end of a genuine smile from him in a while.

"I'm going to run up to my room, too." Aaron smiles at me and then frowns. "Sorry to leave you down here by yourself, Jessica."

"Don't be silly." I shake my head. "I'll be fine. You better hurry, though. You'll have to deal with Monica if you're late."

"She's right. Monica's sweet as pie, until you mess up her plans," Ryan adds, walking past me.

Twenty minutes later we're all reassembled in the hotel lobby. The men arrived back downstairs right before Monica had run out of patience. They've cleaned up nicely and no one would guess they spent the entire afternoon at the bar. With his effortless good-looks and laid-back demeanor, Luke in particular looks like he spent the afternoon preparing for this meeting.

"This afternoon we're heading to De Luca winery. I hope everyone found time to read the information I gave you this morning." Monica's definitely a little amped up. Her jitteriness is going to make everyone nervous. I catch a look Mrs. Bianchi flashes to Luke, causing him to jump in.

"Don't worry, Monica," Luke says calmly, but not in a condescending way. "You can debrief us on the ride. We have a great team here, the last thing we need to do is try too hard to impress them. Everyone just be yourselves, that'll be enough. Bianchi winery is great, but you all are why we wanted to invest in the company. We wanted to work with you and the De Luca's will, too."

Ultimately, this is what Luke's good at. He puts people at ease and builds them up. People are drawn to that and can't help but want more of it. Not to downplay his business knowledge, but I suspect this is the real reason why people want to work with him.

The mood of the group eases as we leave the lobby and walk out to the van. Luke and Aaron sit next to each other again, so Ryan reclaims his seat next to me. This time he doesn't look as happy about it.

"Sorry, I'm sure you can sit by your new friends at dinner." I smile at him.

"It's your fault, you left me with them." Ryan leans in. "I've always liked Aaron, but Luke was different today. You always said there was more to Luke than the over-confident asshole I thought he was. You can't be mad at me for finally agreeing with you."

"I'm glad you're getting along." I pause, debating whether I should ask or not. "So, what did you guys talk about?" I try to sound casual and begin to flip though the bio on my lap for added effect.

"We spent the entire afternoon talking about you." My head jerks up and Ryan laughs. "I'm joking. We mainly talked about the winery, sports…typical stuff."

"That's nice." I look back down at the papers in my lap.

"Luke's a good guy."

I turn my head toward him. "Do you have a man crush, Ryan? He may be interested, you all looked like best buddies when I came downstairs."

"I'm serious. He's sure as hell a lot more fun than I expected."

"He can be." I smile and return to my reading.

When Ryan doesn't say anything else, I look at him again. He hesitates a moment before leaning in again. "He feels awful, you know, about everything that happened with you two."

"I know." I say and turn my attention out the window even though my view only consists of the parking lot.

I know Luke feels awful. I do, too.

Chapter 8

*M*onica and Ryan spend the thirty-minute drive to De Luca winery filling us in on everything we may need to know before we meet our hosts. As we pull up the hill onto the property, all speech halts. The estate is absolutely stunning. The main building is a masterpiece of stone and stained glass. Smaller stone buildings stand to the sides of the main structure, and seemingly endless rows of grapevines stretch out as far as my eyes can make out.

Ryan and I are the last off the bus where an older, grey-haired gentleman, accompanied by a younger man, probably in his mid-thirties, are waiting for us. They're both attractive in their own way, a fact that is amplified by the genuine smiles they wear.

"Welcome to De Luca winery. I am Antonio De Luca, and this is our general manager, Sebastian." It's immediately apparent that our host is friendly and enthusiastic. Luke is the first person to reach him with an outstretched hand.

"We hug here." He grabs Luke in an embrace. I can't help but giggle at Luke's rigid body in the arms of this affectionate stranger.

Mr. De Luca continues to greet Aaron and Chad with hugs and adds a kiss on the check for Monica when it's her turn. She humors him, but I can tell she's not amused.

"You're not going to try to steal my wife this afternoon, are you?" Mr. Bianchi jokes when it's Mrs. Bianchi's turn.

"Oh, no." Mr. De Luca chuckles. He has a fantastic laugh. "I've been happily married to my Valentina, for forty years," Mr. De Luca says, as he kisses Mrs. Bianchi's hand instead. "But you should watch out for this one." He points at Sebastian who looks equal parts embarrassed and annoyed. "Sebastian keeps telling me I shouldn't hug our business associates."

"Or kiss them," Sebastian mutters while shaking Monica's hand.

"I tell him young people today are too uptight. Everyone likes a good hug." Mr. De Luca pulls me in for my turn. Mr. De Luca is animated and uses his hands a lot when he speaks. He's a lot to take in.

"I mean, he is a great hugger, Sebastian," I say, after he lets me go.

"Don't encourage him." His tone is serious, but the smile he flashes at me lets me know he's happy to play along.

"This is the kind of woman you should be looking for, Sebastian." Mr. De Luca leans into me before adding, "he is single, you know."

"Good to know." I nod at Mr. De Luca, but don't look at Sebastian.

After introductions are complete, we follow our hosts through the large wooden door into the tasting room.

"Good afternoon. Welcome to De Luca winery. Feel free to step up to any counter and purchase your tasting tickets."

A young woman in a black skirt and crisp white shirt greets the couple who walked in ahead of us. "Hello, Mr. De Luca. Sebastian." She smiles warmly at the gentlemen, her genuine fondness for them evident.

I pause a moment to take in the room once we're fully inside. It's expansive, about three times the size of our tasting room. And it's packed with people.

"This is impressive," Mrs. Bianchi remarks, her eyes roaming the space.

"Grazie. My wife and I opened the doors thirty years ago and it has grown into this." Mr. De Luca wears an expression of pride.

"It's beautiful." Monica stares at the ceiling. I follow her sightline to the ornate wine bottle chandeliers.

"Beautiful things attract people, brings in the customers." Mr. De Luca beams.

"Such a great atmosphere. It's apparent right away," Mr. Bianchi says to Mrs. Bianchi, but we all hear his comment.

"Yes, everyone is family when they walk in. Everyone is excited to be here." Mr. De Luca waves his arms and wears a wide grin.

"I love it." Mrs. Bianchi speaks louder than normal. I'm not sure if she's allowing her voice to rise above the clatter of the room or if she's attempting to match our host's enthusiasm.

"Make people feel like they are in a special place and they will return." Mr. De Luca nods so quickly he reminds me of one of those bobble head toys.

"Exactly." Sebastian jumps in on the conversation, but his tone is calmer and more business-like. "If everyone is ready, I'd like to get our tour started before the wine production team leaves for the day."

"Sounds great," Mrs. Bianchi says. We follow Sebastian out of the tasting room, through a large set of double doors.

Their wine storage facility is double the size of ours even when counting the additional square footage we recently added. We continue to walk until we reach another set of doors. Sebastian enters a code onto an electronic keypad and the door clicks, indicating it's now unlocked.

"We can bottle up to one hundred and fifty bottles per minute during peak season," Sebastian yells to us over the noise of the bottling machines. "Today we're bottling a pinot noir which has been aging in our barrels for sixteen months."

"What type of barrels are you using?" Ryan asks.

"French oak for the pinot, American oak for everything else," Sebastian responds. "I can introduce you to our wine-maker, Giovanni. His office is right around the corner. He'd be happy to talk shop with another winemaker."

"That would be great." Ryan follows Sebastian leaving the rest our group with Mr. De Luca. He shares some solid advice regarding the industry and growing a business, but with his own colorful style sprinkled in. I look at my phone when it buzzes with a text from Emily asking me to call her later. I'm surprised to see we've already been here an hour.

"How about we continue our discussion over some wine. Sebastian has arranged a private tasting for us." Mr. De Luca breaks from his conversation with the Bianchis to announce the next part of the tour.

Sebastian and Ryan reemerge as we're readying to exit the building and we walk as a group over to the conference room. The table is already set with multiple glasses at each place setting. Glasses of water and individual plates of cheese and crackers are also present.

I walk around the table one way and am happy to see Ryan coming toward me from the other direction. Tasting with Ryan is always educational and fun. Sebastian sits on my other side, while Luke and Aaron sit across from us. This leaves the couples at the other end with Mr. De Luca.

Two servers walk around the table with bottles of white wine, and once everyone has a pour in their first glass, Mr. De Luca raises his. "We're happy to have the great people of Bianchi winery here today and look forward to a rewarding collaboration with you. Salute!"

"Salute!" we all echo.

"So good," Monica hums, after swallowing the dry wine.

"This is our sauvignon blanc. You may pick up notes of green apple and kiwi in this vintage," Sebastian explains.

Ryan hasn't drunk his yet, he's still smelling and examining the pale yellow liquid. He finally drinks it and turns to say something to Mr. De Luca that I don't catch. I look across the table to see Luke and Aaron exchanging notes.

I turn to Sebastian. "How long have you worked here?"

"Almost three years now." He takes another sip of his wine.

"Are you from the area?"

"No, I moved out here for college from Ohio. But I immediately knew California was a good fit for me."

"And have you always worked at wineries?"

"No, my background is in hospitality. I worked for a hotel and well-known restaurant in San Francisco before coming here."

"Napa's quite different than the city. Do you like it?"

"I do. I like the laid-back vibe here. Besides, I can visit the craziness of the city whenever I want."

A server pours another white wine in our second glasses, this one is noticeably more golden in color.

"This is our chardonnay, Mrs. De Luca's favorite. The winery has been producing this varietal for over thirty years now and it's our best-selling white. You may pick up notes of pear and caramelized sugar in this one."

I swirl the wine a little before tasting it. "I definitely taste the pear," I say, to no one in particular.

"Yes," Sebastian agrees, before leaning in to whisper. "This one's not my favorite, but the De Luca's love it and it sells."

"I'm more of a red drinker, myself."

"Me, too." Sebastian smiles. "I suggested to Mr. De Luca we focus on the reds during our tasting today, but as you can already tell he doesn't listen to me much."

Sebastian rolls his eyes in such an exaggerated way that I can't help but laugh out loud. I set down my wine and as I reach for my glass of water, I lock eyes with Luke. I brace for a surge of jealousy from him, but instead he gives me a small smile and turns to resume his conversation with Aaron.

With each sample of wine, the volume of individual conversations rises. At the other end of the table, the Bianchis and Mr. De Luca have added more hand gestures, table slapping and booming laughter into their exchange.

We're on our eighth or ninth taste when the wine really hits me. Wine tasting is like that. You're drinking small quantities of wine at fast intervals and it's hard to keep track of exactly how much you've drank. With these pours in particular being on the generous side and gauging by how I feel, I estimate that we've drank the equivalent of three glasses of wine in the last hour.

"I'd like to give a toast." Mr. De Luca stands suddenly, commanding the attention of the table with his boisterous voice. "I planned on thanking you all for coming to visit us today and toasting to our new business associates, but I changed my mind." Mr. De Luca attempts to look serious before his mouth breaks into a wide smile. "Today we toast to new friends. Salute."

"Salute." We all respond in kind, and clink glasses.

I turn back to Sebastian to resume our discussion about the winery and his experience. I find him and his stories completing engaging. We spend the rest of the tasting exchanging notes on the similarities and differences of the two wineries.

An hour later, after hugs goodbye from Mr. De Luca and handshakes from Sebastian, we're boarding the shuttle to take us to dinner.

"Dinner will be at…" Monica says, before swaying too far to her left and losing her footing. "Oh geez." She rights herself before continuing. "Dinner will be at Brix, assuming we can pull ourselves together."

Mrs. Bianchi giggles. "Serious business is over for the day."

"If that's what serious business looks like to her, I want to be Mrs. Bianchi when I grow up," Ryan says. I think he meant to whisper it but misjudged his volume. Aaron and Luke snicker at his comment from across the aisle.

The ride to dinner goes by quickly as Monica leads a discussion about the De Luca wines. We all agree that their Cabernet was our favorite. Ryan gives a more detailed account of the wine and uses some fancy terms that I'm not even sure the Bianchis are familiar with.

"Showoff." Aaron pretend coughs and we all laugh, even Ryan.

"We're here," Monica announces as the van slows, and we all stand to wait our turn to exit.

"This is the best field trip I've ever been on," I say to Ryan.

"If they would have included winery stops on our field trips, I may have attended school more often," Aaron answers.

"No, you wouldn't have," Luke shakes his head.

"No, you're probably right." Aaron nods.

"Aaron, I'm shocked. I can't picture you being anything other than a studious young man in school." I grab onto the back of one of the seats to steady myself, it feels like the bus is still moving.

"Ah, Jessica, I wasn't always the dashingly handsome captain of industry you see today." Aaron smiles widely. I like buzzed Aaron.

"Oh no?" I tilt my head to one side.

"No." Aaron shakes his head. "I always had big dreams, but...don't tell anyone...but I was actually, just a little bit, lazy." Aaron holds his thumb and forefinger slightly apart.

"Well, I don't believe it." I wink at him.

"It's true."

"And what changed?"

"Andi." Aaron laughs as he's remembering something. "I don't think she knew the extent of my laziness until we moved in together. Let's just say she was having no part of it."

I laugh. "I don't imagine she would." I've only had the pleasure of speaking with Andi a few times, but I've enjoyed every conversation we've had. Andi is opinionated, outgoing, and funny. Based on our interactions I have no trouble believing she wouldn't have a lot of patience for nonsense.

"She came home for lunch one day and found me. I had called in sick to work and was eating pizza and watching a baseball game." Aaron shakes his head. "I remember it like it was yesterday. She stood there with her hands on her hips. She wore a calm exterior, but there was this look in her eyes. She was the scariest, most beautiful woman I'd ever seen. She told me I would pick up after myself and I would get myself to work on time or I could move back home with my mother."

Luke laughs. "I can totally picture it." Luke has described his friendship with Andi as being almost sibling-like, including a fair amount of teasing and competitiveness.

Aaron nods. "That woman changed my life, not putting up with my bullshit." Aaron lets Luke pass him to exit first. Aaron hangs back until Luke is out of earshot. "Kind of like you two." He waves his hand from me toward the front of the van where Luke was a moment ago.

Aaron's back is to me, retreating down the aisle toward the door before I can respond. I follow him outside where the others are waiting for us.

The restaurant is warm and inviting with tall beamed ceilings and stone accented walls. Monica walks up to the hostess station and quickly returns.

"They're getting the room ready for us," Monica says as another hostess walks up behind her.

"Bianchi party?" she asks, wearing a bright smile.

"That's us," Monica responds.

"Allow me to show you back to your table."

We follow the young woman back to an intimate private room. The lit candles atop the long, wood table cause light to flicker across the pair of crystal chandeliers hanging above. I walk the length of the room and start to pull out a chair before realizing that Luke has rounded the table from the other direction and I'll be sitting next to him.

Luke senses my hesitation and pauses from pulling out the chair to my right. "Should Aaron and I switch?"

"No, this is fine." Today has gone really well and I don't want to be the one to make things awkward. Besides, we need to be capable of sitting next to each during a casual dinner.

He nods and takes his seat. I take off my sweater and sit down as well. The waiters arrive with wine already in hand.

"Good evening, Mr. and Mrs. Bianchi and guests. We're ready to begin pouring the wines you preselected for this evening," the blond one says with a flourish, before beginning to pour a sparkling wine into Mrs. Bianchi's glass.

The other waiter, an older gentleman with a warm smile, remains and proceeds to tell us about specials and take any additional drink orders.

"No thanks," I say, when the waiter reaches my glass.

"I'm good," Luke says, when the waiter attempts to pour into his glass.

We both look to Mrs. Bianchi's end of the table where she appears to be giving Aaron marriage advice while sipping on her wine.

Luke asks Aaron a question about their company, effectively saving him from the awkward conversation. I turn my attention to Monica and strike up a conversation about her summer vacation plans.

The table is conversing loudly when the waiter returns. "So, is everyone ready to order?"

"Shoot, I knew I forgot to do something. I haven't even looked at the menu." Mrs. Bianchi laughs again before picking the menu up from the table.

"Give us a couple of minutes," Mr. Bianchi instructs the waiter.

I open the black leather portfolio to find a list of elegant dishes listed in fancy script. I'm trying to decide between the salmon and the steak when Luke leans his head slightly toward me. "Mrs. Bianchi's had a lot to drink today. You've known her longer, is this normal for her?"

I keep my eyes on the menu. "No, this is definitely a first."

"She's not showing signs of slowing down, either."

I peer over my menu at Mrs. Bianchi. She's smiling and rubbing Mr. Bianchi's arm, while reading her menu. "I think the wine just got away from her tonight. She'll be fine."

"Okay, but if she insists we go somewhere else after this I'm faking an illness. I don't need to get trashed on a work trip."

I tilt my eyes up to see Luke is suppressing a playful grin and there is a sparkle of amusement in his eyes.

"We better start working on our alibis. She's very persuasive." I place my hand on his arm as I lower my voice.

The small gesture causes his thoughts to drift for a moment and his eyes soften. He shakes whatever thoughts he was having away and returns to our conversation. "We can tell them I have a headache and you need to go wash your hair."

"What?" I let loose an unbridled laugh before leaning in to whisper again. "That's a horrible excuse."

"Okay, you have cramps, then."

"You are so bad at this."

"Sorry, I don't know a good fake girl excuse." He pauses, and his face turns more serious. "You were right about Ryan, he's a good guy."

"Well, those are words I never thought I'd hear you say."

Luke shrugs. "I admit when I'm wrong."

I don't mean to, but my mind wanders to thoughts of us. For a moment I forget what we were talking about and stare at him.

Luke clears his throat and turns his attention to his glass of water. He takes a big swallow before turning back to me. "As much as I enjoyed hanging out with Ryan today, this is the highlight of my day." Luke points back and forth between him and me with a smile that instantly stirs feelings deep inside me.

I feel the heat rising in my cheeks, so I force myself to look down for a minute. I need a moment to regain my focus.

When I look at Luke again, he's looking down to the other end of the table, and I follow his gaze. I only hear the words "handsome" and "open yourself up." Oh no, Mrs. Bianchi now appears to be giving Ryan dating advice.

"She's definitely going to want to go out after this." Luke smirks.

"I'm sure I'll twist my ankle walking to the car in these heels." I point down to the black pumps on my feet.

"Nice." Luke nods and looks me directly in the eye. "I could always come wrap your ankle if you need me to."

The thought of another time when Luke took care of my injury leads me to think of Luke's warm hands on me which sends an involuntary shiver through me. His grin lets me know he notices, but he doesn't say anything.

"Luke, didn't you used to play college ball?" Ryan yells from the other end of the table. He's desperately trying to save himself down there.

Luke takes another drink of his water before turning to answer Ryan and I turn my attention back to Monica and Chad.

Luke and I engage with the rest of the table for the remainder of the evening. Whatever moment we experienced, I stuff away. I love and hate the things he makes me feel. I have to remind myself more than once that he's not mine anymore, especially when the urge to touch him arises.

I catch snippets of Luke discussing baseball with Ryan and Mr. Bianchi. Monica and I play marry, shag, kill, superhero edition. I tell her she's crazy when she says she would kill Captain America. She threatens that we could never be best friends when I say I would shag Ant-man over Thor. When Mrs. Bianchi announces we should go out after dinner, Luke bumps his knee against mine under the table.

Mr. Bianchi pays the bill when it arrives, and our group slowly vacates the table, still finishing up conversations as we spill out into the cool night air. As we're filing into the bus, I catch sight of Mrs. Bianchi yawning. Looks like I won't have to fake an injury this evening after all.

The thirty-minute drive back to the hotel has allowed everyone to mellow and tire. Monica must have fallen asleep because her hair is a tangled mess as we stand to exit the vehicle for the last time today.

"Good night, everyone." Mrs. Bianchi yawns. "Thank you all for a great day. Get some rest and get ready to do it all again tomorrow."

The Bianchis take off toward their room on the other side of the lobby, while the rest of us get in the elevator. Monica and Chad exit first, followed by Aaron at the next floor.

The next stop is mine. "Good night, boys," I say, exiting into the hallway.

"Ryan, would you please walk Jessica to her room?"

"What?" Ryan and I say at the same time.

"I'm not a fan of women walking back to their rooms late at night by themselves," Luke says, like that explains why he's comfortable with Ryan completing the noble gesture. It shouldn't bother me, but I can't help but wonder why he didn't offer to do it himself.

"Okay," Ryan says slowly. "Is this a test of some kind?"

Luke laughs. "Make sure the lady gets safely back to her room, please."

"Are you sure you don't want to do it?" Ryan sounds as confused as I feel.

I hold my breath. Am I hoping he says yes or no? I'm not sure.

"I'm sure." Luke nods and closes the door to the elevator.

Ryan and I look at each other and shrug our shoulders at the same time.

"I'm fine Ryan, you can take off."

"Luke asked me to walk you to your room, so if you don't mind, I'm going to follow through on his request."

"What is going on with you two? That must have been some serious bro time this afternoon."

Ryan shrugs again. "I may have underestimated him."

I don't say anything hoping he will elaborate without me having to fish for more information. Thankfully Ryan has had enough wine to loosen his tongue and my wish is granted.

"I really thought Luke was only trying to get in your pants when he first showed up. I was trying to be a good friend to you. I mean, I did have some feelings for you back then, but I was mainly trying to detour him." Ryan laughs before quickly adding. "I don't like you anymore."

"Thanks." I pretend to be offended.

"You know what I mean. I think of you more like a sister now and I don't ever want to make out with my sister."

I can't help but laugh. "First of all, ew. Second, I'm glad you're over your battle with Luke."

Finally, at the end of the long hallway, I stop in front of the door to my hotel room.

"Did you have to get the room the furthest away from the elevator?" Ryan pants and places his hands on his knees. I laugh, and he quickly ends his little performance.

"Monica probably put me here on purpose," I say while digging my key card out of my purse.

"Why do you always think she's sabotaging you?" Ryan laughs.

"Oh, I don't, I only like to pretend she's out to get me. Plus giving her a hard time is fun. You know it is."

"It is." Ryan admits. "She's so easily riled up."

"Exactly." I smile triumphantly. "Thanks for the escort. Don't worry I'll make sure to tell Luke you fulfilled your duty to your utmost ability."

Ryan shakes his head and laughs. "I appreciate that." He pauses and looks to be weighing something in his mind. "I didn't get it before, but I think I do now."

"Get what?"

"How he is with you. Luke didn't share details about what's going on with you two, but he did say he misses you and that he wishes he could take away your pain. I mean I always thought the way he watched you was about being possessive, but now I'm beginning to see how genuinely protective over you is. Like tonight, he could have walked you to your room himself, but it wasn't about him, it was about you, so he asked me to do it instead."

My heart aches talking about him and it must be evident on my face because Ryan's face immediately drops.

"I'm sorry, I shouldn't have brought him up."

"It's okay. Thanks again for walking me to my room."

He nods. "See you tomorrow, Jess."

Chapter 9

I sleep in until nine, and as a result wake up in much better spirits than the previous morning. I unplug my phone from the charger and swipe the screen open. I already have a text from Monica.

Morning meeting cancelled. Enjoy your free day. Meet in the lobby at four o'clock sharp for our meeting/dinner at Wilkens Winery.

I decide to start my day with a run and within twenty minutes I'm dressed in workout gear and out the door. I begin to stretch in the elevator until it stops to let a family with their suitcases onboard. I smile at the mom when the young toddler begins to whine about not wanting to leave…we've all been there. A couple of months ago this scene may have triggered a breakdown from me. The reminder is still there, a twinge of loss in my chest, but I don't feel as raw anymore. I know this is something I will always carry with me, but as the months have gone on, I'm able to acknowledge the pain and keep moving forward easier than before.

We arrive at the lobby level and the family waits for me to exit first.

"Thanks," I say as I step out of the elevator and walk toward the front of the hotel.

The sun is already beaming bright and I'm thankful I remembered to grab my sunglasses. I stretch out my limbs for a few more minutes before setting off across the parking lot. When I reach the main road, I look both ways. To my right is a winery in the distance, but to my left are rows of grapevines as far as I can see. I turn left.

I haven't been running regularly, but I had the foresight to think I may want to during this trip. I thought I may need to. Luke's presence was bound to bring with it some level of confusion, so I was expecting to need a run to clear my head at some point. My chest and legs scream at me for a long time, but slowly their protests wane. Eventually, I can't hear them anymore and as my body quiets, my brain speaks up.

Things felt easier with Luke yesterday and I was reminded of what I love about him. When his easy-going charm is on display it balances his confident, driven self in a way that makes him terribly appealing. When I see that side of him and I don't think about our problems, I want what we had back.

Under the blazing light of the morning sun things look different. I have to remember that we do have issues that aren't going away and that his stubbornness is always lurking under the surface. Just like that, the fears and problems look insurmountable again.

I look back at where I've come from. I can barely see the hotel, indicating that I have ventured out far enough for today. I pivot and head back.

By the time I make it back to the front of the hotel, my legs feel weak and my lungs beg for a moment of relief. I pace back in forth in front of the building, watching the valets scurry to retrieve cars for people waiting with luggage. I'm watching a particularly interesting couple argue over whether or not they should eat lunch before heading out of town or wait until they are on the road. They're both dead set on getting their way and it's turning into a bigger argument than the topic warrants.

"Good morning," a familiar voice jolts me from my eavesdropping.

I turn around to see Luke. He is sweaty and breathing heavily, but still manages to pull off one of his heart stealing smiles.

"Good morning." I allow my eyes to move down the length of his body while he turns away for a moment. Why does he have to be so damn attractive?

"Have a good run?" he asks when his eyes return to mine.

"I did. And you?"

"It was good." Luke continues to stretch out his tan, muscular legs. "Yesterday was fun."

"It was." I clear my throat and force my eyes to look at his face. "Mr. De Luca was something else."

"Definitely from a different era." Luke shrugs. "I wouldn't want to work with him every day, but I suppose that's not the point."

"No." I agree. I can handle someone like Mr. De Luca in small doses, but I'm not sure I would enjoy him on a daily basis.

"I really liked Sebastian. He's super knowledgeable about the valley and industry as a whole."

"Yeah, I got that impression, too." I search for something else to say, but I'm distracted by the way Luke continues to stretch and bend his athletic frame.

"The guys were talking about heading over to check out another winery." Luke tilts his head slightly. "You're welcome to join us."

"Thanks for the offer, but I'll pass. I'm going to take advantage of downtime and relax, give Amelia a call later." Plus I need some time to get visions of Luke's sculpted form out of my head.

"How is she?" Luke bends down to retie his shoe and doesn't look at me as he asks the question.

"It's okay to ask about her, Luke." I reassure him. "She's doing good, getting ready to finish out the school year."

Luke looks up and gives me a small smile. "I don't know what's appropriate given the situation."

"I don't, either." I stretch out my neck. My number one goal has always been to protect her. They both miss each other, but I don't know how to fix that for either one of them.

Luke nods. "Well, if you change your mind and want to join, give me a call."

"I will. See you later."

"Later," Luke says, and I watch him walk away. I have a momentary flash back to a time in high school when I did the same and he caught me checking him out. The encounter led to a playful moment when he called me out. It's a memory of him that always makes me smile. I continue to watch him, half-hoping he'll turn around and catch me again, but he doesn't.

I return to my room and take a long shower to cool down from my run and from ogling Luke. Afterwards I put on my bright blue bathing suit, followed by a white, semi-sheer cover up. Some light reading by the pool is my idea of a perfect day. Before I head out, I give Amelia a call.

"Hi, Mom!" she yells into the phone, causing me to pull my phone several inches away from my ear.

"Hi, honey. Just wanted to give you a quick call to say hi."

"Dad and I are at the zoo feeding the birds."

I know exactly what's she's talking about. It's an exhibit where you pay for a cup of nectar and let dozens of birds land on you and clamor for it. I did it once years ago and it completely freaked me out. Trying to watch an active toddler while simultaneously not making any sudden movements that would prompt the birds to bite me was more stress than I was looking for in a trip to the zoo.

"Sounds fun."

"It is." She squeals, and I hear Grant laugh in the background.

"Enjoy your day with dad. I'll talk to you tomorrow."

"Love you, Mom."

"Love you, too." I hang up and take a deep breath. I don't miss being married to Grant, but I miss the family outings.

I follow the signs to the pool area. The sun is on full display now and I slip my sunglasses down over my eyes to shield them. The pool area is small, but quaint. Green hedges and clusters of irises surround the umbrella dotted space. My eyes scan the chairs, searching for an empty one. Toward the back I see a grouping near one of the umbrellas that appears to be unoccupied. I pass by the others, mostly couples, occupying the lounges closer to the pool entrance. When I reach the chairs in the back, I find that they are indeed empty. I'm arranging my towels on my chair when I hear my name.

"Jessica," Ryan says brightly, walking toward me. He's not alone, Luke and Aaron are right behind him.

"Hello, boys."

Ryan proceeds to set his folded towels on one of the chairs and removes his t-shirt.

"How was the winery?" I say, giving a small wave to Luke and Aaron. They nod, and I resume setting up my space.

"It was good. Didn't care for the décor, but the wine was drinkable." Aaron sets his towels down, too.

Luke sets his towels on top of Aaron's.

"Really?" Aaron asks incredulously.

"There are only two empty chairs, what do you want me to do?" Luke laughs. "We came out to swim, anyway."

I glance up from grabbing my book from my bag, to see Luke removing his shirt. There's something unnatural about being this close to a body I'm so familiar with and feeling guilty for even looking at it.

The trio head to the pool and with them preoccupied in the water, I feel less self-conscious. I don't know why I feel nervous to begin with, but the butterflies are present nonetheless. I remove my cover-up and settle onto my towel.

I'm lost in the fantasy world created by the talented author when I register a shadow cross over me. I look up to see Luke grab one of the towels from the lounger next to me. Water droplets drip down his defined chest. I don't think about it when I lick my lips but I'm instantly embarrassed when I see Luke's smirk.

He dries his hair with the towel before lying on the lounge next to me. In an effort to stop staring at his half-naked body, I set my book down and grab my sunscreen.

I smooth the lotion onto every part I can manage. I change approaches several times trying to figure out how to reach the middle of my back. I've nearly done it when Luke interrupts my efforts.

"Do you want some help?"

I don't dare to look at him. He's probably wearing a sexy grin, waiting for me to react to him. "No thanks. I've got it."

"Okay." He drags the word out slightly.

After several more failed attempts to adequately cover my back I realize I'm being ridiculous. There's no harm in letting the man help me with something. "Luke?"

"Yes?" I can practically hear the smile in his voice.

"I think I'll take you up on your offer, after all."

"Sure." I hear him sit up, but still don't look at him. "Scoot closer," he directs, and I scoot across my chair toward him. Neither of us say anything as I pass the bottle of sunscreen over my shoulder. I hear him squeeze some from the tube and I pray he doesn't notice my accelerated heartrate. I focus on remaining calm while listening to him rub the lotion between his hands. I'm in the middle of a deep breath when he places them both on my back. I still have my sunglasses on and take the opportunity to close my eyes without anyone noticing. Luke's hands are warm and strong. I don't mind when he reapplies the lotion to areas I'd already covered. I don't even think of protesting when one of his hands slips under the straps of my bikini top, making sure to not leave any skin exposed.

His hands leave my back and a beat passes before either of us says anything or I even move.

"All done." Luke's voice contains a hint of gravel.

"Thanks." I half turn around to grab the lotion from him, but he's already leaning back in the lounge chair and the bottle is resting on my chair. He gives me a casual smile before I turn and lay back down.

It's a struggle to get back into my book while Luke is this close, but I eventually do. Aaron and Ryan stay in the water the entire time and I read several chapters before Luke speaks up again.

"Jessica?"

"Yes?" I give him a sideways glance, but don't move.

"I know you said you don't want to discuss anything this weekend, but there is something we should talk about."

I'm about to tell him I don't think that's a good idea, when Ryan walks up.

He looks at Luke and freezes. "I'm sorry, I didn't mean to interrupt."

"You didn't." I smile widely at him, no sense for everyone to feel awkward. "I was about to tell Luke it's time for me to head up to get ready. I'll see you all in a little while." I stand and begin tossing my things in my bag.

I glance at Luke before I walk away. He nods, showing no sign of being upset I blew him off.

I take my time getting ready. Between another long shower and taking time to curl my hair, I make it down to the lobby with no time to spare. Luke and Aaron appear to be the only other ones on time.

Luke sees me first. He continues to stare until I'm closer and Aaron hears my approach.

"Hey, Jessica." Aaron looks up from the message he was typing.

"Hi, Aaron. Luke." I smile at each of them. Luke and I gaze at each other for a lingering moment.

"You look amazing," Luke says.

I feel the warmth race through me and my brain suddenly can't think of an appropriate response. Thankfully, I don't have to.

"Hello. Where is everyone else?" Mrs. Bianchi approaches with Mr. Bianchi in tow.

"I'm sure they'll be here shortly," I answer as she gives me a hug first, followed by Mr. Bianchi.

"Too bad our plans for this morning fell through, but it was nice to have some downtime. Did you all have a nice day?" Mrs. Bianchi addresses all of us. It dawns on me that Mr. Bianchi has been more quiet than normal on this trip.

"We did," Luke says as Mrs. Bianchi hugs him. I'm not sure if Mr. De Luca has had an influence on her or if she's behaving more casually because we're away from the winery.

"Wonderful. Were you able to get ahold of Mr. De Luca and work out his contract concerns?" Mrs. Bianchi asks Aaron when she gets to him.

"Yes. After Mr. Bianchi and I sat down this morning and reviewed the material I sent it over to Mr. De Luca. He called me right before I came down here to say he accepts the revised terms. He'll be sending over the signed contract this evening."

"Fantastic." Mrs. Bianchi gives Aaron his hug. "Well, we have something to celebrate tonight then, don't we?"

"Nice work, Aaron. Thanks for making that happen." Mr. Bianchi adds.

"Not a problem," Aaron says as Monica, Chad and Ryan arrive.

"Mr. Bianchi and I feel very lucky to be working with both of you." Mrs. Bianchi nods her head toward Aaron and then Luke, before grabbing Mr. Bianchi's hand. I love how he lets Mrs. Bianchi run the show but supports her at every step. It's not completely unusual for him to take a backseat to her when dealing with the winery, but there's never any question they are a team.

During the ride to Wilkens Winery, Aaron makes the announcement that the De Luca deal is in the final stages of being executed. When he's done, Mrs. Bianchi stands and thanks everyone individually for their hard work. She makes it a point to even thank Chad, who she says serves as a great support to Monica. She mentions that the support that happens behind the scenes is as important as the visual work that everyone sees. I catch the look of adoration she flashes at Mr. Bianchi as she sits back down next to him.

We arrive at our destination right on time and the different vibe the place carries is immediately evident. Besides the building being made of wood, it simply has a more casual feel to it than De Luca did. There's an attractive woman with long dark hair in a logo polo shirt and white capri pants waiting for us. She smiles, revealing perfect, abnormally white teeth.

"Welcome to Wilkens Winery." Her voice is laced with forced enthusiasm and the simple handshake she offers feels more formal compared to the hugs and kisses offered by Mr. De Luca yesterday. I notice when she shakes Luke's hand, she takes extra time, allowing for the opportunity to completely take him in. "My name is Nicolette. I'm the general manager of the winery and I'll be your host today. As I mentioned to Mrs. Bianchi during our phone call, Mr. Wilkens is presently out of the country. He's asked me to show you around today and I'm confident I can answer any questions that may arise."

Nicolette leads us through the large barn style door and I take note of how the feel of the inside matches the outside. There is no one to greet us as we enter, and the furnishings are simpler. Everything is made of wood and while it creates a certain level of coziness, it doesn't feel as special as what we saw yesterday. I really hope Mrs. Bianchi and Monica are taking notes and are planning to incorporate some of the mood created at De Luca winery into our space.

We continue through the tasting room as Nicolette points out key components. "When Mr. Wilkens first opened this place, twenty years ago, he only had the one tasting counter. We added the second one you see here and an additional members-only tasting room toward the back of the property five years ago."

She continues to lead us around the property, through the barrel room, the bottling room and finally the storage room. She is knowledgeable and confident. Her command of the room is impressive. I admire her ability to present herself in such a polished manner, I don't do that nearly as well as she does.

The final room she takes us to is lined with shelves of wine. There are four tables set up with beakers of wine, test tubes and various other scientific looking equipment.

"We thought you might enjoy a little competitive activity as part of your experience here today," Nicolette says once we have all entered the room. "Today you're going to be mixing the five single varietals that we grow on the property. The team that creates the perfect blend will be named the winner."

I glance between Luke, Aaron and Ryan and see their eyes light up.

Nicolette notices it, too, and laughs. "I see we have some competitors among us. I can't tell if this was a very good idea or a very bad one."

"Oh, it was a good one." Ryan smirks.

"This one thinks he's got this in the bag, Luke," Aaron says, nodding his head in Ryan's direction.

"Your cockiness is no match for my experience." Ryan directs his comment at both of them.

"Don't be so sure Ryan. You understand the science, but don't underestimate my ability to be creative." Luke winks at him.

Nicolette giggles and clears her throat. "I'm going to let the ladies be team leaders and pick their partners."

It surprises no one when Mrs. Bianchi grabs Mr. Bianchi's hand and Monica loops her arm through Chad's.

Luke and Aaron immediately start huddling and strategizing.

"Excuse me. I haven't chosen yet," I speak up, and all three men look surprised. Ryan would be the obvious choice, but I have a different plan. "I pick Luke."

No one looks more surprised by my choice than Luke does. He quickly replaces his look of shock with a cocky grin. "She's playing to win today, boys."

"Seriously, Jessica? You do realize this is what I do, right? I'm a wine-make-er." Ryan complains.

"Sorry, Ryan. Luke always figures out a way to win."

Each duo selects a table. When I take my place next to Luke, I see he's still wearing his grin.

"Stop smiling," I say, turning my head so he can't see the edges of my mouth are threatening to curl up.

"I don't think I can," Luke says, rummaging through the supplies on the table.

"Stop it, Luke. Get your head in the game." I playfully chastise.

"You'll only have twenty minutes to create your special blend. I suggest you use your time wisely." Nicolette raises her volume and when I look up, she is looking directly at Luke and me. She's trying to hide it, but I can tell she's frustrated we're not paying more attention to her instructions.

"I hope you're happy, I think we're in trouble now," I whisper.

Luke glances up at Nicolette and gives her a wide smile. She returns it with one that contains a hint of flirtiness. "We're not in trouble. You're unusually competitive today…I like it."

I roll my eyes. "Whatever. Stop distracting me."

Luke picks up the beaker labeled Cabernet. "I like to distract you."

I feel his eyes on me, but instead of looking at him, I grab the sheet of paper from the table and begin reading the descriptions of the wines. "I picked you to win, not so we could exchange witty banter."

"Thank you." He pours the burgundy liquid into one of the test tubes.

"Are you thanking me for picking you or do you think I called you witty?"

"Both."

"You're impossible," I say, pouring the merlot into a small cup to taste.

He takes the cup from my hand after I've tasted it and brings it to his lips. "I can definitely taste the cherries in this one. I think it might blend well with the Cab Franc."

I realize I'm staring at his mouth and divert my eyes back down to the table. Luke pours some of the Cab Franc in a small cup and hands it to me.

"I can't taste the violets." I point to the sheet where the wines undertones have been listed for us. "I still think it would work well with the merlot and cabernet, though."

Luke and I proceed to mix and taste our wines for the next fifteen minutes. We wind up laughing more together than we have in a very long time.

"I think it's pretty good," I say after tasting the final product.

"Hey, you should go over and say hi to Ryan," Luke whispers, before trying the wine himself.

"Why?" I want to make sure his comment isn't stemming for any unresolved jealously. Luke wears a mischievous grin after swallowing the wine.

"Just to be friendly." Luke leans in so his mouth is close to my ear, close enough for me to feel his breath on my neck and I shiver. "If you happen to catch a glance at the percentage of each wine they mixed even better."

I roll my eyes and push him away from me. "Lucas Taylor, we are not going to cheat."

"Finding out what the competition is up to isn't cheating. Stealing their product would be cheating." Luke takes a mouthful of the remaining syrah on the table.

"Time's up," Nicolette announces as she walks around the tables. "I'm going to take your labeled finished product. Our winemaker, Antonio, and I will be the judges."

"This should be interesting." Mrs. Bianchi laughs when she sees the looks flying between the men.

"My money's on Ryan," Mr. Bianchi speaks up.

"Thank you, Mr. Bianchi, always the voice of reason." Ryan nods is his direction.

"I'm going to have to go with Luke. Sorry, Ryan, I think Luke wants it more than you do," Chad chimes in.

"I'll remember that, Chad." Ryan frowns.

"Nope. Ryan's got this one," Monica disagrees.

"You've always been my favorite, Monica." Ryan picks up a glass of wine and drains the remaining contents.

"You know I did help, too." Aaron complains.

"We all know who the brains of that operation is." Luke points to Ryan.

"Traitor." Aaron shakes his head. "Jessica is clearly the brains of your group, so does that make you the beauty?"

"Nope, she's that, too. I'm merely lucky she picked me." Luke winks at me and I feel the warmth spread across my cheeks.

We continue to debate what we think the outcome will be. After several minutes, Nicolette clinks a glass with her pen to get our attention.

"So, we have a split decision. To break the tie, we're going to ask Mr. and Mrs. Bianchi to come up here and do a blind taste to determine our winner."

"You're putting me in a bad situation, Nicolette," Mrs. Bianchi jokingly groans as she follows Mr. Bianchi up to the table where Nicolette and Antonio are. Nicolette pours samples from the two remaining blends. They taste each one and huddle together to exchange notes.

"No question, the first one is the winner," Mr. Bianchi says as Mrs. Bianchi nods in agreement.

"That blend belongs to…" Antonio looks down at his paper. "Ryan and Aaron."

"Yes!" Ryan pumps his fist in the air as Aaron grasps his shoulder and gives him a congratulatory shake.

Luke hangs in head in pretend shame as he walks over to Ryan. When he gets to him, he stands up tall and smiles. "Congratulations, man," he says as he slaps Ryan on the back.

"And me," Aaron reminds him with a smug grin on his face.

"I refuse to believe you had anything to do with this win." Luke shakes his head.

"You may be right, but I'm still sharing in the victory." Aaron throws his arm around Ryan.

"Thank you, Nicolette and Antonio. This has been a lovely afternoon," Monica says. When I look at the time, I realize she's trying to get us out of here in an attempt to arrive at our dinner reservation on time.

"Thank you. It was so nice to meet all of you," Nicolette says before shaking hands with Mrs. Bianchi first.

We all say our goodbyes to our hosts and start to make our way back to the van. I walk with Ryan while he recounts how he decided how much of each wine to blend to achieve his victory. His explanations can be long winded, but certainly educational.

We're about to climb on the bus when Monica looks around. "Where's Luke?"

"Nicolette grabbed him as we were headed out. Wanted to talk to him for a minute." Aaron says absent mindedly while typing out a text.

We all board the vehicle and wait for Luke. I remind myself that Nicolette could have wanted to talk to Luke about any number of things. No matter what rationalization I come up with, I don't like it. I don't like how she was looking at him or that she wanted to talk to him alone.

A few long minutes later, I see Luke running across the parking lot. He's out of breath when he takes his seat next to Aaron. He doesn't look back at me and I try not to let my imagination veer off too wildly.

We arrive on time for dinner at Zuzu, a Spanish tapas restaurant, and are promptly led back to our table. We aren't in a private room this time and the buzz of the restaurant adds to the excitement of our group. We talk and laugh loudly while waiters pour glasses of wine ordered by Mr. Bianchi. Tonight, Luke is sitting at the other end of the table and I realize I'm disappointed I won't have the opportunity to talk to him throughout dinner.

Our salads are being placed in front of us when Mrs. Bianchi starts a conversation with Luke and Aaron. I strain to hear over the clatter of the busy restaurant.

"What do you think our chances are of putting together a good deal with Wilkens?"

"Nicolette said they're definitely interested in doing business with us," Luke says.

"I'm worried their pricing may come in a little high for us," Aaron adds.

"They may, but it would be nice to have some options." Mrs. Bianchi sets down her fork and picks up her wine glass. Mrs. Bianchi stands and the table quiets down quickly.

"I'd like to say a few words. I'd like to toast all of you. You've all gone over and beyond what we expected from each one of you. I truly enjoy working with each of you and consider you family." Mrs. Bianchi chokes on her words and reaches up to wipe a tear away. Mr. Bianchi grabs her free hand and gives it a gentle squeeze. I'm not sure if the alcohol is causing her to be overly emotional, or if it's merely seeing her vision for growing the winery nearly complete. Either way, seeing Mrs. Bianchi be so sentimental makes me tear up. I catch sight of Monica as I'm dabbing the corners of my eyes and hers look glossy as well.

"I want to say thank you. Thank you for everything you've done for us and the winery." With that, Mrs. Bianchi moves her glass toward Aaron's. We all quickly grab our glasses and join in, clinking them together.

I notice several times throughout the evening that Luke and Mr. Bianchi are talking more than usual. I can't make out what they are saying, but it appears to be semi-serious based on their body language and facial expressions.

If someone asked me, I wouldn't be able to tell them why, but something about it gives me an uneasy feeling.

Chapter 10

On the ride back to the hotel, Aaron tells us the story of the first time he took Andi camping. In-between bouts of laughter, he describes the scene of her unpacking her bag inside their tent. He barely gets out the word "hairdryer" while trying to catch his breath as we pull up the circular driveway of the hotel.

Once we're all off the bus, Mrs. Bianchi wraps one arm around Mr. Bianchi's waist. "We're headed up for the evening. Our meeting tomorrow isn't until after lunch, so enjoy the rest of your evening and tomorrow morning."

"Good night." Our voices mingle in the crisp night air.

Chad claps his hands together. "It's early and I could really go for a drink other than wine. First round's on me."

We walk as a group into the lobby bar and quickly snag an area in the corner. Chad asks what everyone would like and goes to order our drinks from the bartender.

I take one of the big comfy chairs closest to me, while Monica reserves the loveseat for her and Chad. Ryan sits next to me, leaving Luke and Aaron to sit across from us. We argue about which winery had better wine, but all agree that we preferred the overall ambiance of De Luca.

When Chad returns with a tray full of drinks, Monica stands and passes them out. After grabbing his old fashioned, Ryan leans back in his chair and addresses Luke. "So, let's hear it."

Luke grabs his phone from his pocket and begins to scroll through. I recognize that strategy of distraction. "Hear what?" he asks, without looking up.

"Why did Nicolette pull you off to the side before we left?" When Ryan whispered to me on the bus that he was going to ask Luke about it, I half hoped he wouldn't. Unfortunately, the other half of me was dying to know, too.

"She was asking about the deal…" Luke trails off as he sets his phone on the table in front of him.

"And?" Ryan prods.

"And she asked me to join her for dinner." Luke's eyes dart over to me for only a brief second. "Obviously I told her I wasn't interested."

Aaron laughs. "I think we finally found the one person that can make Luke feel uncomfortable."

"And you are clearly enjoying that a little too much." The corners of Luke's mouth curl up as he points at Aaron.

"Must have been a little more than a simple invitation to dinner?" Thankfully Chad is thinking the same thing I am and asks the question I can't.

"She was a little aggressive." Luke takes a drink of his gin and tonic.

"Nothing wrong with being an aggressive woman," Monica says defensively.

"Absolutely. In the right context, when a woman goes after what she wants, it's downright sexy." Luke catches my eye for a split second before returning his attention to Monica. "This was not one of those times."

Ryan gives me a sideways glance before returning his attention to Luke. "You don't strike me as the type to be thrown off by a woman asking you out."

"I'm not, but I'm not comfortable with a business contact…never mind. We may be doing business with this woman, so I don't want to say anything else. I would appreciate it if this doesn't get back to the Bianchis, either."

"Sure," Ryan and I say at the same time.

"I can respect that, Luke." Monica nods.

"One misstep doesn't make her a bad person," Luke adds.

"No, of course not," Monica agrees.

Everyone is quiet for a beat, before Aaron changes the subject. "I thought the blending activity was a lot of fun. Any thoughts on us doing something similar at Bianchi?"

"I think our customers would really enjoy the opportunity to do something like that." Monica looks excited about the prospect of planning a new event for the winery.

I didn't get all the details of Luke's interaction with Nicolette, but at least the change of subject affords me the opportunity to actually participate in a conversation. "It was a lot of fun. Is anyone else in the valley doing something similar?"

"Not that I'm aware of, but I can find out," Ryan responds.

The conversation moves forward onto less serious topics such as baseball, upcoming summer plans and the latest movies everyone has seen. When the topic changes again, this time to how the vineyard is looking after experiencing heavier rains than normal this last winter, I excuse myself to use the restroom.

"I'll go with you." Monica rises, too.

We walk side by side until we reach the door where Monica looks back at me as she pushes it open. "That must be difficult."

Her look tells me she's referring to Luke and I take a guess that she's referring to the Nicolette encounter. "Luke's a good-looking man, women flirting with him is nothing new."

"Not that. Well, not only that. I'm talking about how hard both of you try to pretend to not want each other."

I shake my head. "Monica—"

"I know we're not best friends or anything, but we've worked together for a while now and, as the only other female in the group, I feel an obligation to share my observations."

I laugh nervously. Monica and I have always had a strictly working relationship, so I'm not sure what to expect from her in this situation. "Okay."

"I'm not sure if the others notice it, too, but I catch all the little looks you give each other."

"There's a long history there. We still care about each other," I admit.

"Obviously. He was really uncomfortable talking about Nicolette. He kept glancing at you."

"I know." I saw it, too.

Monica sighs. "I've had a lot of wine, so I'm just going to say it. I know a lot has gone down with you two, but you are so obviously still into each other. It's exhausting watching you two try to fight that connection."

I think about denying it, but ultimately, she's not wrong. "It is exhausting."

Monica gives me a knowing smile. "If fighting what you're both feeling isn't working, maybe you should stop."

I give her a half smile before she turns and enters a stall. We don't say anything else until I push the door leading out into the hallway open. I turn back when Monica begins to speak.

"I hope I didn't overstep too much in my observations." She smiles and her eyes motion behind me.

I turn back around to see Luke leaning against the wall. This dim lighting makes his eyes appear a deep shade of midnight blue, but there's still a sparkling quality to them. He wets his lips with his tongue causing me to stare at his mouth.

"Hello, ladies." Luke greets us both, but his eyes are focused on me.

"Bye, Luke." Monica laughs lightly as she walks away, leaving me alone in the hallway with that mouth.

"Hey." Luke's husky voice makes me shiver and I pull my sweater tightly around me.

"Hey." I try to sound casual, but my high-pitched voice gives away my nerves.

"I wanted to tell you what happened with Nicolette."

"It's not my business." I wave a hand in dismissal.

Luke lets out a frustrated sigh. "Can we not do this tonight? Will you please let me explain the Nicolette encounter without reminding me how badly you want it to not matter to you?" His words are pained as he stares straight at me the entire time he speaks.

"I obviously care, Luke." I rewrap my sweater around me. "I don't feel entitled to ask."

Luke nods and relaxes his shoulders again. "I don't owe the others any more information about what happened with Nicolette, but I'm not going to put you in a situation to wonder.

She pulled me aside and asked if I'd like to have dinner with her. I sensed she didn't mean in a strictly business sense, but I tried to keep it on that level. I told her I'd have to pass, that we had plans to have dinner as a group. She then suggested I come over after, said something about our chemistry being instantaneous. She wanted to negotiate the final terms of the contract with me privately."

Luke pauses, and I feel like I have to say something. "What did you say?"

Luke dips his chin slightly. "I politely told her I preferred to keep business separate from my personal life. She said she understood completely and apologized if she was too forward. I reassured her it was fine and that there were no hard feelings. I went to shake her hand and she came in for a hug. I was hesitant, but after Mr. De Luca…I don't know…there was a moment where I thought I should go with it, that maybe she was just a hugger. When she pressed up against me, I quickly realized this was not a friendly hug. As I tried to pull away, she tightened her grip and whispered something about having talents beyond running a winery and that she would never tell anyone about anything we did. I admit I was caught off guard. I may have panicked a little." He cringes at the memory.

I can't help but let out a small laugh. "What did you do?"

"I pushed her away, mumbled something about not needing any new talent at this time and ran away."

I try to suppress my smile.

"It's not funny." Luke smiles while he says it, but then his face actually turns serious. "Not only is she a business associate, she's a family friend of the Bianchi's."

"I didn't realize that."

"They don't want everyone to know. They told Aaron and me but asked us not to say anything. They wanted to let everyone form their own opinions about her."

"And now she hit on you and you pushed her and ran away," I state matter-of-factly.

"Do you have to say it like that?" Luke cracks another smile.

"Isn't that what happened?" I give him a puzzled look and try to keep a straight face.

"Yes, but I thought you may offer a female perspective that would make me feel better."

"I'm sorry. She was really unprofessional." I place a hand on Luke's forearm.

"What are the chances she'll forget it ever happened?" Luke cocks his head to one side.

"Here's the thing, I doubt she's going to tell the Bianchis, but she's not going to forget about it, either. If a man pushed me away, I'd be mortified."

"I don't get the impression that Nicolette gets embarrassed or deterred easily." Luke takes a step closer to me. He gazes into my eyes for a lingering moment. "And for the record, I can't imagine any man pushing you away."

He brushes his fingers against my forearm and my skin heats from the contact. My brain is still trying to catch up to what my body is experiencing, when Luke drops his hand. I follow his eyes to the other end of the hallway.

Ryan is frozen in place. "Sorry, guys."

"I...I was heading back," I stammer.

"Me, too." Luke follows my hurried escape from a moment which felt dangerously right.

When we arrive back to our corner, Chad is returning with a tray of shots and Monica is grinning at me. I gladly take one.

"Should we wait for Ryan?" Monica asks.

"No," I say quickly, my nerves are shot at this point and I have high hopes the little glass in my hand can help.

"To good friends." Chad raises his glass and we all follow. "And good tequila."

After another round of tequila shots, everyone is smiling more than normal and feeling more relaxed with each other. No one brings up anything else to do with work or the winery, instead beginning to ask more personal questions. Monica and Chad have just shared the story of how they met through a mutual friend. Apparently, she wasn't interested at first, but Chad was taken with her right away.

"How did you two meet?" Monica waves a hand between Luke and me.

"In high school," I state plainly, and shrug my shoulders. I'm not too drunk to know we're entering dangerous territory here.

"I know that, but like how? I'm assuming this one was a real player in high school." Monica points toward Luke, her volume has risen proportionally to how many drinks she's had.

"That hurts, Monica." Luke places a hand over his heart.

"I can't imagine you falling for some cute boy's cheesy lines, so I'm dying to know how it happened." Monica is undeterred by Luke's fake upset.

"You're right. Cheesy lines would've never worked on Jess. She was way too smart for that. I had to appeal to her kindness."

"He asked for help in a class we had together," I add, my heartbeat increasing at the memory of that day.

"I practiced how to ask her for a week. I knew I had one chance to get it right, to get her to say yes. If she thought I was full of shit, she'd never give me another chance."

I look at Luke and I don't know if it's the nostalgia of the memory or the tequila, but I swear he looks the like the teenage boy I fell for back then. "I didn't know that." I scrunch my nose at him.

"I was totally nervous." Luke looks surprised that I didn't already know this piece of the story. He turns his attention back toward the rest of the group. "She was way out of my league."

"I was not." I laugh. "I was quiet and didn't know how to talk to boys at all."

Luke shakes his head. "She was smarter than the other kids and more interesting than the other girls. The thought of asking her out was daunting."

"Please, Luke, no one here is buying that you were afraid to ask a girl out. You were every bit as confident back then as you are now." I roll my eyes and grab my glass from the table.

"You've always underestimated the effect you have."

I feel the heat rise in my cheeks. I take a big drink of my water, trying to cool myself down and as I glance over at Monica, she gives me another deliberate grin.

"I love hearing how people met." She winks at me before continuing. "How did you meet your wife again, Aaron?"

Aaron tells the story of how he met Andi at a party in college, but between all the alcohol coursing through my veins and the set of intense blue eyes which catch mine more often than they should, I'm having trouble concentrating.

An hour and several stories later, Monica yawns and slaps Chad on the hand he has resting on her knee. "Alright, guys.

Time for us to head up." She wags her eyebrows at Chad and any resistance he may have been ready to put up instantly falls away.

"Good night, everyone," Chad says quickly before heading to the bar to close out his tab.

"Yeah, it's late." Aaron rises out of his seat. "I have to go close out my card, too."

"Me, too." Ryan looks a little clumsy getting out of his sunken in chair.

"Good night boys. I'll see you tomorrow." I give a small wave after I have finished standing.

"I'll walk you to your room." Luke rises quickly and I swear my heart stops for a few seconds.

I remind myself that he had Ryan walk me to my room last night, and that I shouldn't look for too much meaning in it.

We reach the elevator and I push the button. When the door opens, Luke puts his hand on the small of my back and leads me into the elevator, an action hard to not read into.

Once inside the elevator, I lean back against the wall to steady myself. Luke leans against the adjacent wall and smiles at me causing my body to flood with warmth.

My eyes move down his body. His relaxed stance shows off his confidence as much as his flexed arms resting on the rails show off his muscles.

I know he's watching me, but the alcohol fills me with an unusual boldness. When I raise my eyes back up to his face, I see his sexy smirk. I wait for a snarky comment, but he doesn't offer one.

He holds my stare until the elevator dings and the doors open. I step off and feel Luke follow me. The long walk down the hallway feels even longer than it did last night. I reach my door and insert my key. I don't open the door when the light flashes green, though, instead I turn around. This may not be a great idea, but I'm suddenly hit with the thought that I'll regret it if I go in that room alone.

I step toward him and close the space between us. I only hesitate a moment, working up the courage to ask the first question that comes into my foggy brain. "Do you want me, Luke?"

His eyes widen for a moment. I like that I've caught him off guard, it gives me a rush of confidence and I know I want to see that reaction from him again. I fight the urge to look away and instead stare into his eyes waiting for an answer.

"Every piece," he whispers, his voice laced with desire.

I take another step toward him and place my hand on his chest. "I've really enjoyed the last couple of days."

"Me, too." His breathing shallows as his voice deepens.

I take one more step, our bodies as close as they can be without touching. I raise my chin and he instinctively lowers his mouth to mine. The kiss is slow and tentative, like we're learning our way around each other's lips and mouths for the first time.

I'm about to deepen the kiss, when he places his hands on either side of my face. He slowly pulls his lips away from mine but stays close. "As much as I'm enjoying this, we've both had a lot to drink." I see the battle in his eyes. He wants this, but he doesn't want to take advantage.

"You were the one who said you liked aggressive women." I lean back and smile at him, but he still looks unsure. "Luke, I know what I'm doing. I'm not that drunk."

He backs up against the hallway wall, pulling me with him. "Come here." He runs one hand through my hair while the other remains firmly grasping my hip. I gasp when he pulls my body against his. "I want to do lots of really bad things to you right now," he whispers in my ear, but then pulls back again. "But we should talk first."

He's probably right. No, I know he's right, but his grip increases on my hip and I can feel his excitement pressed up against me. I take a deep inhalation to try to calm myself down. His cologne invades my nose and it makes me want to bury my face in his neck.

"Luke…" I say as I reach my hand down and begin to stroke him through his pants. I'm emboldened even more when I feel his chest still, holding in a breath. "For one night can you allow me to not overthink everything?"

Luke's head lands with a thump against the wall behind him in a cross of frustration and pleasure. "Jessica," he moans my name, and it only increases my hunger.

"I want you, Luke." I place a soft kiss on his neck and I feel him growing harder beneath my palm. "I want you to take me into that room and remind me why you're the man I can't get over."

"Jesus." Luke groans and pushes us off the wall. He grabs my hand and pulls me over to the door of my hotel room. He reinserts the key card I left there and opens the door, pulling me inside with him.

The door shuts with a thud and he spins me around so my back is to him. He slows his pace as he slides the zipper of my dress down my spine and I shiver. My long curls are swept to one side, as he pushes the dress off my shoulders and I watch as it falls in a pool around my feet. His warm mouth makes contact with the sensitive skin on the back of my neck, sending a tingling sensation through my body. When he reaches around and massages my breasts through my lace bra, I let out a whimper.

He doesn't say anything but takes the cue. After unhooking my bra and sliding it off, he trails kisses down my spine until he reaches the hem of my panties. He hooks his fingers through the sides and slowly pulls them down. I step out of them, his hands trailing back up my legs as I do.

"I want you to kneel on the bed," he says in an authoritative voice. I look back to see him removing his shirt.

"My shoes…"

"Leave them." He kicks off his shoes and tosses his wallet onto the bed. His pants and underwear come down in one movement. I enjoy the site his body flexing as he undresses. I continue to watch as he retrieves a condom from his wallet and puts it on. When he's standing there naked and ready, he repeats his command. "On the bed."

I'm not usually a big fan of being told what to do, but in this moment, it's definitely working for me. I climb onto the bed and Luke grabs my hips and pulls me closer to the edge. He moves his fingers between my legs until they find the spot that makes me moan.

"I love that you're ready for me." He rubs my wetness around with his fingertips. "And I get so hard when you make sounds like that."

"Luke…" I pant as he pushes his fingers inside me.

"Say it again." Luke's voice is ragged behind me. "Say my name again."

"Luke…" I breathe out. I'm already beginning to feel the pleasure building. This man knows exactly how to touch me and exactly what to say while he's doing it.

"Again." He continues to work his fingers inside me and outside in a slow, rhythmic fashion. I'm right on the edge of my orgasm until he pauses for a moment before repeating the sweet buildup again.

When I feel like I can't take anymore my voice comes out hoarse. "Luke, I want you inside me."

Without hesitation Luke climbs on the bed and pushes me forward. He grabs my hips and thrusts into me. My body and mind are overwhelmed by him and I cry out. He thrusts again, but harder this time.

He continues to pound into me until we're both panting and on the verge of climaxing.

"Luke…" I murmur.

"What, baby?" He never calls me that and it somehow makes the encounter feel less intimate.

"Don't call me that." I say more sternly than intended and he stops.

He leans down and kisses the back of my neck. "What, Jessica? What do you need?" He whispers, his breath tickling my skin.

"I need you," I say, and immediately wish I didn't. Not because it isn't true, but because those words are laced with too much meaning for tonight.

Luke pulls out of me. My body aches and my drunken brain scrambles for the words to salvage the moment, but before I have a chance to jam my foot any further down my throat, Luke grabs me and flips me over. He swiftly reenters me, and I gasp.

"I want to watch you come apart for me. I want you to see me when I can't hold back any more." Luke lowers his head and raises by breast to his mouth. The suction is enough to send me over the edge.

I moan deeply and arch my back. When I half open my eyes, I see Luke. He's studying me as he continues to slide in and out. Soon his pace increases and with a final push he joins me with his own release.

He slumps on top of me and we lay there trying to catch our breaths. After a few minutes I gently push on his chest and he rolls off of me. I retreat to the bathroom to get cleaned up and immediately begin to wonder what this meant to me. What did it mean to him? Is he sleeping here tonight? Should I be mentally prepared for him to head back to his own room now? Do I want him to?

I apply my facial cleanser and rinse it off with cold water. My mind continues to swirl as I brush the taste of alcohol and Luke from my mouth.

I return to the bed to find Luke laying on his back, his eyes closed. He could be asleep, or he could be pretending.

As I climb into bed, a warm hand encircles my wrist.

"Come here." Luke's voice is raspy as he pulls me down toward him and wraps his arm around me.

Once I am lying against his naked chest, he begins to stroke my hair.

We don't say anything else. I didn't know until this moment that this is ultimately the closeness I was looking for tonight.

"Jessica," Luke groans.

My head feels as groggy as his voice sounds. I roll over and tuck the blanket tighter around my neck.

"Jessica, your phone is ringing." Luke rubs my shoulder.

I struggle into a sitting position and take note that the room is still completely dark. The clock on the nightstand indicates it's only four in the morning. I untangle myself from the blankets and drag my heavy body from the bed. I pause for a moment trying to remember where my phone is. Luckily, it begins to ring again giving away its location somewhere on the other side of the room. I follow the tune and finally realize it's still in my purse from last night. By the time I pull it out the call has gone to voicemail.

My brain wakes up when I see that I have three missed called from my mom. I press the buttons to call her back. She doesn't answer, so I hang up and try again.

"What's going on?" Luke rubs his face as he sits up.

"I'm not sure, but my mom called three times in a row. She's not answering her phone now." I finish my sentence as my second call goes to her voicemail. My stomach churns with uneasiness. I immediately call her again.

This time she answers after the second ring.

"Jessica." I'm not sure if it's my imagination or not, but she sounds weak.

"Hi, Mom. What's going on?"

"I'm in the hospital."

"What happened?" I do my best to maintain a calmness in my voice even as my entire body tenses.

"I was having some pain in my chest and some difficulty breathing. They're not exactly sure, but they think I may have had a small heart attack."

I'm fully awake now.

"They're running more tests. Not sure if I'm going to need surgery or not. I'll call you back when I know more." She sounds out of breath.

"Okay." I'm careful to keep my voice steady. "I'm in Napa, but I'll get back there as quickly as possible."

"Okay." The fact that she doesn't tell me not to worry or try to convince me to stay where I am is unlike her.

"Call or text me when you know anything." I want to keep her on the phone until I can see her face, but I know she needs to rest and communicate with the doctors.

"See you soon," she says and hangs up.

"Shit." I press the end button and quickly enter a search for the phone number for the airlines. While the screen loads, I frantically go through my laptop bag looking for my plane ticket.

"What's going on, Jessica?" I hear the concern in his voice, but I don't have time to stop and answer him. I find my ticket and turn to face him.

"I have to get…" I start to respond to him, but someone answers at the airline.

"Thank you for calling. How may I assist you today?"

"Good morning. I need to reschedule a flight."

"I can help you with that. Where are you flying from and to what destination?"

"My current reservation number is E887695." I wait until I hear the typing stop. "I need your next available flight out of Oakland or San Francisco, to San Diego or Ontario." I pace while the person on the other end loudly punches keys on their keyboard. I walk to the window and turn around to find Luke standing in the middle of the room. He looks as worried as I feel. I raise a hand to let him know I'll explain in a minute.

"I have room on a flight out of San Francisco to San Diego at four o'clock this afternoon."

"Four o'clock? That's too late. You don't have anything for this morning?" My voice reaches a higher pitch in frustration. I'm not upset with the airline, just anxious to get to my mom.

"I'm sorry ma'am. That is the earliest flight I have room on."

I let out a frustrated sigh. "Thank you. I'll figure out something else." I hang up and start to pull up another airlines information when Luke gently places his hand on mine.

"Let me help. What's going on?"

"My mom's in the hospital. They think maybe a heart attack. They don't know. She mentioned she may need surgery. I have to be there if she needs surgery. The airline didn't have any available flights until this afternoon. That will be too late. I could drive a car there quicker, except I can't, because I think I'm still drunk from last night." I ramble off my thoughts.

Luke grabs me gently by the shoulders. "I got this. You get a shower and pack up your stuff. Be ready in an hour."

This is the part where I would normally tell him that I appreciate his offer, but I'll figure things out. Not this time.

"Okay."

Luke quickly throws on his clothes, his phone already to his ear as he walks out of my hotel room.

An hour later I'm putting my final toiletries in my bag when there is a knock on my door. I open the door to find a freshly showered Luke with his duffel and garment bag. "

"The car is about thirty minutes out," he says, looking at his phone. When he looks up and sees the confusion of my face he continues. "My driver, he's going to drive us back to Temecula. Even with the private plane, avoiding the airports ended up being the quickest way to go. I'm going down to grab us some breakfast to go. I'll meet you down there?"

His company owns a plane, but I didn't expect him to use it for this. When he said he had this I figured he'd make some calls to other airlines. I feel bad he's waking up his driver this early on a Saturday, but I need to get to my mom, so I accept the offer. "Thank you."

"You're welcome." He nods and leaves.

It dawns on me as I run around the room, throwing my belongings into my suitcase, I've never had a man in my life take care of me the way he does.

Chapter 11

"Wake up, Jessica, we're here." Luke's warm hand grips my shoulder.

I push myself up to a seated position and glance around in order to get my bearings. We're in the parking lot of the hospital.

"I can't believe I fell asleep," I say, checking my phone for missed messages and putting my shoes back on.

"I'm glad you did. It's why I asked Dean to bring the limo, more room to lay down."

"I hope you did, too," I say, eyes still on my phone.

"I didn't, but that's okay. I kept an eye on your phone to make sure you didn't miss any calls or texts."

"Thank you." I text my mom to see if there's been any developments or if she's been moved to a different location. Our texts ended around six in the morning when the nurse demanded she get some rest. At that point she didn't have any of the results from the tests they ran. When I don't receive a response after a few minutes, I get out of the car and Luke follows behind me.

Images of our night together and its undetermined meaning, flash through my brain. I might feel embarrassed if I wasn't so preoccupied with my mom. "Thank you again for getting me here."

"Anytime. I'm happy I could help."

"I'll give you a call later." I give him a hug and he holds me a beat longer than a friendly version.

"I'm going in with you," he says as he releases me.

"You don't have to, you've done enough." Part of me wants him to stay, but it's not fair for me to. I've already muddied the waters with my actions last night.

"I need to be here," Luke says earnestly, and motions for me to lead the way. "Let's get you in to see your mom."

I don't have time to argue, so I let him walk beside me toward the large stucco building. Despite everything that's happened between us, there is something about his presence that is still comforting.

We step through the large sliding glass doors and it hits me. It's not the same waiting room, not even the same hospital but the room feels dreadfully familiar. I'm suddenly very warm and my legs feel heavy as memories of that awful night creep back in. I freeze and try to catch my breath.

"I've got you," Luke says quietly as he takes my hand and leads me to the check-in desk.

"May I help you?" A woman with remarkably long fingernails asks without looking up from the papers she's writing on.

"I'm looking for my mother, Jill Adams. She came in last night. I don't believe she's been moved out of the emergency room yet."

The woman punches a series of keys on her keyboard and appears to be reading something on the screen.

"What's your name, honey?" she asks using a more polite tone this time.

"I'm her daughter, Jessica Rogers."

Her nails click loudly against the keyboard as she enters additional information. She stares at her screen longer than makes me comfortable.

"Ma'am, I'm going to ask you to have a seat. The doctor will be out to speak with you in a few minutes."

"Why is the doctor coming out to see me?" The panic causes my pitch to elevate.

"Ma'am, it's normal protocol. The doctor will be able to give you more information." Her face remains neutral, giving nothing away.

"Will you please tell me what's going on?" I beg, but the woman only offers me a sympathetic look.

"Thank you," Luke says politely, and leads me to the other side of the room. "She's not allowed to say anything. It doesn't mean..." Luke doesn't finish that thought.

"Ms. Rogers?" A deep voice calls from the doors that have been pushed open.

"Yes. That's me." I walk quickly to where the distinguished looking, bearded man is standing.

"Hello, I'm Doctor Evans. Come with me."

Luke follows us, his hand on my back, as Doctor Evans leads the way to a private sitting room.

I pause in the door frame and hold both sides for support. I don't want to go into this room. This seems like a place where bad news is delivered.

"Ms. Rogers," the doctor says as he takes a seat in one of the chairs facing the door, and motions for me to take the seat across from him. His expression changes from serious to apologetic when he sees my face. "Mrs. Rogers, your mother is upstairs being prepped for surgery. I'm going to insert stents into two blocked arteries. She may need additional procedures in the future, but for now the stents should open up the arteries and she should start to feel better."

"Oh, thank goodness." My body slumps in relief. Considering where my mind had wandered to, this is good news. I take a deep breath and finally take the seat across from the doctor and Luke sits beside me.

The doctor explains what he's planning to do, but my foggy brain isn't able to grasp all of what he says. I do take note when he mentions she'll need to change her diet and get more exercise.

"It's a fairly straightforward procedure," he assures me. Luke places his hand on mine sitting in my lap. "Would you like to see her?"

"Can I?" I perk up.

"Yes, you and your husband can go see her." He inaccurately assumes the status of my relationship with Luke, but I don't correct him. "I'll send someone down to get you in a few minutes."

"Thank you," I murmur as he exits the room. I lean back and close my eyes. When I reopen them, Luke is leaning forward in his chair with his head in his hands.

He must sense me looking at him because he sits up quickly, shaking off his own emotions. "She's going to be all right."

"Yeah," I say as a nurse pokes her head in.

"Mrs. Rogers, I can take you and your husband to see your mother now."

"Oh…" I'm unsure how I should proceed.

"I'm not Mr. Rogers, just a friend." Luke squeezes my shoulder as he stands. "Can you point me back toward the way we came in?"

"Jessica," my mom's voice is frailer then I've ever heard it.

"Mom," I say as I approach the hospital bed. There are a multitude of tubes and wires connecting her to various machines and sensors.

"Hey, honey. I'm glad you're here," she says with a little more strength, and I nod. "Sorry you had to cut your trip short."

"You know I don't care about that. How are you feeling?"

"Like crap." She gives a small laugh. "But I suppose no one comes to the hospital because they feel good."

"No." I smile at her. Her sense of humor being intact is a good sign.

"I'm fine, or at least I will be," she says confidently.

"You better be." I take her hand in mine.

"Tell me about Napa? I've always wanted to go there." My mother has never liked too much attention directed her way. I'm sure the fact she's lying in a hospital bed with me staring at her is making her uncomfortable.

"It's really beautiful." I want to know more about her right now, but she clearly is looking for a distraction. "Rolling hills, grapevines everywhere you look, you'd love it."

She yawns, and I immediately feel guilty for not getting off the phone with her earlier this morning.

"All right, ladies, it's time to go down." A nurse I haven't seen before enters and begins to rearrange some of the tubes and wires.

"I'll be waiting outside." I give my mom's hand a squeeze. "Let's get you fixed up and then we can plan a mother-daughter trip to Napa."

"That would be lovely." My mom squeezes my hand back. "I love you, Jessica."

"I love you, too." I kiss her on the forehead and give her hand one final pat.

When I enter the waiting room, Emily is waiting for me. I texted her as soon as we started the drive back and knew she would show up here at some point. Vivien is in Palm Springs with Ed for the weekend. She offered to drive back, but I told her that wasn't necessary. Knowing that she may come back to check on me anyway, I made her promise not to cut her time with her husband short.

She stands and wraps her arms around me. "How is she?"

"She's good. The doctor said it's a routine procedure."

"Jill's a tough lady. She'll be fine." Emily gives me another hug.

"Yeah. I was worried the whole way here but seeing her was good. I'll be a little anxious until I can get her home, though," I say as I relax into the embrace.

"Of course." Emily releases me and shifts her attention to the doorway with an icy glare. "What are you doing here?" Her sudden anger surprises me and I whip my head around to see Luke wearing the same look of shock I imagine is displayed on my own face.

"Nice to see you, Emily. I gave Jessica a ride back from Napa." Luke tucks his hands in his pockets.

"Why the hell would you do that?" Emily sneers.

"Emily?" I know her well enough to know she must have a reason for the hostility, but I can't for the life of me place where it's coming from.

Luke raises his hands in front of him. "I'm not here to cause any problems. Maybe it's time for me to leave."

"That would be great." Emily gives Luke a hard look. I look back and forth between them. All indications are that Emily wants to cause bodily harm to Luke and he has no idea why.

"What's going on?" I direct my question at Luke.

"I don't know." He shakes his head. "Whatever it is can be discussed later. You deal with your mom. Try to get some rest and I'll call you tonight." Luke kisses me on the cheek and I hear Emily mumble next to me.

"What?" I look at her with wide eyes.

"I said 'fucking asshole'." Emily enunciates every syllable while crossing her arms across her chest.

I glance around the waiting room. There's only one other family in here. They don't turn in our direction, but they had to have heard Emily's comment. They deserve to deal with whatever they have going on without having to listen to our drama.

"Both of you, outside, now," I order as I push Luke back toward the door and pull Emily along with me.

Neither of them say anything as we exit the building. It's late spring and the temperatures in Temecula have already shot up into the high eighties. I pull off my sweatshirt layer and stare, waiting for one of them to say something.

"Well?" I throw my hands up in front of me when they exchange more looks instead of speaking.

"I don't know what's going on, but whatever it is doesn't need to be hashed out while Jill's having surgery." Luke frowns at Emily.

She glares at him before turning a softer look at me. "I'm sorry, Jessica. As much as I hate it, he's right, this isn't the right time."

"It's a little late for that." My volume raises out of frustration. I look at Emily, who continues to glare at Luke. I catch him shake his head at her, indicating he still doesn't think this is the right time for her to bring up whatever has her so worked up.

"You tell her, or I will." Emily shoots more daggers his way. "You wouldn't be here right now if you already had."

Recognition dawns on Luke's face. "This really isn't the time, Emily."

"No, it isn't, but she deserves to know."

"And I'm going to tell her." Luke runs a hand through his hair. "You're making this sound like a bigger deal than it really is."

"Not a big deal?" Emily sucks in a quick breath and pulls out her phone. We all wait while she searches for something. "I'm sorry, Jessica. I was looking through Instagram this weekend and came across this." She hands me her phone.

"Jessica. I'm not sure what Emily has seen, but there is something I need to tell you." Luke says while I stare at the picture of a woman staring out at a cityscape.

"You, shut it." Emily chastises. "You had all weekend to tell her."

It takes me a minute to take it all in. The blonde in the picture has her back to the camera and is angled in a way that

I almost didn't notice her pregnant belly. I look at the name on the account ClaireBear88.

"Thanks Emily, I really don't need to see another picture of her." I try to hand the phone back to Emily, but she shakes her head.

"Look again," she insists as she pushes the phone in my hand back toward me.

I sigh and reluctantly return my eyes to the image of Claire. My chest tightens, being forced to look at her, the woman who has what I want. I know Emily wouldn't insist unless it was important, so I try to see what she's trying to show me. Claire has her back toward the camera and is looking out over the city. She looks happy, peaceful even. My heart starts to race. I was so caught up in the sight of her I didn't notice before.

"Only one more month until we bring our little guy home." I read the caption aloud. "Why is Claire in your apartment?" I question without taking my eyes from the phone screen, a surge of jealousy courses through me.

"This was obviously not how I planned on showing this to you," Emily says from beside me, but I don't look at her. "Not with your mom in the hospital. Not with him here."

I hold the phone up to Luke. "Is Claire living with you?" The words feel rotten and cloying in my mouth.

"She's not living with me, she's staying in the guest room for a few months." He opens his mouth to continue, but I speak before he can get any other words out.

"Are you serious?" Up until this moment I was still holding out hope that this was some sort crazy mix-up.

"She had some plumbing problems with her apartment and with the baby being due soon, we decided her staying at my place made the most sense. She doesn't have to stress about bringing a newborn home to a hotel room and I can help out with the baby. It seemed like a good solution." He shrugs his shoulders as if he told me he bought a new piece of furniture.

"Unbelievable." Emily huffs out a breath.

I glare at her, letting her know her work here is done. I keep the glare in place when I look back at Luke. "When did she move in?"

"This weekend, while I was in Napa…with you." Luke eyes me steadily.

"And you didn't think this was something you should tell me?" I knit my eyebrows together.

"There never seemed to be a good time. I tried to tell you by the pool."

Luke mentioned we needed to talk, but I thought he wanted to rehash old issues, not introduce new ones. "I didn't know you were going to tell me that Claire had moved in with you." I realize I'm blinking too much and force myself to stop.

"It really isn't that big of a deal. She's staying in my guestroom for a little while," he states calmly, but his jaw tenses.

This is the dark side of Luke's confidence, when he can't admit he's wrong. "It is a big deal, Luke, don't act like I'm the one being unreasonable here," I raise my voice in an effort to get him to hear me.

"It's only a big deal if you make it one. Nothing is going on with Claire and me, end of story." Luke's gesture that the conversation should be done only irritates me more.

"You don't get it. It really doesn't matter if you're sleeping with her or not, she's your priority now." Saying the words aloud makes them hurt even more than they did when they were merely running through my head.

"No, she's not, but my son is." His frustration causes his volume to rise as his eyes fix on mine. "Up until this weekend you've wanted nothing to do with me. If you want more say in the choices I make, you need to actually be a part of my life."

My entire body tenses. "You're right, I'm not a part of your new life with Claire and the baby. Thank you for reminding me."

"That's bullshit. You're only not part of it because you don't want to be. You've made it clear, it's not worth it to you." Luke stares at me hard, daring me to disagree with him.

"You're right, it's not worth it for me to be a part of a relationship filled with secrets and lies."

Luke throws his hands up. "This wasn't a secret. For the record, I even tried to tell you again last night. You were the one that didn't want to talk, remember?"

"I didn't want to repeat the same argument we've been having for the past four months. I was enjoying remembering the parts of you that I used to love." My use of the past tense was meant to sting and by the look on Luke's face he didn't miss it.

Luke nods slowly. "Yes, you made it very clear in the hallway what parts of me you missed. I wanted to tell you, but bringing up another woman's name while you were grabbing my dick seemed inappropriate."

My mouth hangs open and I see Emily out of the corner of my eye slink away. I had forgotten she was here.

"Well, you had your fun, now you can go home to your family." I lift my chin and try to hide the hurt.

"For fuck's sake." A humorless laugh escapes Luke's throat and he runs a hand down his face. "I thought we made some progress this weekend."

"Sex isn't progress." I shake my head at him. "Besides, everyone knows you're not opposed to the meaningless variety." I throw his bachelor past back in his face even though we both know last night could never be mistaken for being meaningless.

Luke narrows his eyes. "I'm sorry to hear you say that. Last night meant something to me, but clearly it didn't to you."

Working to keep the tears in requires all my energy, so I just shrug instead of answering.

Luke takes my silence as confirmation and his eyes tighten. "Well, you sounded like you were enjoying yourself last night, so you're welcome."

"You're such an asshole." I turn to walk away, but Luke grabs my elbow. "Let go of me." I yank my arm away from him.

"You act like you hate me, until we're in the bedroom and you're moaning about how much you need me."

I take one step toward him and stop. "I admit I wanted you last night, but you will never be the man I need."

Luke's arms fall to his sides as he admits what we both already know. "Last night was a mistake. You're not ready to move past this."

"Move past which part, Luke? My baby dying or the part where you moved on with your new family?" My voice trembles as I near the depths of my resentment.

"I didn't want to move on without you. Claire is having my baby and whether we like it or not she has to be a part of my life."

I notice my hands are shaking as I brush loose stand of hair from my face. "You're right, she does, but I don't. There's the bright side. We don't have a baby, so we don't have to be together. Like you said, our baby simply wasn't meant to be."

Luke flinches. "I never meant it like that." His expression reflects how I felt when he would say that to others. Maybe now he'll finally understand.

"It makes much more sense in hindsight. I thought when you told people you would move on and have another child, you were talking about with me, but it turns out you weren't. I didn't know you already had your backup baby coming from someone else."

Luke stares at me like he doesn't recognize me, with a mix of sadness and disgust.

I take a deep breath and slide my hands in my pockets in an attempt to stop the trembling. "I wondered why you didn't care as much as I did. I wondered how you couldn't understand my grief, how you weren't completely gutted like I was."

"That's not fair. Just because I showed it differently, doesn't mean I wasn't hurting, too." Luke looks away from me.

I ignore his comment and continue with my rant. "And you kept trying to get me to move on quicker. But it was easier for you, you weren't as devastated as I was because you already had your recovery plan in place." My heart races, begging me to stop, but I need to get the anger out of me before it explodes.

"Jessica…" Luke's voice has an edge of warning to it.

"You said it before, everything works out how it's supposed to. Everything always works out for you, Luke. I mean it's probably a good thing, actually, two babies would have been too much. Luckily you only have to be a dad to one now." I don't know why I expected to feel better after releasing such ugliness. I should have known I would only feel worse.

"That's enough," Luke says sharply, and I flinch. He clamps his eyes shut and I feel like I'm going to throw up. "I'm going to say this as calmly and as kindly as I can." He takes a deep breath and fixes his eyes on mine. "Don't you ever suggest that us losing our baby was in any way a good thing for me. There is no bright side to it and I sure as hell don't think I can replace one child with another."

Luke appears to have run out of words. His stormy blue eyes search mine. I don't know what he's looking for, a glimmer of hope, a sign of regret maybe, but I give him nothing. I have nothing left to give.

Luke looks confused. "I kept hoping that if I loved you hard enough, you'd come back to me."

"You don't love me. You love the idea of me, the idea of us." I look down at the concrete.

"How can you say that?"

I can't look at him, but I can hear the hurt in his voice. "I knew we would never work."

"You knew we would never work? Why were you going to marry me, then?" The hurt in his voice is replaced by a flash of anger.

When I don't answer, Luke makes his own assumptions.

"I didn't ask you to marry me because you were pregnant, but maybe you said yes because of it."

It's not true, but too much damage has already been done, this is merely a symbolic nail in the coffin. "It doesn't matter now anyway."

When I look up at Luke, he looks at me with an expression that gives me chills. "I thought you could never do or say anything to me that would make me not want to be with you, anything that would make me not believe in us, but I was wrong. I loved the woman you became even more than the girl I first loved in high school, but I don't see her anymore. She's gone, and I'm done."

Luke turns from me and walks back to his waiting car, not stopping once to look back as I crumple on a nearby bench and allow the tears to flow.

Chapter 12

*M*y mom's procedure, to have cardiac stents inserted, went well and the doctor only kept her in the hospital for one additional day before sending her home. The next week revolves around hospital visits, paperwork and conversations about after-care. She isn't exactly excited about her new diet and exercise requirements, but she promises she'll try her best.

Despite the stress and over-tiredness, I enjoy focusing on my mom for a change. It's an added bonus when I'm too worn out at the end of each day to beat myself up too much over my fight with Luke.

With my mom settled in at home and her slow adjustment to her forced reduction in activities in effect, it's time for me to return to work. Mrs. Bianchi suggested I take the entire week off, but I insisted that working on Friday will make for an easier Monday next week.

"Good morning Linda," I say as I juggle my purse, laptop bag, lunch cooler and an extra-large coffee.

"Good morning. Let me help you." Linda rises from her chair.

"I got it, but thanks. Anything urgent I need to know about?"

"No, but Mrs. Bianchi did ask me to have you call her when you got in. How's your mom?"

I give a small laugh. "She's good. She's already complaining about not working. It's going to be a long two weeks."

"Well, I hope her being antsy is a sign that she's feeling better."

"I think it is."

"Ryan said the trip to Napa was successful and fun. Did you have a good time? I mean before you got the call about your mom."

"Did I have a good time in Napa?" I repeat the question, giving myself time to think. "I did, then I returned to Temecula and reality and the bubble burst."

Linda gives a sympathetic frown. "Are you referring to something with Luke?"

"Of course."

"I'm sorry. Want to talk about it?"

"Not really, maybe later." The truth is I'm embarrassed by a lot of what happened. Our fight at the hospital was disgusting and in hindsight, I shouldn't have slept with Luke, not without any real resolution to our issues. I let myself get swept up in the moment and will now have to pay the price for my lapse in judgement.

"I'm here if you need an ear."

"Thanks." I continue my walk to my office while talking. "I should make that call to Mrs. Bianchi."

I unload my arms and turn on my computer. Once everything is up and running, I dial her number.

"Hi, Jessica." She sounds weary.

"Hi, Mrs. Bianchi. Linda mentioned you wanted to speak with me?"

"Yes. Can you come by my office please?"

"Of course. I'll be right there."

I grab a pen and notepad and head to her office. When I arrive, the door is shut. I knock, and Mrs. Bianchi calls out, "come in."

When I enter the large office, I find her sitting at her desk. She looks like maybe she's coming down with something, pale and fatigued. "Hi, Jessica. Have a seat."

I sit and smile, even though my gut is telling me I should be prepared for bad news.

"I hate that this has to be a rushed conversation, but things are moving quickly and I'm making a big announcement at the management meeting this afternoon. I didn't want you to walk in unprepared."

"What's going on?" She averts her eyes for a moment. Her nervousness is making me uncomfortable.

"We're selling the winery." There is unmistakable sadness in Mrs. Bianchi's voice.

"What?" Nothing could have prepared me for this news. I close my mouth when I realize it's hanging open.

"I know it's a shock." Mrs. Bianchi looks at me thoughtfully.

"But why? You love this place." I can't think of one reason Mrs. Bianchi would be selling this place.

"I do, but some things are more important." Mrs. Bianchi pauses. She appears to be searching for words. "Mr. Bianchi's sick."

"Oh no." The words are so inadequate to describe the sinking feeling in my stomach.

"Prostate cancer, stage four." Mrs. Bianchi fiddles with the pen in her hand.

I don't know much about prostate cancer, but I know that stage four almost never leads to a great outcome. "How's he doing?" I ask fighting back tears.

"He's trying to be strong for me, for the kids. The only thing he's asked for is to move to Texas to spend what time he has left with our kids and grandkids." Mrs. Bianchi grabs two tissues from the box on her desk and hands me one.

"You don't have to sell it. You could take some time away. I can help run it while you're gone." Walking away from the winery is probably something she never foresaw doing.

"I appreciate the offer and I thought about that option, but I don't want to come back and run this place without him. I know most people think of me when they think of this place, but he handles so much behind the scenes, things I never wanted to be involved in. It's been ours, together, this whole time and I can't imagine it any other way."

I nod, knowing no words to make this even a tiny bit easier.

Mrs. Bianchi dabs her eyes. "We talked it over with the kids and since none of them have any interest in stepping in, we decided that selling it made the most sense."

The Bianchi's two sons and daughter all live in Texas. Their daughter married a man serving in the army and relocates her family every few years. Last I heard, they were stationed at Fort Hood. One son is a successful pediatrician in the Dallas area. The other son got married a few years ago and they moved to Austin to be near his wife's family. Mrs. Bianchi and I had a laugh about how they all ended up completely different, but within a few hours of each other. Now, it's apparent that this was a blessing.

"Are you sure you want to do this?"

"I'm sad to leave this place, but I'm positive it's the right decision. I'm getting older and spending time with family isn't something I've been able to do a lot of over the years. My grandchildren are thrilled I'm coming to live near them and that makes me happy." Mrs. Bianchi presses the tissue to the corners of her eyes again. "I can't stay here without him."

I stand up and walk around the desk. I don't know what else to do other than wrap my arms around her. We stay that way for a few minutes before I return to my seat, wiping my damp eyes with my crumpled tissue as I do.

"So, what's the plan? How can I help?"

Mrs. Bianchi takes a deep breath. "Well, I hired a general manager."

Mrs. Bianchi mentioned hiring one a few months ago. Someone who could potentially lighten her work load.

"That's great. I didn't realize you had already started the interview process for that position."

"We didn't. You met Nicolette at Wilkens. She's agreed to move down here and take the position."

"Oh." I try to sound excited about it.

"She's Mrs. Everett's granddaughter and she has great experience. I think she'll be a great addition to the team." Mrs. Everett is a long-time friend of the Bianchis. She's even invested in different projects at the winery over the years.

"I'm sure she will." I nod and remind myself I should keep an open mind. Nicolette seemed very capable. Maybe I'll end up really enjoying working with her. I plaster a fake smile on my face. "When does she start?"

"Next week. She'll be spending the next month working closely with me to learn the operations side of things, but she should spend some time with you, Ryan and Monica, too."

"We can definitely work out a schedule. When do you leave for Texas?"

"In a month. It's not a lot of time, but…" I don't blame Mrs. Bianchi's reluctance to verbalize there may not be a lot of time left for Mr. Bianchi. "The winery may take a while to sell, but at least I can leave knowing the day to day operations will continue with minimal interruption. The sale can be finalized without me here."

I can't believe we're having this conversation. I try my best not to burden her with my sadness about the situation. "Do you have any buyers in mind?"

"No, but I've asked Luke and Aaron for some help. I know it's not something they would normally handle, but I trust them, and they've agreed to give it a shot as a personal favor. The thought of selling this place to the highest bidder makes me sick to my stomach. I want this place left in good hands when I'm gone."

"I'm sure Aaron and Luke will be able to find someone suitable."

"I hope so."

Mrs. Bianchi's phone chimes with an incoming text, it's a good time to excuse myself.

I rise from the chair. "Thank you for telling me before the meeting. Please let me know if you or Mr. Bianchi need anything."

Mrs. Bianchi smiles softly. "Thank you, Jessica."

I nod and leave the office, sickened by the news.

I return to my office and get started on cash reports Mrs. Bianchi asked for last week and I've yet to complete. I'm doing a final check of balances when I hear the door to the office open.

I hear low voices but can't make out what Linda or the person who entered is saying. I'm looking at my doorway, as if that will somehow give me superhuman hearing capabilities when Luke walks through, causing me to startle.

He closes the door and takes a seat. "Mrs. Bianchi said she met with you."

I clear my throat and adjust myself in the chair. "She did."

"It's awful." Luke looks around my office, anywhere but directly at me.

"It is." I set down the pen I was nervously tapping on the desk.

Luke shifts in the chair. "Mrs. Bianchi called on Monday and asked if we could rearrange our schedules to be out here yesterday and today. I had no idea this was why."

"She said you and Aaron are going to help find a buyer?"

"We're not brokers, but we're going to try to guide the process for them. She feels we have a good understanding of this place and the type of person who she would want to sell it to."

"Right." I say tapping my nails on the desk.

We're both quiet for a long time.

"How's your mom?" Luke is the first to break the uncomfortable silence.

"Better. Reluctantly resting. She's getting restless and bored." My hands move to my stomach were a dull ache is building into something more.

"Sounds like Jill." Luke's eyes shift down to my hands. "About the other day at the hospital—"

My stomach sinks even further. "Luke, I said some things that day—"

Luke raises a hand to stop me. "It's fine. That's not the way you should have found out about Claire staying with me. I wish I could go back and have that conversation go differently." Luke keeps his voice steady and controlled.

"Right." I look down at my desk. "I shouldn't have said...a lot of things." I can't bring myself to repeat anything I said that day.

Luke clears his throat. "I'm not proud of myself, either." When I look at him his eyes turn away quickly, examining the plaques and artwork hanging on the walls. "We should focus on our working relationship for the remainder of the time I'm associated with the winery."

"Remainder of the time?"

"When the winery is sold, Aaron and I will be bought out. We won't be investors here any longer. Then we won't have to see each other anymore." Luke looks away, pretending to be distracted by his phone.

"Of course." A sudden chill in the air makes me grab my sweater from the back of the chair.

"I'd like to set aside our personal feelings and get this winery sold for the Bianchis." Luke is looking at me when I turn back around. He's sitting up a little taller in his chair. "Aaron and I would like for you to sit in on meetings with potential buyers. You know the Bianchis better than we do and can offer some deeper insight into the daily operations."

"No problem." I purse my lips together.

"Great. I don't think anyone could ever replace the Bianchis, but I look forward to working together to find someone who will love it and its people." Luke abruptly rises and gives me a nod. "Aaron or I will be in touch." He walks out before I can respond.

I lean back in my chair and look up at the ceiling, trying to reconcile all that's happened.

"Hey, Mom," I call out as I let myself in.

"Hi, Grandma." Amelia sings out, making her way past me and into the house.

"My favorite girls." My mom is standing in the kitchen pulling a cookie sheet from the oven.

I frown at her and keep it plastered on my face until she sees me.

"Don't give me that look, they're not for me, they're for Amelia." Amelia squeals and my mom sets the tray on the counter before pulling her in for a big hug.

"Fine, but you're also supposed to be resting, not baking cookies." I take a seat at the counter and she hands me an oatmeal raisin cookie. I take a bite and smile. She really does make the best cookies.

"See, these cookies are healing. They even made you smile." She winks at me before going to the fridge to pour Amelia a glass of milk.

"Grandma?" Amelia says in her sweetest voice.

"Yes?" My mom echoes her tone.

"Can I please take my cookies into your room and look through your jewelry box?" Amelia wraps her arms around her grandmother's waist.

"Sure." She rubs Amelia's back for a minute, then loads her up with several cookies on a plate. Definitely enough to ruin her appetite for dinner.

I grab another cookie from the sheet as I pass by on my way to the fridge. As expected, my mom has a half empty bottle of rosé in there. I grab it and pour myself a glass. "You're not supposed to be drinking wine, either."

"I haven't, that's from last week." She raises her hands in a surrender pose. "I promise I'm trying to be a good patient."

I take a big swig. It's too sweet, but I'll take it tonight. "That's what they say right? Doctors and nurses make the worst patients?"

"Assholes of any profession make the worst patients."

I laugh. "How're you feeling?"

"Good." She answers too quickly, causing me to raise an eyebrow at her. "I'm more tired than usual, but otherwise I feel back to normal."

"Good." I pour more wine in my glass.

"So, when were you going to tell me about your fight with Luke?" She leans back, her arms crossed over her chest.

"Who told you I had a fight with Luke?" I ask, but I already know. "Emily." I answer my own question.

"She stopped by yesterday to say hello."

"Traitor." I don't really mind that Emily said anything. I planned on filling my mom in once things settled down with her health.

"She figured you'd already told me." My mom shakes her head. "But I told her no, that apparently you were holding out on me. Is this what getting older feels like, being left out of things because everyone assumes you're too frail to handle it?"

"Nobody's going to mistake you for a brittle old woman anytime soon." I take another sip. My taste buds have already started to dull to the overly sweet liquid.

"What happened?" Her look of concern indicates she's done joking.

I try to stretch the tension out of my neck. "Luke had her move in."

"Had who move in?" She looks confused for a second and then realization dawns. "His baby mama?"

"You aren't allowed to say that ever again." I shake my head. "But, yes, he had her move in."

"Why? They aren't together, are they?" The pain in my mom's voice echoes what I feel in my heart.

"He says no, that he's only trying to be there for her and the baby." I fiddle with the edge of the placemat on the counter. "She's only supposed to be there for a couple months."

"One might say that's a nice gesture." She shrugs as I peer over the top of my glass at her. She quickly shakes her head. "I'm not one of those people, though. Having her move in seems inappropriate."

"Tell me about it." I sigh.

"So, he told you about it and then you fought?" my mom says cautiously. She's right to assume there's more to it.

"No, he didn't tell me. Emily figured it out on social media and confronted him about it."

She lets out a rush of air. "I don't think he goes looking for it, but that boy sure does know how to find trouble."

The way she says it causes me to snort and choke on my wine. My mom's laughter joins mine momentarily before the mood returns to the serious one the conversation warrants.

"What are you going to do?" She looks at me thoughtfully.

"Nothing." I sigh.

"Nothing?" My mom sounds incredulous.

"Nothing for now. When we talk about it, we both end up more angry. Honestly, this entire year has been overwhelming, and I need some quiet. Luke is not quiet."

My mom twists her mouth and looks at me thoughtfully.

Before she can say it I add. "I know he didn't plan this and part of me respects he's trying to do the right thing, but it doesn't mean this is the right situation for me. Maybe we're simply very different people at different places in our lives."

"Maybe." My mom looks sad.

"The fight at the hospital was bad, Mom. I said some really mean things. Luke said he's done. The only reason we're even talking is because of the business of selling the winery." I lean back. "I don't know how to not be angry with him right now. I thought I was close to forgiving him until I found out about her moving in and all the resentment rushed back in."

"Are you really worried about her?"

"I don't know. It's not even that I think something's going on between them. I don't want to sit around and wait for him to…" I trail off.

"To what?" My mom frowns waiting for me to continue.

"What if he picks her someday? What if he decides he wants to try to have a normal family with her? Luke's going to do anything to be a good dad, what if he decides that means being with his baby's mom." I stare at my now empty glass.

"You have to trust he won't do that." My mom sighs. "That's the inherent risk to loving someone, you have to be vulnerable and believe they won't hurt you, at least not on purpose."

"He didn't set out to hurt me, but he did."

"I know and that doesn't set the foundation for a good relationship."

I look up in surprise. "I thought you liked Luke."

"I adore him." My mom smiles at me.

"But?" I urge her to continue.

She places her hand on mine. "You've been handed a set of extraordinary events that would test the most solid of relationships. The fact that you and Luke haven't learned to work as a team yet makes it nearly impossible. That was the problem between your dad and me, too." My parents divorced when I was young. We don't talk about it often, but I know the catalyst for their split was their inability to communicate and reach a mutual decision regarding my mom's education.

"I would love to be a team, but it's hard when the other person always thinks they're right." I roll my eyes.

"Yes, Luke puts on a very manly front, always has an answer, always rushing in to save the day. I wonder why he does that?" My mom tilts her head in thought.

I wait for her to answer, but she doesn't. "Are you going to fill me in?"

"I have theories, but I don't know. You should know better than me. I will say, no matter the reason, Luke is obviously a protector. He enjoys being in charge and taking care of you, but you want to be independent and often push his help away. I know it's hard for you and it's probably hard for him, too."

"How very caveman of him." I roll my eyes again. "So, you're suggesting I become a submissive housewife?"

"Of course not. My guess is your independence is two-parts attractive one-part frustrating to Luke. He loves that you're strong, but he wants to feel needed."

I cringe internally thinking of when I told him I would never need him.

"In my experience, some men need to be allowed to lead the way or at least think they are." My mom smirks at me. "Neither one of you is wrong, just different visions of what a relationship looks like. You'll have to figure out a compromise if you want it to ever work between you."

"Maybe, but I think I finally pushed him far enough away that compromising isn't an option any more, even if Luke was capable of it." I sigh. "Can I ask you something?"

"Always." My mom takes a sip of her tea.

"Did Luke seem sad when the baby died?" It sounds like a silly question once I say it aloud.

She sets her tea down and appears to be thinking of her answer. "Men react to these things differently than we do. I don't know if it's biology or heightened emotional intelligence on our part," she winks at me before continuing, "but we show our feelings on the outside more than they do. I've seen it a lot in the hospital."

"He seemed to be okay a lot quicker than I was. I try not to be, but I'm really resentful about the whole thing."

"I see. Well, to answer your question, yes, I think Luke seemed sad after the miscarriage. Actually, helpless may be the better word to describe what I saw."

Before I can respond Amelia bounces back into the kitchen wearing enough jewelry to add at least five pounds to her small frame. "Ready to watch a movie?"

"Absolutely." I catch my mom popping a cookie in her mouth out of the corner of my eye. I laugh when she sees me and stops chewing. "I wish your ability to follow doctor's orders was as good as your advice-giving abilities."

"Can't be good at everything." She smiles with cookie still in her mouth.

"Good morning, Linda." I walk into the office and instantly get a whiff of chocolate. "You brought treats? What about fitting into your dress for the wedding?"

"I brought chocolate croissants and they're not for me. I thought you may need a little pastry therapy today." Linda looks sympathetically at me, but quickly reads that I don't know what she's talking about. "An email went out this morning."

My face drops as I instantly know what she's referring to. "Thanks, Linda." I grab a croissant and go to my office. I stare at my desktop while my computer warms up. It's impossible to prepare yourself for something like this, so I just focus on my heartbeat and breathing.

When the computer screen lights up, I pause only a moment before opening my email. I only have a few unopened emails from this morning, so the one I'm looking for is easy to spot. I open the one titled "Baby Taylor" and rip the Band-Aid off before I can think about the sting too much.

The email is originally from Luke, but it's been forwarded to the winery by Aaron. The email indicates that everyone is doing great and that Finn Taylor arrived weighing eight pounds, three ounces and is twenty-one inches long. I scroll down to see two pictures have been included in the email. There's a close-up picture of Finn. Even with his eyes closed and his little face still red and scrunched up, I can tell he's a beautiful baby. The second picture is of Luke holding his son. Behind the tiredness in his eyes is an undeniable twinkle, something that says this is the happiest day of his life.

I wipe away the tear that has slipped down my cheek and place my hand against my heart, as if that will somehow ease the ache there.

Chapter 13

"It's a no from me." Luke leans back in the chair after the young man leaves the conference room. "Not enough experience, plus his finances aren't as robust as the business is going to need to properly execute the planned growth. Best case scenario, the winery is limping along in a year. Worst case it's completely out of funds."

"As the new owner, he could decide to scale back the growth," Aaron offers.

"We've already discussed this, Aaron. Finding a buyer who will finish out the plans that have already been laid out is our goal." Luke sounds slightly irritated. "I thought we both agreed that it was the right thing business wise, but also the right thing to do for the Bianchis."

Before the three of us started meeting with potential buyers, we sat down and discussed what we were looking for. I appreciated that Luke in particular had a strong interest in preserving the vision the Bianchis have for this place. It's obvious that this isn't merely another business deal to him. At first, I didn't understand why the Bianchis asked Luke and Aaron to handle the sale, but their caring, personal approach to it became apparent early on.

"I know, Luke, but we also need to get this place sold. We may have to compromise some of our ideals to make it happen. We're never going to find the perfect buyer." Aaron matches Luke's frustration. Aaron cares about this deal, too, but he thinks the Bianchis would be better served by finding a buyer quickly.

"I disagree. We'll find someone." Luke turns to me. "What did you think, Jessica?"

"I agree with you, he's too inexperienced for an operation this size." Once again, I find myself agreeing with Luke, something I've been doing a lot lately. Working together the past few weeks has gone better than expected. He even sat in on a meeting I had with Nicolette, brainstorming different management structures we could go forward with after the Bianchi's imminent departure. He was able to provide some valuable pros and cons for each scenario we ran based on what he's seen at the variety of companies he invests in.

For Nicolette's part, she's been nothing but professional and so far, seems to be a good addition. I look forward to spending some one-on-one time with her after she's done shadowing Mrs. Bianchi.

"Ultimately, I agree with both of you, but we may need to rethink what we're looking for," Aaron says as he answers a text on his phone. "I hope the meeting this afternoon goes better."

"The next one looks good on paper. Good experience, finances are adequate and in order." Luke studies the packet in front of him.

"I hope so, but we've had several who've looked good on paper and we always find fault with them." Aaron looks up from his phone. "Sorry, I can't be here for the next one. If it feels right, feel free to move forward without me."

"Okay." Luke doesn't look up from what he's reading.

"You need anything from me before I leave?" Aaron puts the folder in his bag.

"No. I think we're good here." Luke still doesn't look at Aaron, instead he's intently focused on what he's reading.

"Let's talk tomorrow after the meeting." Aaron stands. "By the way, is Nicolette still pissed off?"

Luke finally glances up at Aaron. "She's fine."

"Good." Aaron turns his attention to me. "Don't let his crankiness derail the effort, we'll find someone."

"Thanks, Aaron." I begin to gather my papers as Aaron walks out of the conference room. "Why is Nicolette mad?" I ask Luke.

He sets the papers aside and gives me his attention. "She was upset she wasn't asked to be a part of this process. She didn't understand why you were, and she wasn't."

This is the first I've heard of this. "What did you tell her?"

"That her time would be better spent with Mrs. Bianchi and that you were asked because of your knowledge of the finances and your familiarity with how the business has been run for the past several years."

"And she was okay with that answer?" I assume that she wasn't.

Luke shrugs. "If she wasn't, she didn't say anything else to me about it." Luke pulls out the financial package I put together for these meetings. His eyebrows scrunch together.

"Is there a problem?"

"No, I was just thinking."

"About?" I raise an eyebrow at him.

Luke looks up at me again. "Nothing." He places the sheets back into the folder and stands up. "The meeting is at three?"

"Yes."

"Then I'll see you back here around a quarter to?"

"Sounds good." I reply, realizing Luke isn't in the mood to discuss Nicolette or the deal at the moment.

"Good afternoon, Mr. Harney. My name is Jessica Rogers, I'm the controller, and you've already spoken with Luke Taylor, one of our primary investors."

"Nice to meet you both. Please call me Jim." He extends his hand to me and then Luke before we all take our seats at the conference table.

"Thanks for coming out to meet with us today, Jim."

"My pleasure. I'm obviously here because I heard enough to pique my interest. I'm still not clear as to why a long-term owner would be trying to sell off a profitable business."

I give Mr. Harney a warm smile. He's testing to see if I'll spill something we didn't previously disclose. "As I mentioned before, it's simply a matter of the owners having some emergency personal issues to deal with, prompting their desire to retire. They simply want to move on to the next stage of their lives as quickly as possible."

Mr. Harney smiles tightly back at me. "The financials you sent me look promising. Established business, solid revenue streams with growth possibilities. The debt is the only real concern."

"As we discussed during our earlier phone conversation, the debt is understandably a potential roadblock," Luke jumps in. "My partner, Aaron Bennett, and I are the primary investors here and we feel confident the right owner can bring the full expansion of the winery to fruition. The current owners have nearly completed stage one in the projected growth model, but it's the continuation of the expansion that will really generate the profits this business is capable of. We've mapped out projections on how we think, with a proper focus on building additional revenue streams, the debt would be a short-term problem, not a long-term one."

"Understood, but the debt will make it difficult to secure the size of loan that the large scale expansion you're suggesting would necessitate," Mr. Harney says.

"Correct. As investors, Aaron and I are willing to work with the new owner to secure whatever funding is necessary to expand this business properly, potentially even reinvesting ourselves." When the possibility for Luke and Aaron to reinvest in the company came up during one of our planning meetings, I was surprised that I felt relieved by the idea. I convinced myself the relief was for the business and not personal reasons.

Luke takes over the meeting from here. His negotiating skills shine as he lays out the vision and what it's going to take to make this deal work. He then highlights why he thinks Mr. Harney would be a good fit and how his experience in the restaurant industry would be valuable. I pay attention to what is being said as much as I pay attention to Luke's charismatic presentation style. Mr. Harney listens intently when Luke speaks and asks a lot of thoughtful questions. He definitely came prepared. He smiles at me from time to time, even though I stay quiet for a good portion of the discussion. I offer financial information as necessary, but I have to admit the fast paced back and forth between the men is intimidating to me.

After an hour of dissecting the merits and potential drawbacks of the deal, the pace slows.

Mr. Harney pulls out his phone. "You've given me a lot to think about. Excuse me for a moment while I step outside to make a phone call."

"Of course," Luke says. We wait until the conference room door closes to look at each other.

"What do you think?" I feel like Mr. Harney could be our buyer, but I can tell by the way Luke's tilting his head from side to side that he's undecided.

"I'm not sure. He has potential." Luke stops and runs a hand through his hair. "I like that he's onboard for putting some effort and money into the growth."

"But?" I drag the word out knowing Luke has more to say.

"I can't pinpoint it, but something feels off." Luke narrows his eyes trying to focus and figure out what he's missing.

"He's the best option we've come up with so far." I try to think of what Aaron would say in this situation. Convincing Luke of anything takes finesse.

"Maybe." Luke studies Mr. Harney's bio in front of him.

"He marks all the boxes of what we said we're looking for." I remind him. Mr. Harney may not be perfect, but he's certainly not a bad option at this point.

"I can tell he wants it." Luke smirks while still reading over the paper.

"You think?" I sound too eager, too excited. I would make a horrible negotiator.

Luke gives me a knowing smile. "He probably stepped outside to call his accountant to make sure he's ready."

"Don't be overconfident." It's more a reminder for me not to get my hopes up.

"He's going to make us an offer." Luke leans back in the chair and steeples his fingers by his mouth.

"And we're going to take it?" I prod.

"Maybe—" The door to the conference room opens, halting Luke's thought.

Luke maintains his relaxed posture in his chair as Mr. Harney walks back in and takes a seat.

"You're motivated to get a deal done." Mr. Harney leans back in his chair and rubs his chin for a moment. "Buying a company with this much debt is risky. A risk most buyers are going to shy away from."

"Shyness has little place in business." Luke leans forward slightly. "This company is solid and has growth potential you've been dreaming of since you heard about it. It's an opportunity to build something big. You know it, it's why you're here."

I glance back and forth between the two men, neither of them giving much indication of what the next move is.

Mr. Harney is the first to break the silence. "You sent me last year's statements. Can I have a look at the current year to date financials?"

"Of course," Luke says. "They're preliminary at this point, but you're free to see them.

"I'll go grab them." I rise quickly to retrieve them.

Due to my heels slowing me down, it takes a few minutes to reach the office. "Hey, Linda. Do you still have the year to date financials through June that I just gave you to file?"

"I already filed them." Linda stops typing on her keyboard.

"I'll get them. You're almost too efficient." I laugh as I open the file cabinet.

"How's it going in there?" she asks.

"I have no idea. I've never had this much trouble reading a room. Luke thinks he's ready to buy."

"Well, Luke has good instincts."

"Honestly, it's impressive to watch him maneuver through these meetings. I'd be completely outmatched in there by myself. I'm glad he's here." The words hang in the air. I look at Linda and she just raises her eyebrows at me. "You know what I meant."

"I know exactly what you meant," Linda mumbles under her breath.

I don't have time to defend my comments as I leave in a rush, not wanting to take any longer than necessary. I take a deep inhalation to catch my breath before pulling open the heavy wood door to the conference room. I smile as I enter the rich red colored space, but it quickly fades.

"Did Mr. Harney have to step outside again?" I ask as I return to my seat. Once I've lowered myself into the soft leather, I look at Luke. He looks tense.

"No," he says calmly, but this is a different type of calm. He must have misread Mr. Harney and he doesn't look happy about it.

"He wasn't interested?" I ask, careful not to sound too disappointed.

"He was interested." Luke wears a wry expression as he loosens his collar. "I told him to fuck off."

"Luke!" I gasp, causing the corners of Luke's mouth to turn up slightly.

"Relax, I didn't use those exact words."

"But you told him no? What the hell happened?" My voice comes out louder than intended.

"We got to talking more about what direction he would like to take the winery and he said the first thing he would do would be to bring in some of his top people."

"He wanted to fire people?" I'm shocked. I didn't pick up on that during the conversation at all.

"Not everyone, the management team." Luke looks straight at me.

"Oh." I stare at the table for a moment. When I open my mouth to speak again Luke interrupts.

"Before you say it, I didn't make this decision for you."

I turn my eyes up to his. "I was just going to say thank you."

Luke's eyes widen slightly, surprised by my reaction, before he regroups. "It's the right decision. No way in hell I'm selling this company to someone like that. Mrs. Bianchi would be heartbroken if we did."

I nod and let out a sigh. "Where do we go from here? When are you back here next?"

Luke's posture relaxes. "Not sure. We don't have any other appointments set up as of now." Luke looks at his phone. "I have to go, but we'll talk sometime next week."

"Okay." I let out another sigh, this day has been exhausting.

"Don't worry." Luke says as he stands. "I have to get to the airport and I have an important phone conference this evening for another project, but I'll give this some more thought over the weekend."

I walk to the door ahead of him but turn back around before I pull it open. "How's the baby?" Luke and I haven't talked about his son yet and I've been looking for an opportunity to bring him up. I sent him an email congratulating him and I've been around when others have asked about him, but this is the first time I have brought him up to Luke directly.

Luke freezes and swallows hard. "He's good. Claire has moved back into her apartment, so I don't get to see him as much, but he's good."

I nod and give a small smile. I internally congratulate myself for my maturity.

Luke moves like he's going to touch me, then lowers his hand back down. He gives me a half smile instead. "Thanks for asking."

"Have a safe flight, Luke." I escape the conference room; my damp eyes not being detected.

I spent the weekend with Amelia planning her upcoming birthday party. She insisted the theme be turquoise unicorns and after trips to just about every store in town we finally found party supplies she liked online. In between our search for the elusive unicorns, I worried about what is to come of Bianchi Winery.

Luke didn't contact me over the weekend. I typed out a dozen texts to him, each one deleted before being sent. They all sounded too panicked. The closest I got to not sounding fearful about the situation was still laced with neediness, looking for reassurance that everything is going to work out. I had to remind myself multiple times that Luke is doing his best, but ultimately it isn't up to him to ensure everything with the sale goes according to the Bianchi's plan. He's already taken on enough of the responsibility without me putting additional pressure on him.

My anxiety about the entire situation continued to fester into the work week. I was comforted by the fact that even with the increased stress I didn't experience an attack, a fact that reassured me I'm coping a lot better than I was a few months ago.

Luke's text on Tuesday afternoon didn't offer any specifics, only indicating that I shouldn't worry, and he is working on a plan. I texted back asking him to elaborate, but he said it was too early to discuss.

That was two days ago, and the anticipation of what Luke is up to is proving to be as distracting as Amelia is today. She woke up with a low-grade fever and a sore throat and with no one else available I kept her with me. After resting at home this morning, she was feeling well enough for me to bring her to work with me for a little while. Linda loves when I bring her in, but I don't get a lot done with her here. Nonetheless, squeezing in a couple of hours' worth of work will be better than nothing, even if they aren't the most productive.

"I'm sorry, but we're not in a position to extend your terms. We did that six months ago under the condition that you would get your account up to date, which never happened. Your account is nearly ninety days past due." I hate making collection calls, fortunately I don't have to do it very often, except with this customer. Ryan does some consulting for a smaller startup winery in the valley, splitting the money earned with the winery. It's a pain to manage, especially when the owner is strapped for cash and I have to chase down payment every month. I'm listening to the owner prattle on about his cash flow issues, things I hear every month, when I hear the outside door to our office open.

"Well, hello there." Linda sounds more chipper than normal.

"Good morning. Here, this is for you." His voice is unmistakable. My heart starts to race when I remember Amelia is here, too. "I didn't expect to see you here today."

"Luke!" Amelia practically screams.

"Nice to see they finally hired an assistant for Linda. When did you start?" I can hear the smile in Luke's voice.

Amelia giggles. "I'm sick, so mom brought me with her today. After she's finished all her work, we're going to get ice cream. Want to come?"

Amelia's missed Luke. Part of me warms hearing the two of them together, but I also worry it's not the smartest idea. Amelia thrived during the divorce, but I still carry a lot of guilt. Removing Luke from her life was another blow that I wish wouldn't have happened.

"I wish I could, but I have meetings this afternoon." Luke lowers his voice to a loud whisper. "Did you ever take your mom to our favorite place?"

"No. I'll see if she wants to go there today."

"Are you going to get orange honey again?"

Amelia giggles again. "I get it every time."

"Are you ever going to try a new flavor?"

"Probably not, I like that one too much."

Luke laughs. "Fine. When you go, tell your mom to try the chocolate lavender. She'll like that one."

I realize the owner is done pleading his case, the one I haven't been listening to, the one I already have memorized from our previous conversations. "I'm sorry, Larry, but you need to get me some sort of payment by the end of next week or we won't be able to send Ryan out to consult this month."

"All right. I'll make it happen, don't cancel Ryan's visit," Larry gives in.

"By next Friday." I reassert my position as Luke walks in my office and sits down across from me.

"Next Friday, got it. Thanks, Jessica," Larry says sincerely.

"Thanks, Larry." I hang up the phone.

"You look tired." Luke looks bright eyed and bushy tailed this morning as he hands me a paper cup. Amelia runs into my office.

"It's before ten." I take a sip of the chai tea.

"Mom, you didn't tell me Luke was here." She frowns at me like I've been keeping a secret from her.

"I didn't know. Hey, Luke and I have business to discuss, can you go hang out with Linda for a few minutes?"

Amelia frowns at me again.

Luke playfully taps her arm. "After we're done, if it's okay with your mom, you can walk with me up to the tasting room to deliver some paperwork."

"Can I?" My heart clenches when her eyes light up.

"Sure," I say, not confident I'm making a good choice.

Amelia returns to Linda's portion of the office and Luke quietly shuts the door to my office.

"Thank you for this." I raise my cup.

"You're welcome. She's sick?" Luke looks concerned.

"Just a virus. She's obviously full of energy and up for ice cream, so I think she'll be fine." I take a quick sip of tea. "What brings you to the winery today?"

Luke fidgets in his seat. "I have news. News you should hear from me first."

My heart races and in a split second I start to mentally prepare for every worst-case scenario I can think of. I stop when I realize he looks really happy. "What's the news?"

"I'm buying the winery." He takes a sip of his coffee.

Those words were not part of my mental preparedness and I find myself at a loss for words. I stare at Luke blankly trying to come up with a proper emotion.

Thankfully, he starts talking again. "I don't know why I didn't warm up to this idea sooner." Luke smiles like this is the best plan he's ever had.

"Luke, you're a venture capitalist, not a winery owner." I tread carefully.

"I know, but I'm a quick learner." He shrugs.

"And Aaron's onboard with this?" I try a different angle.

"Aaron's not part of this. This is my deal."

I remind myself to breathe. "I thought we agreed this place needs a present, actively involved owner? Don't take this the wrong way, but I think Mrs. Bianchi wanted to turn this place over to someone with hospitality experience."

Luke sets his cup down. "It was actually Mrs. Bianchi's idea. I told her I wasn't interested at first, that I don't know anything about running a winery, but she was very encouraging. The more I thought about it, it's really what I want. I was already looking for ways to reduce my travel, to work a more traditional schedule, be more present for Finn."

Oh, dear lord, this isn't good. "Luke, this is crazy. You can't just decide you want to buy a winery."

"Actually, I can." Luke shrugs again. "I have on offer on my apartment, so now I'll just have to find something here, probably closer to San Diego." Luke listed his apartment after we got engaged. I assumed he had pulled it off the market, but in the chaos of the breakup and everything else I never bothered to ask.

"Why San Diego?" I spit out the questions flooding my brain. "What about Finn? You can't spend more time with him if you're down here." I realize the answer before Luke says it. Finn won't be in San Francisco.

Luke looks at me thoughtfully. "Claire mentioned a few months ago that she had an opportunity to transfer to her company's office in San Diego. We talked this week and she found out the position is still available. She'll be moving in a month. It's kind of amazing how all the pieces have come together."

I try to process it all, but the fact that Luke is looking at me like I should be happier than I am is distracting.

"I know it's a lot to take in, but this is a good thing, for everyone," Luke states confidently.

"Is it?" I mumble, and lean back in my chair.

"We can talk more about this later." Luke stands up.

"Where are you going?" I blurt out.

"Mrs. Bianchi's office to drop off the contract. I think she's going to make an announcement later today or tomorrow."

No! Stop! Don't! I scream in my head, but my mouth doesn't move. There's nothing I can say to stop this. Luke has made up his mind and is clearly thrilled with his decision, there will be no convincing him otherwise.

"Smile, Jess. This is a good thing." Luke tosses me a reassuring smile and leaves my office. "Ready, kiddo?"

"Yep." I hear Amelia jump from her seat and follow Luke out the door.

I hide at my desk for the next two hours, trying to calm my nerves. I go so far as to fake being on a phone call when Luke returns Amelia. Around noon I take Amelia to get ice cream at the place her and Luke were discussing. It's all homemade and the chocolate lavender flavor is delicious.

I receive texts all afternoon from Linda, Ryan and Monica after Mrs. Bianchi makes the announcement about Luke becoming the new owner. I answer them calmly, reassuring them that Luke will do a great job, but my stomach is in knots. Amelia and I curl up on the couch and watch movies, both attempting to feel better.

Amelia's fever spikes in the evening, so I give her more medicine and put her to bed early. I sit in the quiet house and face my thoughts about today's events.

First, I think about Mrs. Bianchi. Selling this place is emotional for her and this is probably as good of a solution as she's going to get. She's fond of Luke, but more than that, she trusts him.

Luke seems really excited and his lack of experience isn't as worrisome as it may be with someone else. He'll figure out how to run the winery. He's built that way, he'll work hard and be eager to learn all he can. Failing isn't something Luke takes lightly.

The real question that's haunted my afternoon remains. How does this affect me?

I grab my laptop off the island and turn it on, the glow from the screen illuminating the dark room. I stare at the screen while I think.

With the deal finalized, the Bianchis are officially out of the winery. Their move to Texas is scheduled for a week from Monday. Mrs. Bianchi will be in and out of the office next week, and then the next week she'll be gone. This place won't be the same without her. I won't be the same without her here.

I type out the email and reread it once to make sure I've kept it professional. I stare at it for a long time, debating whether I really want to send it or not.

Working with Luke has been better lately, but it's always going to be difficult. Everything with us seems to be. I have too many feelings for him, good and bad. The fact that I still find myself wishing things were different between us is painful and often confusing. Seeing him on a limited basis has been somewhat manageable. Having to work with him, see him, on a daily basis would be an unnecessary level of punishment.

I take a deep breath and with one click of a button, the email is sent. Nothing to do now except await the aftermath.

Chapter 14

The pounding at the door prompts me to set down my bowl of cereal and turn off the movie I'm only halfway through. I was hoping he wouldn't read the email until he was on the plane back to San Francisco tonight.

I don't bother to look through the peephole. I open the door to find my new, very angry boss glaring at me. "Hi, Luke."

"What the hell is this?" He holds up his phone as if I need reminding about the email I sent him only a couple of hours ago.

I sigh and step aside. "Keep your voice down, Amelia's sleeping."

Luke storms past me toward the kitchen. Once there, he places both palms on the island and leans forward as I rest against the counter on the opposite side.

"Well?" he asks, even though it's clear he's not going to like any answer I'm going to provide to him.

"Don't make this harder than it needs to be." I cross my arms across my chest.

"I'm making things harder?" Luke widens his eyes at me.

"Luke, you had to know this was coming. By the way, you showing up here, after business hours, to yell at me about

something work related is exactly why this could never work."
I wave my hand back and forth between us as I try to appeal
to his sensible, business side.

"Is that why you're quitting? You don't like the idea of me
being your boss?"

"Of course I don't like the idea of you being my boss," I
say matter-of-factly. "Did you think I would?"

Luke rubs the back of his neck. "I thought we reached a
good place in our working relationship."

"We have, but we've only been required to interact with
each other for moments every week or so. Working together
on a daily basis would be different."

"Once the shock wears off, you'll realize this is a good
solution. The winery gets an owner dedicated to its success,
I get to spend more time with my son, and you get to stay
at the company you love." Luke's chin is raised slightly, his
jaw set.

"I don't belong there anymore." I plant my feet and
straighten my stance.

"Like hell you don't." Luke's anger flashes for a moment,
but he composes himself quickly. His Adam's apple moves
as he swallows. "I don't want to run the winery without...a
controller."

I shift my weight to one foot. "I'll stay on until you find
my replacement."

Luke doesn't say anything immediately and I wait for
his frustration to be unleashed. Instead, he looks at me with
a scrunched brow and keeps his voice calm. "Is this because
I've never run a winery before? Mrs. Bianchi seems to have
confidence I'm capable."

"No, I'm sure you'll do great," I concede, his reaction confusing me. I expected to argue, not to tap into some insecurity hiding below Luke's confident exterior.

"Isn't this what we all wanted? For someone to come in and run the place with the same vision the Bianchis had. I'm going to do that. This decision was about me and what I wanted, but that doesn't mean you can't reap the benefits as well. The winery has been important to you for years." Luke runs a hand through his hair. "Besides, replacing the controller during the middle of all the changes already happening is going to make things even more complicated."

"I can't believe Aaron didn't talk you out of this." I sigh and shake my head.

"Aaron and I had already begun conversations about me stepping back, although when we first started them it was more about me finding a better balance between work and family, not because I was going to run another business. The plans to get Christina more involved have been in the works since last year."

Last year he would have been planning for our baby. The sick feeling in my stomach instantly returns. "You're lucky Claire is willing and able to uproot her whole life for you." The bitter words escape before I can trap them in my brain where they belong.

Luke tilts his head at me and shakes it. "She's excited about her work opportunity. She was offered more money and a title increase to make the move."

"You don't owe me any explanations." I stalk off toward the family room.

"What do you want from me, Jessica? I'm damned if I do, damned if I don't. I don't tell you what's going on and you don't trust me. I do tell you and I'm an asshole for bringing it up." There's confusion in his voice and when I turn around, he's rubbing his forehead. "We're not together, but we're not merely business associates. I don't know at this point what I should share with you and what I shouldn't." He looks at me like he's waiting for me to tell him what to do. He looks more helpless than angry.

It's the moment I realize he's right, I wouldn't have been happy either way. "I don't know, either, Luke." I try to swallow the lump in my throat. "I feel like I want to know, but every time you mention her, I get this hollow feeling in my stomach and no matter how hard I try, no matter how badly I wish it away, it's still there." My voice catches on the last word and I struggle to hold back the emotions brewing inside.

Luke takes a cautious step toward me and I squeeze my eyes shut, willing them not to release any tears. I startle when he wraps his arms around me, but he doesn't let go, instead he holds me tighter.

"Tell me, Jess." He rests his chin on top of my head. "Tell me how I can make this better for you."

"You can't." I gently push away from him and wipe my eyes. I don't tell him how desperately I want him to. "Please don't fight me on this, Luke. I need to move on."

Luke's arms fall limply at his sides and he lets out a big exhale. He studies me with concerned eyes. Finally, he says, "give me six months."

"For what?"

"To get my bearings. By then I'll have a better game plan and more knowledge. At the very least, I'll be in a better position to hire a new controller." He tilts his head at me. "Come on, Jess, six months to make sure Bianchi Winery gets a proper new start."

I hate to admit it, but he's right. I don't owe this to him, but I do owe the Bianchis. "I'll give you six months."

Luke nods and swallows hard. "Thank you."

"And then you'll let me go?" I ask, my voice small.

"Then I let you go." His voice is thick and his eyes hold mine momentarily before looking away. "It's late, I should leave."

"Okay." I move toward the door and Luke follows.

"Tell Amelia I hope she feels better."

"I will." I open the front door and Luke walks past me.

He stops in the doorway and I think he may turn around to say something else, but he remains facing the street. "Good night, Jessica."

"Good night, Luke."

"Hello, ladies." Emily slides into the booth Vivien and I have been occupying for the last thirty minutes.

Vivien glances at her phone. "You're late, even for you."

"I know, I'm sorry. Rob asked me to help him pack. I texted you."

Vivien and I finally got to meet Rob a couple of weeks ago. He was friendly and funny and we both instantly liked him. Emily practically beamed when we both told her we thought he was a good match for her.

"Another work trip?" I ask.

"Yeah. He's meeting with some bigwigs at the corporate office. I don't know, some meetings about the project he's been working on." Emily shrugs before raising her arm to wave down a waitress. "Glad one of us is successful at being employed."

"Job isn't going any better?" Vivien asks.

"No. I've really tried, but it's just not the right fit. I can't believe I'm saying this, but I need something more challenging than fetching coffee and breakfast burritos for a bunch of twenty somethings."

"Why can't you believe that?" I take a sip of my tea. While Emily has a fun, carefree side, she's always struck me as being a hard worker and very capable. Beyond that she has a quick wit and the ability to talk people into doing things they wouldn't normally do. I've always thought her talents weren't being fully utilized in the positions she's previously held.

"I'll take a pot of oolong and a beer." Emily turns her attention momentarily to the waitress who just approached our table.

"Double fisting tonight, huh?" I tease. We always order tea when we meet for Chinese food, it seems like a necessity.

Emily winks at me. "Don't get me wrong, I like the people at work, but it's a very young crowd." Emily shakes her head and pretends to slap it. "Seriously, what the fuck is wrong with me and why do I sound like a middle-aged woman all of a sudden?"

"You're getting older, more mature?" Vivien pours more tea into the small porcelain cup in front of her.

"Bite your tongue! I'm not nearly as old as you two." Emily likes to remind us often that she's a full two years younger than we are.

"For what it's worth, Emily, I think fetching breakfast and coffee is fine, but I can see you doing a lot more than that." I blow on my tea, so it doesn't scald my tongue.

"Me, too," Vivien adds.

Emily looks genuinely surprised and I feel a pang of guilt in my gut. We all give each other a bit of a hard time, but it hurts my heart that this is apparently the first time Emily is hearing that we think she's capable of greater things. I need to do a better job of telling people how great I think they are.

"How's your job, Jess? Mrs. Bianchi's completely gone now?" Vivien changes the subject.

"She left a little more than a week ago. It's going to be a big adjustment not seeing her every day."

Emily nods in understanding. "How's your new boss?" She's been careful not to say too much about Luke since the incident at the hospital instead simply listening and offering support.

"He's been busy, so I haven't seen him much. We did have a mini budget meeting last week." While Luke's been agreeable and respectful in his new role, I can tell the budget is going to be a continued point of contention between us.

"What happened?" Vivien halts her cup halfway to her mouth.

"Just some arguing about what should be spent this year," I sigh. "He's frustrated by the budget."

"Luke doesn't strike me as the type of man who likes restrictions." Vivien twists the corner of her mouth.

"Maybe not, but that's the point of me staying for the six months, to make sure things transition as smoothly as possible. Sticking to an annual budget is going to help him and the business remain successful."

"He probably likes that, though." Emily takes her beer from the waitress. "Even someone like Luke needs one person that will stand up to him."

I laugh. "I don't know if he likes it, but he definitely needs it."

Emily raises a finger. "Hold that thought, I have something to tell you. I'll have a bowl of the wonton soup and an order of the chicken lettuce wraps."

"I'll get that right in, so it comes out at the same time as their food." The waitress nods toward Vivien and me.

"I can't believe you ordered soup, its one hundred degrees outside." Vivien shakes her head.

"You're both drinking hot tea, same thing. Plus, it's cold in here." Emily rubs her arms with her hands. "I hate that about summers here. If you dress for outside, you're freezing inside in the air conditioning. If you try to dress to be even remotely comfortable indoors, you'll break a sweat walking from the parking lot into the building."

"That's the nice thing about my office, since it's just Linda and I we set the thermostat up a little bit." I feel a moment of sadness at the thought that this time next year I'll be sharing an office with someone new.

"I work in an office which is ninety percent male, so I freeze all summer." Emily rolls her eyes.

"Jess, you really think you'll leave after six months?" Vivien wrinkles her nose.

"Yeah, it's time." I turn to Emily. "What were you going to tell me?"

"Shit, I almost forgot to tell you again." Emily clears her throat. "Luke called me."

I freeze holding a fried green bean mid-air. "What? When?"

"A couple days ago. I was going to call you right away, but it was late and then I sort of forgot." Emily twists her mouth.

"What did he want?" I pop the bean in my mouth.

"To apologize…about the hospital." Emily waits for my reaction.

Luke and I haven't talked again about that day and I have to admit I'm surprised he called Emily. Luke Taylor isn't always the most apologetic man. "What did he say?"

"He said he completely understands what it looked like, but he wasn't hiding anything. Said the more he thought about it he realized I was being a good friend. He apologized for putting me in a bad position where I needed to bring it up at that time. He sounded sincere." She shrugs before taking a sip of her beer.

"Well, that's…surprising." I shake my head.

"I thought so." Emily shrugs. "And I have to say my bullshit meter didn't go off once during our conversation."

"Maybe he's growing up a little?" Vivien suggests.

"Maybe," I say, thinking about the changes I've seen in Luke lately, in particular the increased patience.

The waitress drops off Emily's soup giving me the opportunity to change the subject. "You're both coming to Amelia's party this weekend, right?"

"Yep, I even found a unicorn bathing suit to wear." Emily wiggles excitedly in her seat.

"Wow, you're really dedicated to this theme." Vivien laughs.

"I'm dedicated to my friends." Emily winks at me, reminding me that I'm really lucky to have these ladies in my life.

"Thank you so much for spending the morning with me." Nicolette begins to organize her papers that are now strewn across my desk, a result of our training for the last three hours.

"No problem. I know we covered a lot in a short amount of time, so please don't hesitate to ask me to revisit any of this later. Once you have more context, it will make a lot more sense."

"I will." Nicolette places the stack of papers in her folder. "Do you have lunch plans today?"

"I don't."

"Want to join me, then?"

I hesitate a moment before answering. "Sure. Can you give me a couple of minutes to answer a few quick emails?"

"Yep, I'll meet you out front in twenty?"

"Perfect."

Fifteen minutes later, I step out onto the tasting room porch where Nicolette is already waiting.

"I'll drive," she announces once she sees me. "Are you good with Thai food? I've been wanting to try Tasty Thai," she asks as I follow her to her car.

"That's over on Winchester isn't it?" If we're going over to the other side of town, lunch is going to take longer than I was planning.

"Luke won't mind if we take a little longer." She presses the button on her key fob and the lights flash on the black BMW a few cars away from us.

I round the side of the vehicle and open the passenger door. I notice immediately how clean her car is inside and out. Mine probably has leftover snacks from Amelia's soccer game last weekend still in the backseat.

On the drive to the restaurant I find out that Nicolette has two sisters back home in Santa Barbara, she's allergic to dogs and cats, and she's learning to speak Italian via some online courses. She dominates the conversation, but I don't mind, not ready to share too much about myself until I know her better.

We arrive and are quickly seated, beating the lunch rush.

Our waiter takes our drink order right away and we remain quiet while examining the menu. A few minutes later, he returns with our iced teas.

"Are you ready to order?" the middle-aged man asks.

"Yes, I'm going to have the pad thai," Nicolette leads, while I scan through the rest of the menu in order to make a quick decision.

"And for you, ma'am?"

"Can I please have the yellow curry?"

Nicolette smirks.

"Great." The waiter says leaving us to resume our small talk. I look at her after he steps away.

"Sorry, just a personal thing of mine." She shakes her head as she puts her napkin on her lap.

"What is?" I tilt my head to one side.

"I find it interesting when people ask if they can have something at a restaurant, like the waiter is going to say, 'no, you can't have that today.'"

I don't like that she's managed to make me feel embarrassed by my politeness. "Just a habit, I suppose."

"Oh, of course. I totally get it. I just try to imagine a man asking permission to order what he wants. I mean, would Luke ever ask if it was okay to order anything?"

No, he wouldn't.

Nicolette puts her hand up to her chest. "I didn't mean to make you uncomfortable. I just notice these things, how it's socially acceptable for a man to behave in certain ways, but not a woman."

"I understand what you're saying." I still don't like the way she's made me feel, but I do get her point.

"I suppose that's why I try to be very direct. You know what it's like to work in the male dominated wine industry."

"Sort of a 'if you can't beat 'em, join 'em' mentality?" I ask.

"Exactly, if you want men to respect you in this industry you have to learn to play by their rules." She nods like we're agreeing on something.

I don't agree with Nicolette, but this is too heavy of a debate for a first lunch, so I change the subject. "What made you want to move down this way?"

"I suppose I've always been somewhat of an adventure seeker. I spent my junior year of high school in France and after that I've had a yearning to see as much of the world as I can."

"You went to school back East right?" I overheard her mention missing her college stomping grounds when Monica mentioned traveling to New York to see Chad's family.

"NYU. I love New York. There's always something going on. We'd spend free weekends and breaks driving to different states and experiencing as much of that coast as we could."

"What a great experience that must have been. Did you stay there long after you graduated?"

"No, after graduation I traveled through Europe for almost a year before moving back to California. I was offered a job at a winery and I've been in Napa ever since."

"I would think Napa would be a little too slow paced for you after all that."

"Anywhere can be exciting if you want it to be." Nicolette shoots me a naughty smile before taking a drink of her tea. "I had a good time in that valley, but I'm definitely ready for a new challenge. What about you, Jessica? Have you had the opportunity to travel much?"

"I haven't. I grew up in the San Diego area but settled in Temecula with my ex-husband while he was completing dental school."

"Wife of a doctor, huh? Impressive."

I can think of a lot of things I'm proud of, marrying a man I was in love with who also happened to be interested in dentistry isn't one of them. "It's not nearly as glamourous as it sounds."

Nicolette raises an eyebrow. "Then you managed to nab San Francisco's hottest, most notoriously single bachelor."

My eyes widen a little, taken aback by her comment.

"Yes, I know about you and Luke and, well, everyone knows about Luke and his reputation. I have lots of friends in the city and in social circles of a certain age group, he was talked of often." Luke's big reputation has a way of rearing its head even when we're not together. "I'm assuming you know I asked him out when you all were in Napa."

I'm not used to her forwardness and it's admittedly jarring. "He mentioned it."

Nicolette laughs. "I hope you won't hold it against me. I was just curious what all the fuss was about. Obviously, I didn't know you two had something going on at that point."

"Obviously," I respond simply. She doesn't strike me as the kind of woman that it would have made any difference to.

"You don't have to answer this if you don't want to, but I have to ask. Does he live up to the hype?" Nicolette has a gleam in her eye. I'm not sure if she's more interested in the details of Luke's reputation or in watching me squirm.

"Luke is our boss. I'm not going to discuss anything about him or our past relationship at work." I would under no circumstances tell this woman anything about Luke, but this is the most polite answer I can come up with on the spot.

Thankfully my message is received enough for Nicolette to at least pretend to be apologetic. I get the distinct impression this woman is never truly sorry for anything she says or does.

"I'm sorry. I didn't mean to strike a nerve. I've seen you at work and assumed you were both completely over each other." She stresses the word completely.

"It's complicated." A simplification, but I'm not going to give her any of the details she's hungry for.

"I'm sure it is." I recognize Nicolette's tone as the one I use with Amelia when I'm trying to let her pacify her need to be heard. "I didn't realize you still have feelings for him, you hide it well at the winery. It must be difficult working so closely with him, day in and day out."

I'm not interested in analyzing my unresolved feelings about Luke with this stranger. "It can be, but we share a common goal of ensuring the success of the winery."

"Of course." Nicolette smiles and something about it bothers me.

"Here you go, ladies. The pad thai and the yellow curry." The waiter sets down our respective dishes. "Can I get you anything else?"

"We're good," Nicolette answers sweetly, and he walks away. "I won't bring up your personal relationship with Luke again."

"It's not relevant, we've been able to maintain a good working relationship."

"Gotcha." Nicolette pauses to take a bite of her food. "Speaking of Luke, he's a hard read for me. In order for me to be successful in my position I need to be able to interact with him well. What do you consider the most difficult part about working with him?"

I use the fact that I just took a mouthful of food to buy me some time and choose my words carefully. "Luke is very driven, but really fair and intelligent. I'm sure you'll enjoy working with him."

"Well, that was a very politically correct answer," Nicolette scoffs. "Despite legend, I'm sure he's not perfect. I'm sure you must butt heads over something?"

I sigh and think of what I can say. I don't want to say anything I wouldn't say to his face and I certainly need to keep my comments professional. "Luke is very opinionated and can be a bit stubborn when he believes he's right. Having said that, he has great business insight and is often correct. The area we sometimes disagree on is the budget. We simply have different roles, different philosophies. As a controller, I'm required to be more conservative with spending. Luke subscribes more to the adage of you have to spend money to make money."

"And he doesn't respect your opinion?" Nicolette raises one eyebrow over her fork.

"I wouldn't say that. It's difficult sometimes, but we can usually work out a compromise."

"And if you can't?"

"Well, he's the owner, so ultimately I concede to what he wants to do. I consider it my job to convince him my position is correct, but he has the final say."

Nicolette give me one last catlike smile as she takes another bite of her noodles.

Chapter 15

"Linda, want to go grab some lunch?" I send off what I hope is the final email to Monica regarding ordering supplies for this year's harvest event. She's been emailing me all morning with additional questions about last year's expenses.

"I'm sorry, I have to go find shoes for the wedding. I'm running out of time." Linda will be gone all next week to go help her daughter with final preparations.

"All right. I'm craving Mexican food."

"Great, now I'm going to be thinking about tacos for the rest of the day."

I laugh. "Sorry." Linda's mission to trim up for the wedding has led to me dropping a few pounds as well, but a diet of smoothies and salads can only be sustained for so long.

I grab my purse and log off my computer. "I have a meeting with Luke and Nicolette at one, so I won't be gone long. I'll just pick something up and bring it back. You want me to bring you something?" I say once I reach Linda's desk.

"No, I'm good. I tried my dress on last night and it fits perfectly. Tacos are not going to help me maintain that."

"You look great." I think back to the feelings I had right before my wedding with Grant. "Chloe is going to be a beautiful bride."

"She is." Linda beams. "Oh my gosh. She called me the other day so excited. For a moment I got hopeful she was going to tell me she was pregnant." Linda pauses and pulls a face. "No. She was ecstatic she found the perfect outfit for the dog to wear."

The edges of my mouth curl up. "Your grand-doggie."

"I refuse to call him that. Don't get me wrong, I like the dog, but is it really necessary to have him carry the rings?"

"I think it's kind of cute." I shrug.

"If it was only him maybe, but they're bringing their bird now, too." Linda shakes her head in disgust.

"What? You didn't tell me about this." I smile widely.

"I didn't? Oh yeah, they're placing the bird's cage on the table where everyone gets their table seating cards because they wanted him to be part of the day, too."

"Is this the same bird who says 'I've been a bad boy'?" I can't stifle my giggles. This bird has been a recurring source of laughter for us ever since Chloe adopted him. He obviously had a very interesting previous owner.

"Yes. And don't forget he also says 'harder, baby.'" Linda stares at me with wide eyes.

Ironically, I laugh harder. "That's right."

"Laugh all you want, I have to witness this nonsense first hand. I will die of embarrassment if that bird says anything in front of the pastor."

"What does Richard say about all this?" I've met Linda's husband multiple times. He's always appeared easy-going to me, but I know from Linda's stories that he's a serious guy.

"She's his princess. His little girl can do no wrong in his eyes."

"Well, I can't wait to hear all about it." I snicker.

Linda rolls her eyes again and shoos me away. "Go get your tacos."

"I'll be back," I say, walking out of the door.

I smile at guests on my way up to the tasting room. I decide to stop by and see if Monica wants anything for lunch. Ryan is off site today or I would stop by his office as well.

I'm heading up the stairs when I hear a woman laughing. It takes me a moment to realize it's Nicolette.

"I don't think getting Luke to agree is going to be a problem." Another laugh. "Let's just say, him and I speak the same language. I'll get him to approve to it."

I continue up the stairs to find Nicolette in Monica's office.

"Hi, Jess," Monica calls out when she sees me.

"Hello, Jessica." Nicolette turns around in her chair to give me a big fake smile. "Thanks for the info, Monica."

Nicolette hurries past me and I shut the door to Monica's office. "What is she going to get Luke to approve?"

Monica is rifling through her desk drawer trying to find something. "Nicolette? She was asking me if I had money in my budget for updated pamphlets and stationery. I told her no, that I would help with the design, but the costs would be part of her rebranding budget." Luke, Monica and I came up with a budget to do a brand update for the winery. He was reluctant at first, but Mrs. Bianchi insisted he should at least add his name to the winery. With Monica being bogged down with harvest event planning, Luke decided to loop Nicolette in and asked her to come up with some ideas of how to refresh the tasting room. "I'm beginning to think asking for her help was a bad idea."

"She's going to ask Luke for more money? She's already overspent on this rebranding as it is."

Monica shrugs her shoulders and shakes her head letting me know this was not her doing.

"But we already agreed to a budget weeks ago." I frown causing Monica to raise her hands in surrender.

"That's what I told her, but she seems to think she has some pull with him. Said something about not being as intimidated by him as the rest of us are, that she knows how to handle powerful men." Monica rolls her eyes. "For the record, I am not intimidated by Luke."

I can't help but let out a small laugh. "I know you're not."

"I'm sure you didn't come up here to listen to my complaints about Nicolette. What can I do for you, Jessica?" Monica stops her search and smiles sweetly at me.

"I'm picking up food from El Ranchito. Do you want anything?"

"No, I brought lunch today, but thanks for asking."

"No problem." I say at the same time my gut tells me working with Nicolette is definitely going to be a problem.

"Thank you both for meeting with me." I set variance reports in front of Luke and Nicolette. "You've both been here a little over a month now, so I think it's time we start to take a closer look at our costs."

Luke examines the report thoughtfully. "I know these numbers don't look great on paper, but we need to understand the underlying causes here."

"I realize with the change in personnel and in some cases philosophy, there was bound to be some spending we didn't anticipate. I'm less concerned with the capital expenditures and employee costs. However, I would like to take a closer look at operating expenses." I point to the highlighted section of the report.

Nicolette sets her papers down and smiles at Luke before addressing me. "Luke and I have discussed these expenses at length and deemed them necessary to propel this business forward." Nicolette uses a condescending tone I immediately take offense to.

"Spending ten thousand dollars on new linens for the restaurant is necessary?" I read from my notes. "Another eight thousand on business cards, letterhead and other logoed office supplies…all necessary?" I keep my voice even. I don't want to escalate the situation too quickly, but she needs to be held accountable.

Nicolette sits up tall with perfect posture. "We already agreed about the need to rebrand and generate some renewed excitement for this place."

"Yes, and I believe we also all agreed to a budget several weeks ago. A budget that has already been spent." I look at Luke who is still staring at his pages. "I haven't even seen bills for the new signage, the website update or the wine club member's barrel tasting party."

Luke sets down the reports and slides a spreadsheet across the table to me. "We agreed to those numbers in good faith, but as we started thinking about it more, we realized there was more we wanted to do. I'll take the blame for this one. I had a vision and after talking with Nicolette I realized some costs were left out of the original budget."

I reluctantly pick up the report, my mouth twists as I read the newly revised budget for the rebranding project. A budget I clearly was not asked to assist with.

"Jessica, we want to do this right out the gate. I'm sure you agree that we don't want to look back and regret trying to save a few bucks." Nicolette pushes her dark curls back over her shoulder.

I raise an eyebrow at her. "I'm not trying to save a few bucks. I'm trying to ensure this winery stays profitable." I set down the ridiculous new list of must have items that includes new photography of the site and all the employees.

"The Bianchis managed this place a little differently. I don't mind spending a little more now and seeing the benefit later," Luke explains as he folds his hands on the table. His tone and gesture give the impression his mind is made up.

Nicolette clears her throat causing us to both look her direction. "You've said it yourself, Jessica, your job is to be conservative with the money and I totally respect that. But our job is to attract customers, to sell an experience. Sometimes to do that you have to spend some money. You may need to loosen the reigns and let us do our job."

I don't like that she's referring to Luke and her as some sort of team, but I like it even less that she's painting me as their opponent, as some type of money miser. I feel the heat rising in my chest and realize I need to calm down before I have another conversation with Luke about the finances.

"Fine. I've presented the numbers and given you my opinion on where the numbers need to land to make sense financially." I begin to gather my papers. "Your choice if you use that information or not." I regret instantly that my words sound as irritated as I am.

Luke studies me a moment. "I understand your position and I take full responsibility for the fall out of not listening to it this time."

"Great, well, I think we're done here then." I stand to leave; this conversation will need to be continued another day.

"I need another few minutes of your time. Nicolette, you can go." Luke looks back down at the reports in front of him, giving no hint as to what his current mood is.

I steal a glance at Nicolette, her face sour from being excused so unceremoniously. She gathers her stuff and walks out without saying another word. I toss my papers on the table and sit back down.

Luke studies my face for a moment. "It's not personal, Jessica."

"Of course not." I physically bite my lip to prevent myself from saying anything else.

"You're obviously pissed. I'm trying to figure out if you're angry about the budget or if you're mad because you think I'm siding with Nicolette." Luke keeps his eyes focused on mine.

I narrow my eyes slightly at his implication that I'm jealous of Nicolette. "Definitely the first one."

"Are you sure? Because Nicolette mentioned you seem intimidated by her."

I stand up again. "I don't have time for this."

"She mentioned other things, too." Luke raises his voice slightly, so I stay standing in front of him. "Did you warn her I'm difficult to work with?"

"That's not what I said. I said sometimes we disagree and sometimes it's difficult." I knew I needed to watch what I said to her.

"Isn't that the same thing?" Luke's face tightens.

"No, it's not. Bottom line, I didn't say anything to her that I wouldn't say in front of you."

Luke raises his eyebrows. "Did you tell her I'm not qualified to run this place and that you're only sticking around to make sure I don't ruin it?"

I sit back down, my blood starting to boil at her made up accusations. "Absolutely not." She's really stooped to a level I didn't expect her to. "You think I'd say that to her?"

"I hope not." Luke's face remains passive.

"I wouldn't." I look him straight in the eye and hope he can see the truth. "I don't know what game Nicolette is playing or why you suddenly value her opinion so highly, but I was not bad mouthing you. If you want to believe her over me, that's your mistake."

Luke looks taken aback "I didn't say I believe her over you. I'm trying to understand why you don't like her so much."

"I don't trust her," I clarify.

"She's had nothing but nice things to say about you," Luke offers. I roll my eyes, but he continues. "She's been helpful, a great resource in dealing with the managers and setting up new goals for each department."

"I should have guessed," I mutter under my breath.

"What?" Luke frowns.

I sigh and lean forward in my seat. "Fine. I was going to try to stay out of this and let you two sort out the operations side of things, but you should know I've been hearing a lot of complaints. You currently have a lot of very unhappy employees."

"Complaints from who?" Luke looks genuinely concerned.

"I don't want to name names, but I've had several managers and employees come talk to me."

"Can I get some specifics?" Luke furrows his brow.

"Did you adjust the sales team's goals last week?"

"I did." Luke nods.

"Why?"

"With the projected growth during the fourth quarter, Nicolette and I felt their goals were too easily obtained. We decided it would be good to give them a little push." Luke leans back and crosses his legs.

"Did you discuss this with them or just deliver the news?"

"We had a meeting to discuss it."

"And did anyone talk at this meeting besides you and Nicolette?"

"No one expressed any concern about the new goals if that's what you're asking."

I sigh. "You're the new boss Luke and even when you don't try to be, you're intimidating to some people. Did you tell Luis he had to come up with a whole new menu for the restaurant?"

"Not a whole new menu, but I did tell Luis I thought the menu could use a little tweaking."

Luis is prone to exaggeration, but the details aren't what's important here. "And what gave you that idea?"

"Nicolette suggested—"

I interrupt him. "You do realize that Luis has been our head chef, coming up with menus and running that kitchen for the past five years."

"So, he can't take any constructive criticism?"

"Not really." I shake my head vigorously. "He's a chef, Luke. He considers himself an artist and prides himself on his food. Food that keeps our restaurant with a healthy need for reservations and our Yelp reviews consistently at four and five stars. Why do you think you or Nicolette suddenly know more than he does? Mrs. Bianchi trusted her managers' talents."

"So, your advice is to come in and keep everything how Mrs. Bianchi had it?" Luke scowls.

"No, but I do think you should let the dust settle before you take a leaf blower to the mound. Get to know your people. Trust them. There will be plenty of time to put your mark on this place, but if you're not careful you may end up losing some really good people." I brace for Luke's reaction. He's been patient up until this point, but I know he doesn't agree with me. I'm assuming he's about to unleash his frustration with my disagreement any minute.

Luke looks up at the ceiling and rolls his shoulders back. "I appreciate your opinion, even if I don't agree with it. I need people who want to be here, so I appreciate your feedback and will consider it as I move forward."

I'm stunned into silence for a moment. This is not the reaction I was expecting. I can tell he's holding back his frustrations, but nonetheless he's listening patiently. "They'll want to work for you once they get to know you, but you're coming in too hot. Too many changes too quickly. Give people time to adjust."

Luke nods, but doesn't say anything. I can't tell if he's trying to control his reaction or if he's actually considering all I've said, I suspect he's doing a little of both.

"Luke, you have a lot of qualities that are going to make you very successful here. I'm only trying to help."

Luke stands, so I do, too.

"Thank you," his deep voice vibrates through the room.

"I mean it. You've got this."

He gives me a small smile before walking out ahead of me. It's not clear how my words were received by him. I don't know what Nicolette is up to exactly, but I hope someone figures her out before she has the opportunity to inflict too much damage.

Chapter 16

I'm thinking about the upcoming weekend, about finishing back to school shopping with Amelia, as I walk up the path to my office. Monica is waiting for me, pacing in front of the door to the small building. It's only Wednesday and it's already been a long week without Linda here. By the look on Monica's face, it's about to get longer.

"What's going on, Monica?" As I enter my code into the keypad, I notice she's curling and uncurling her fingers.

"I messed up, Jessica."

"Whatever it is I'm sure we can fix it." I attempt to calm her as she follows me into the office.

As I round my desk, Monica has a seat on the other side. She twists the bracelet on her wrist waiting until I've taken my seat before beginning. "I had a meeting with Nicolette on Monday evening to discuss last minute details about the photo shoot. It was getting late and we were spit-balling ideas about the image and what message we wanted to send to our patrons."

"Okay?" I press the button on my computer and it beeps indicating its attempt to wake up.

"We discussed how we want the winery to retain its family feel. It's the vision the Bianchis had and one that has served us well." Monica clears her throat and clasps her hands together to quiet them. "We talked about the shoot and how we wanted to get updated shots of the grounds with the new logo in place as well as new pictures of the staff, including Luke. She mentioned we should do something on the website to introduce him as the new owner."

"Sounds good." I have no idea where this is going, but based on the sickly look Monica is wearing, it's clearly about to take a sharp turn.

"I don't know what Nicolette did after our meeting, but I think maybe she called her." Monica's eyes widen.

I give a small headshake. "Back up, called who?"

Monica stares at me a moment before continuing in an apologetic tone. "Claire. She's in the tasting room. She's here with the baby."

I feel the color drain from my face.

Monica places a hand on her chest. "I can't imagine this was Luke's idea. The only thing that makes sense is Nicolette called and invited her. I'm not one hundred percent sure, but if this wasn't Luke's idea, he's going to be pissed. If she tells Luke this was my idea, I'm going to knock her right out of her expensive stilettos."

I can't help but crack a smile at the image of Monica engaging Nicolette. Monica is a slight, little thing, but she's feisty. Nicolette may have a good four inches on her, but my money would still be on Monica.

"Maybe it was Luke's idea? Nicolette has his ear for the moment, maybe she convinced him this was a good idea."

Monica's right, if Nicolette went behind Luke's back he won't be happy, but I wouldn't expect such a large miscalculation on her part.

"I doubt it." Monica looks a little embarrassed. "I asked if he was inviting Claire to something months ago and got an earful about how inappropriate that would be." Monica waves a finger at me. "If that woman even tries to throw me under the bus for this, things are going to get ugly. I can't believe you haven't called her out yet."

Nicolette has undermined me in front of several people, but I'm not the type to confront her in public. My discussions with her after the fact always feel productive, but haven't produced any lasting effects. During our last conversation about something she said during a meeting with Monica, she apologized for me misunderstanding her comments. "Nicolette's showing her true colors all on her own. I don't need to sink to her level."

Monica leans forward. "I don't know what your plan is, but you better not leave me here with her."

Luke and I decided not to tell anyone of my plans to leave until closer to my departure date, we didn't want it to affect any else prematurely.

Monica is quick and reads my pause as an admission of guilt. "Shit, you are leaving, aren't you?"

"Monica, you can't say anything. I'm not leaving yet, but yes Luke and I have discussed my plan to exit." I take a deep breath. "I've talked to Luke about Nicolette, but he thinks I'm being jealous. I'm afraid for the time being there's little I can say to him. He's going to have to figure her out on his own."

"Well, I hope he does sooner than later." Monica stands and prepares to leave. "I'm sure having Claire here sucks for you. If she would've mentioned it to me, I would've tried to talk her out of it, not only for Luke's sake."

"Thanks, Monica, but his son is his family and having his picture taken with him for the business isn't a horrible idea." I lean back in my chair and rub my temples. "Is it too late to call in sick?"

Monica smiles sympathetically. "I won't rat you out if you come down with a sudden case of 'gotta get the hell outta here.'"

An hour later, I reluctantly walk over to the lawn where other employees are beginning to congregate. One of the photographers is setting up her equipment, including a tall ladder for a group shot.

I glance toward the other side of the lawn where another photographer is taking pictures of Luke. He's posing by himself, but Claire and the baby are standing behind the camera waiting.

"All right, can I have everyone's attention?" Monica is speaking into a bullhorn even though she could get away with not using it. "I need everyone over on the lawn for the group photo. After that's done, we will be breaking off into groups for department photos."

People slowly make their way to the lawn and await further instruction.

"Hey, Jess." Ryan approaches with Simon, the assistant winemaker, who nods his good morning greeting before veering off to join his friends, a group of tasting room servers.

"Good morning, Ryan."

"What's that about?" Ryan nods his head in Luke's direction.

"Family image shoot," I say, staring at Luke. He's now holding his son and smiling into the camera.

"His idea?"

"Not sure. There's some speculation it was Nicolette's doing."

"That makes more sense. I'm surprised she could talk him into it, though."

I pull a face, prompting Ryan to lean in closer. "Spill it. What do you know?"

"There's a rumor that maybe she didn't ask him."

"Really?" Ryan's eyes grow large and he shakes his head. "If that's true, that's not going to play out well for her."

"Monica's afraid she's going to paint it as her idea."

"I don't think Luke will buy that and he definitely won't like Nicolette interfering in his private life. He's already concerned about her overstepping."

"He is?" The pitch of my voice rises.

"Yeah, he confided in me last week that he was beginning to suspect she was intentionally stirring the pot. He asked me to let him know if I witnessed anything underhanded."

"He needs people he can trust, I'm glad he's talking to you."

"I had to talk Luis down the other day, he was about to quit. I quietly gave Luke a heads-up. I think he had a meeting with Luis and they got whatever was going on sorted out because Luis came to me to work on some wine pairings and seemed back to his normal, grumpy self. A slightly disgruntled Luis is the best we can hope for." Ryan smirks.

I laugh. Luis is never going to win any congeniality awards, but he makes a mean paella and runs that kitchen like a boss.

"Come on, everyone, don't be afraid to squeeze in," Monica yells, causing Ryan and I to abandon our conversation and join the group. "Closer," she prods as everyone slowly inches toward the center.

I see Luke hand the baby back to Claire. They laugh about something, before he turns and looks at the group in front of him. His eyes find mine and I look away.

"One more step in, everyone." Monica's voice booms above the clatter. Luke takes his place at the front of the group and Nicolette scoots over to make sure she is standing next to him. From my view I see him give her a tight-lipped smile, but I can't read his demeanor.

The photographer on the ladder gives Monica a thumbs up. Monica hands the megaphone to the second photographer and takes her place in the group.

"Okay, Bianchi-Taylor winery, on the count of three everyone say, wine and cheese. One…two…three."

The crowd repeats the words enthusiastically. We do this several more times, until everyone's attention is wasted, and the photographer indicates she has enough shots.

With the group photo done, I get in line to have my individual one taken. I'm almost to the front of the line, when I hear him behind me. I'm not sure how I'm supposed to react in this situation, so I pretend not to hear him and buy myself some time.

"I'd like to get a management group shot, too," Luke says.

"Sure, we can do that," Monica answers.

"You, me, Ryan, Jessica and Nicolette," Luke says, and I force myself not to turn around. "Jessica?" I instantly know it's him when he places a strong hand on my shoulder.

"Oh, hi, Luke," I say over my shoulder, hoping I sound surprised.

He squeezes my shoulder a beat too long then awkwardly shoves his hands in his pockets. "I'd like to get a management picture of us."

"You're the boss." I meant it to sound light, but it comes out with an edge to it.

"Next." The photographer calls and I take my place for my individual shot. Ryan joins the waiting group while I try to look cheerful and relaxed in my photo, two things I'm definitely not feeling in this moment. Nicolette runs up just in time for me to knit my brows as the flash goes off.

"Sorry, one more?" I shake my sour mood and smile brightly. This time the photographer gives me a thumbs up, letting me know this one was better.

"Next," the woman in black calls out again, and Luke and the others step forward. "Let's have Luke in the center, flanked by the two taller ladies. Monica you can stand here." The photographer places Monica on the other side of Nicolette. "The other gentleman can stand next to the woman in the blue shirt." She's talking about me.

Luke stands next to me and although I can feel his eyes on me, I don't dare look at him.

"Woman in blue, stand a little closer to Luke, please." I scoot closer and immediately realize my mistake in standing next to him. I'm too close, I can feel the heat coming off his body. I hold my breath, plaster a fake smile on my face, and pray I look somewhat normal in these pictures.

"Wouldn't it be better for Jessica to be on the other side of Ryan? Her shirt is very similar in color to Luke's," Nicolette says sweetly.

I didn't notice it before, but Luke and I do look like we coordinated our outfits a little too closely today—royal blue shirts, black pants, and black shoes.

"No, this is perfect." The photographer places the camera in front of her face and begins in snap what feels like a hundred photographs.

"All right, done," she says, only a few minutes later. I take a step to move away, but Luke touches my arm. His eyes are pleading, he opens his mouth to speak but no words come out. Whatever he's about to say will have to wait until we're alone, not in front of the entire company.

Nicolette taps him on the shoulder. "Luke, I need you over with the other photographer. We need to look at the shots of you and your family to make sure we got some you're happy with." Nicolette feigns innocence while Luke pins her with a cold glare.

I quietly turn away from the uncomfortable triangle that's been created and head toward my office. A stop in the ladies' restroom to straighten myself out is in order first.

I open the door and instantly recognize the woman already in there. Unfortunately, this entire day is proving to be too much and I fail miserably at hiding my surprise at coming face to face with Claire for the first time. "Oh!" I squeak out, and before I can run away, she looks up from the baby she's nursing, her and Luke's baby.

"Jessica?" She smiles tentatively at me. "Nice to finally meet you, I'm Claire."

I give her a polite, closed-lipped smile back. "Yes, I know who you are. Nice to meet you." Nice isn't exactly the word that comes to mind, but what else am I supposed to say?

"Sorry, I would shake your hand, but..." Her voice is shaky as she tilts her head to the feeding baby cradled left arm.

"I didn't mean to interrupt." I attempt to steady my breathing and walk over to one of the sinks.

"I hate feeding him in public places, I'm so awkward at it." Her reflection smiles nervously at me in the mirror.

"Was Luke's office occupied?" If she wasn't here, I would probably splash some cold water on my neck, but I don't want to look any more uncomfortable than I undoubtedly already do.

"I didn't ask." She laughs nervously. "He's not happy today."

I feel a twinge of jealously at her comment of Luke's mood. There are plenty of people here today that know he's not, but the fact that she knows is a reminder of their closer relationship. "I haven't talked to him much today. He seemed fine out there."

"He's mad I'm here." Claire offers another nervous laugh. "He's going to be furious when he finds out I spoke with you."

"He didn't invite you?" I take the opportunity to ask the question I've been wondering about all morning.

"No." Claire shakes her head. "It's my fault for not thinking it through more, but when Nicolette called and explained the plan to surprise Luke with an opportunity to have some pictures with Finn...anyways, I should've run the idea by Luke first."

Claire looks genuinely apologetic for her presence and I have an urge to ease her discomfort. "Nicolette can be very persuasive. My guess is she's more to blame for Luke's unhappiness than you are." I grab a couple of paper towels, throwing them in the trash once my hands are dry. "I'm sure once he sees the pictures with Finn, he'll be happy you came."

Claire nods and a piece of her now chin length blond hair falls in her face. She pushes it back and sighs. "Since Luke's already upset, can I speak with you for a few minutes?"

My initial reaction is to say no and run back to my office. Upon further consideration I realize this woman has been nothing but pleasant to me so far. Besides, she's holding her infant son, I think there's a low risk of anything getting too heated. My split second analyzing of the situation and my innate politeness cause me to sit in the stuffed chair next to the pretty blonde.

Claire tries to readjust herself in the chair to better face me and struggles to adjust the baby underneath the breast-feeding cape.

"Don't worry, I never got the hang of the whole feeding in public, either. I'd love to tell you it gets easier, but it didn't for me."

"Yeah, I'm not sure it will for me, either." She shifts her arm and they settle into the new position. "I know I'm probably the last person you want to talk to, but I've wanted to talk to you for a while now. This is an awkward situation for all of us, but maybe I can help answer some questions you may have."

I swallow and focus on the hem of my shirt.

Claire takes a deep breath. "When I found out I was pregnant, I wasn't exactly happy about it, I didn't even know Luke all that well after only a couple of months of dating. He had just broken up with me, telling me he wanted to be with someone else, this paired with his reputation of being, well, not boyfriend material...I didn't have high hopes of how he'd react to finding out there was now an unplanned baby on the way."

I nod, but don't say anything. I was nervous myself in telling Luke when I was pregnant. Our baby was unplanned, too, but at least I knew Luke loved me and would be there for us. Claire didn't have that.

"I was mad at myself, embarrassed, actually. Here I was, a twenty-eight-year-old-widow about to become a single mom."

"Widow?" The word catches me off guard.

"Yes, my husband, John, died three years ago this fall." The reopening of the wound causes a flash of pain to spark in Claire's eyes. "He fell while on a hiking trip with some friends."

"I'm so sorry." Her loss is evident in her face and the way her body shifts uncomfortably. I can't help but feel sympathetic.

"Thanks." Claire takes a deep breath. "Anyways, I considered adoption, but then I saw the ultrasound." Claire looks down at the baby in her arms. "Something immediately changed in that moment, and I knew I would be a single mom no matter what sacrifices I had to make."

She pauses a moment before continuing. "Time went on and I still hadn't told Luke. I wasn't sure if he'd want to be a part of it and I honestly wasn't sure I wanted him to be. After the appointment when they told me I was having a boy, I knew I had to tell him. I knew this little boy deserved the opportunity to know his father."

"That's when you called Luke?"

She nods. "I hadn't talked to him in months. He didn't want to talk to me at first, ignored his cell phone, refused my calls at work, but I persisted, and he finally agreed to talk to me. I remember thinking how tired he looked when we met for coffee, how troubled. It was clear he was dealing with something, but it wasn't my place to ask questions."

This would have been after the miscarriage. I think back to that time, but I don't have a clear picture of Luke. I was too wrapped up in my own suffering to fully register his.

"It took him a minute to notice my belly. When he did, he grew very quiet. He just sat there for a moment, thinking, before saying he wanted to be involved. He didn't say much else that day, but he came to my next doctor's appointment with me a couple of weeks later. He didn't seem happy to be there, but insisted he wanted to be."

When I found out about Luke's son, I had a vision of him meeting up with this other woman and them celebrating their miracle while I mourned the loss of mine. "I wish he would've been able to enjoy those moments more."

"Me, too, but once he shared more about what he was going through I understood his hesitation to enjoy those moments more. Eventually he became more engaged at the appointments, although it would always take half the visit before he would allow himself to show any kind of genuine happiness about it. I tried to talk to him about it a couple of times, but I stopped when he told me it wasn't something he could talk about with me."

My heart hurts knowing that Luke struggled through this on his own. I wish I could have been there for him during this, even though I know it's not realistic that I could've been.

"Jessica, Luke has always made it very clear that us being a couple isn't a possibility, but I want you to know that it's not what I'm looking for anyway." The baby moves and Claire pulls back the cape, revealing her son…Luke's son.

I haven't seen him up-close and in person before. He has Luke's bright blue eyes. I can't help but stare. "He looks a lot like Luke, but he has your nose."

"He does." She places the alert, wide-eyed boy in his carrier seat. "Finn wasn't planned, but he is loved. He added something to my life I didn't even know was missing."

"I remember feeling the same way when my daughter was born." Amelia was a surprise during college for Grant and me, but she's the best thing I've ever done.

"Luke's a great father. Even though we both thought we'd have children with someone else, life had other plans."

I feel an unexpected ease with this woman and am surprised when I decide to ask her to share more. "Did you and your husband want kids?"

She laughs. "John wanted six, I wanted one, so we settled on a plan for three. He would've been an amazing dad. He was kind and fun and could always make me laugh, even on our worst days."

The loss is apparent in her voice when she talks about him and it makes my heart ache for her.

"I'm happy Luke is Finn's dad, but he's not John. I'm not in love with him and he's not in love with me. We're turning an unexpected situation into something good."

"I can see that." I sense nothing but sincerity from Claire.

She takes a deep breath. "This has been a hard year for all of us. I don't know you and I won't pretend to know anything about your relationship with Luke. He doesn't tell me much and it's not my business, but I thought if you met me it may ease your mind some. I don't want my or my son's presence in Luke's life to make you feel like there's not room for you. No mother loves the idea of sharing her child with another woman, but for Finn and Luke's sake I think we could make it work."

I hate the thought of Amelia being around Grant's new girlfriend, but she's right, for their sake I try to make it as comfortable for everyone as possible. "I appreciate the sentiment and I understand how hard it is, my ex-husband has a new girlfriend, but Luke and I aren't together."

Claire gives me a small smile. "I think you may be more together than both of you admit."

"Luke and I have a tangled-up mess right now, but once I'm away from the winery we'll be able to move on." I bite my lip, the thought of leaving the winery always leaves causes mixed emotions in me.

Claire nods and then stands as a group of waitresses walk into the restroom. "Well, I need to get going if I want to get home before it's time for Finn to go down for his nap, otherwise I'll be driving around with him in the car for the afternoon."

"It was really nice to meet you, Claire." I realize I'm saying the words because they are true, not merely out of politeness.

"You too, Jessica. Under different circumstances I think we might have been friends." Claire smiles at me before swinging the diaper bag over her shoulder and lifting the baby carrier with her other arm.

I walk slowly back to my office, thinking about my conversation with Claire. She's so different than what I pictured. It's confusing, but I think I actually liked her.

I open the door to the office and proceed to my desk.

"Luke!" I'm startled to find him waiting for me. "What are you doing here?"

"You disappeared after the group picture." He watches me as I round the desk and sit.

I'm not ready to tell him about my conversation with Claire. "What can I help you with?"

"I'll just get right to it, I had nothing to do with Claire and Finn coming today. I wouldn't spring them on you like that." Luke leans forward. "It all happened so fast, I didn't get a chance to come and see you once I found out they were here and…I'm sorry."

"I know you wouldn't surprise me like that, it's okay, I'm okay. You should have some pictures of your son at your winery." I give him a small smile to prove my point.

Luke visibly relaxes. I want to mention Nicolette's hand in this but decide to tread lightly until I know where he stands with her. Only a week ago he was defending her, but I know he can't be happy with the stunt she pulled today.

Luke opens his mouth to say something else, but the outside door to the office opens. A couple of seconds later, Nicolette peaks her head in.

"Hi, Jessica. Luke, I've been looking everywhere for you. We need you outside for some casual shots around the winery."

"I'll be there in a minute," Luke says, without looking at her.

"Luke, the photographer has limited time, we really need—"

Luke turns around to her. "I said, I'll be there in a minute." His voice is stern, and Nicolette blinks a few times.

"Okay." She frowns for a split second before spinning on her heels and leaving.

"She's driving me crazy." Luke runs a hand through his hair, a habit of his when he's frustrated.

I'm careful to keep my face neutral. "How so?"

Luke tilts his head and squints at me with one eye, the act reminding me of his younger, less intense self. "You were right."

Relief floods through me, he finally sees it. "What was that, I didn't catch what you said?" I cup my hand behind my ear.

Luke sits up straighter and smirks at me. "You were right."

"You don't say?" I gloat, just a little.

Luke smiles at first, but the look is quickly replaced by a serious one. "Did you say that it may be a better idea to have budget meetings with only her from now on?"

"Of course not," I scoff. "Even when we disagree, they're part of my job and you're the owner. You need to be there."

"I didn't think so." Luke runs a hand over his face. "I don't want you to dread your meetings with me. Can we carve out some time to look at everything, just the two of us and formulate some sort of compromise we can both live with?"

"Of course, but won't Nicolette be offended if she's not included?" I can't help but respond with a snide comment, still a little injured that he previously dismissed my concerns about her.

Luke frowns. "I'll deal with her. I didn't see it before, but I do now. She tries to manipulate the other managers and tries to monopolize my time. I don't like to be managed."

I've never seen anyone try to handle Luke how Nicolette has, but I could have guessed it wouldn't yield good results. "Have you talked to her?"

"I did."

"And?"

"She seemed receptive at first, but then gave indications she wasn't happy about it."

"What sort of indications?"

Luke hesitates, then leans in slightly. "Jessica, you should probably steer clear of her as much as possible."

I dismissively shake my head. "I may not particularly like her, but I'm not intimidated by her, Luke."

"I don't think you are, but she definitely has a problem with you."

I purse my lips. "Why?"

"I don't know, may be as simple as she wants power and sees you as an obstacle to that." Luke looks down at my desktop for a brief moment. "You capture more of my time and attention than she would like."

I shrug, knowing full well that, as hard as we try not to be, Luke and I are big distractions to each other. "Well, I'm not afraid of her."

Luke wears a serious expression. "She's made accusations about your professionalism and I don't want you to fuel her fire."

"What?" I seethe, my heart pounding fiercely in my chest. "How have I been unprofessional with her?"

"It started with comments about how you and Linda are always laughing and goofing off when she comes back here. Now she's saying you spend an awful lot of time meeting with various employees instead of working."

"Linda and I handle more back here than she has any clue about and I've been meeting with employees who are frustrated. I've talked more than one out of walking out, so you're welcome." My words come out angrier than I would've liked, and Luke raises his hands in surrender. "Sorry." I add realizing my irritation is misplaced.

"I'm not saying I agree with her. I'm merely telling you what she's saying. By the way, I hear you about how I'm being perceived by everyone and I'm working to fix that. I don't think you'll have to deal with those complaints going forward."

"Everyone will enjoy working for you more if you include them in your decision-making process. I've seen you rally a team and build the confidence of those around you. I know you can do that here."

Luke smiles at me. "I'm definitely going to try." He cocks his head to one side. "Can you play nice with Nicolette for a while?"

"I'm always nice. I can tiptoe around her if that's what you're asking me to do."

"I don't want you mixed up in her drama more than you already are. Can you trust that I'll take care of it and lay low?" Luke wears a serious expression.

I think carefully before answering. "I can do that."

"Good. I'm interviewing human resource managers next week."

I can't blame him for not wanting to be mixed up in this nonsense. "That makes sense. I always told Mrs. Bianchi she should, but she was weird about it, thought it would make the place seem too corporate."

"I want to keep the family vibe, but I also need this to be a place I want to come to every day. I need someone else to handle certain aspects of the business, so I can focus on what I'm good at." Luke gives a small smile. "Well, I better report back to the warden."

"Is that your nickname for her? Can I start calling her that?" I flash a mischievous smile.

He shakes his head and gives a deep throaty laugh. "No. Not unless you want me to report you to HR."

"Fine. No new nickname. I'll just have to keep using the one I already have for her." I pretend to get back to work.

"And what's that?" Luke's amusement is apparent in his voice.

I look at him and suppress a smile. "Sorry, can't tell you. Don't want any HR problems."

Luke rolls his eyes and stands. "Be good." He winks at me on his way out and I can't help but feel like something has shifted.

Chapter 17

"Grandma!" Amelia screams, and runs into my mom's arms, causing her to stumble back.

"Amelia, not so rough," I gently remind her.

"She's fine, Jess." My mom squeezes Amelia and kisses the top of her head. "How's third grade treating you?"

"It's good, except I have to sit by Ayden."

"And what makes you not a fan of Ayden?"

"He's awful. He pokes me with his pencil and calls me names."

"Not cool." My mom allows Amelia to lead her to the kitchen. "Did you talk to your teacher about it?"

"I did, and she told me to try to make the best of it. Sam's mom told me that maybe he likes me that sometimes boys don't know how to act around girls they like."

My mom looks over her shoulder and frowns at me. "Any boy who doesn't treat you kindly, doesn't like you, he's just being a jerk."

"That's what I said!" Amelia sits at the island and my mom does the same.

"You look good, Mom." It's reassuring to see her not looking so tired and weak.

"Thanks, I feel better working, even if it is only part time for now." My mom loves being a nurse and taking time off was hard for her, but I was relieved when she told me she was only going back half-time to start. I agree with the doctor that she needs to rest and fully heal before jumping back into her normally busy schedule. "What's for dinner? I'm starving."

Besides the reduced hours, my mom's been sticking to her new diet better than I thought she would. "I'm grilling chicken and vegetables. If it's cooled off enough outside, we can sit out there and eat."

Amelia keeps my mom entertained with stories of school and soccer while I cook dinner. When a light breeze picks up, we decide to eat in the backyard.

"This is delicious, Jess." With Luke around I learned to cook leaner meals that still had a lot of flavor. He didn't ask me to, but I know he adhered to a very healthy diet when I wasn't around, and I didn't want to disrupt his habits too much.

"Thanks. I'm glad you like it."

We discuss more details of third grade and all its drama before switching to what Amelia is going to dress up as for Halloween.

"May I be excused?" Amelia asks. "I want to get a shower and then can I watch a show before bedtime?"

"That's fine. Please take your dishes to the kitchen on your way, though."

Amelia walks away, my mom watching her.

"She seems even older than when I saw her a couple weeks ago."

I sigh. "I know."

My mom takes a sip of her water. "So, how are you? How's work?"

"It's good. The new human resources manager, Mindy, seems nice. She seems to already be establishing a good rapport with the staff."

"That's good. Is that woman still there?"

"Nicolette? Yes. I don't know what Luke meant when he said he'd handle her, but for now she's still there."

"Any other issues with her?"

"No, I've haven't seen her or Luke much." I'm not avoiding Luke, he's simply been busy. The interactions I have had with him lately have all been pleasant.

"I wonder what he's up to." My mom thinks aloud.

"I don't know, but he asked me to stay clear of the situation, so I am." As I say the words, I realize something. He asked me to, not told me to.

"Still think you'll leave when the six months are up?"

"That's still my plan. Luke and I are working well together right now, we even made some headway in establishing a reasonable budget of the remainder of the year, but who knows if the peace will last."

"And he's fine with you leaving?" she asks suspiciously.

"By the time I leave he'll be ready to really make his mark on the place without my interference."

"It's sounds like your interference helped him keep half his staff."

"Maybe." I take a sip of my water and try to picture how Luke will run things differently without me there. I remind myself that moving on from a company they've been at for years would make anyone feel sad.

"Good morning, Linda." I arrive Monday morning with coffee for both of us.

"Have I ever told you how much I love working with you?" I confided in Linda last week about my plans to leave in a few months. Ever since she's been subtly and not-so-subtly, reminding me of all the reasons I should stay.

"Every day." I laugh. "Hold that thought, I hear my phone."

I hurry to my office and grab the receiver right before it goes to voicemail. "Hello?"

"Hi, Jess."

"Good morning, Luke. What can I do for you?"

"I'm calling to let you know that I hired a new VP of Operations. You remember Sebastian from De Luca Winery?"

"I do. I mean, he's great, but why do we need a VP of Operations?" During our budget negotiations Luke agrees to curb some of the operating expenses if I agreed to give him free reign to hire staff as he saw fit. I thought he may hire a new assistant and maybe some additional tasting room staff. I didn't think he was going to hire new executive positions.

"I have a solid vision for Sebastian's role here." Luke lowers his voice slightly. "Trust me."

"Okay." I understand now. Sebastian is either here to manage Nicolette or replace her. "I look forward to working with him."

"Me, too." I can practically hear Luke smile through the phone. "Have a good day."

"You too, Mr. Taylor." I've taken to playfully calling him that from time to time.

I spend the rest of the morning working on compiling the month end financials. My productive streak continues until Nicolette barges in right before noon.

"Good morning, Linda." Nicolette doesn't wait for Linda's answer before she hurries into my office and shuts the door.

"Did you know about Luke hiring Sebastian Baldwin?" she fumes.

"No, I only found out about it this morning."

Nicolette studies my face, looking for any indication I know more than I'm letting on. She's intense with her pursed lips and slightly bulging eyes. I'm not a great liar, so lucky for me I'm telling the truth.

"And his title? VP of Operations? What's that? Am I reporting to him?" This is the first time I've seen her look unsettled and I resist the urge to smile.

"I really have no idea, Nicolette. I found out about Sebastian and the new position this morning. As far as reporting, that's something you'd have to discuss with Luke. Ever since Mindy started, the organizational chart resides with her." I'm starting to understand how taking me out of the equation with regards to hiring (and hopefully firing), was a calculated move on Luke's part. He wasn't simply easing my workload by hiring Mindy, no matter what he said when he announced her arrival. Shifting certain duties to a true human resources manager has now created a situation where Nicolette and her complaints need to be directed to a neutral party.

"Well..." She taps her manicured nails rapidly on my desk. "This is ridiculous. I'm going to go to Luke's office and get this straightened out." She huffs as she springs up from the chair.

"Sounds like a plan."

Nicolette gives me one last sideways glance before running off to find answers she may not be happy with.

I'm sitting at my desk wondering what came of yesterday's bombshell announcement that Sebastian would in fact be overseeing all of operations, including managing his second in charge, Nicolette. Rumor has it that when Luke told her, she stormed out of his office, slamming the door behind her.

"Good morning, Aaron." I answer my phone quickly, recognizing his number.

"Hey, Jessica, do you have a minute?" His grave tone halts my typing.

"What's wrong?"

Aaron clears his throat. "Luke's dad died last night."

I gasp. "How?"

"Car accident." I've never heard Aaron sound so somber.

"How's Luke?" I ask quickly.

"Not great. They were finally getting to a good place in their relationship."

"He mentioned they had started talking again." Luke shared at the end of our last work meeting that he took Finn to meet his dad. It went better than he anticipated, and they made plans to get together the following weekend to catch a baseball game.

"He's taking it pretty hard." Aaron doesn't hide the concern in his voice.

"What can I do?"

"I would come down there if I was in San Francisco, but Andi and I are actually on our way to Seattle for the weekend." He pauses for a moment. "I know it's a lot to ask, but can you check in on him? Maybe even go down to San Diego?"

I doodle on the notepad in front of me. "I'll give him a call."

"Even though he'll probably resist it, I think he needs someone to lean on right now."

He's right, Luke's not really a leaner. "I'll see what I can do."

"I think he'll be happy to hear from you." Aaron's voice lightens a little.

"Thanks for letting me know."

"Thanks, Jessica. Talk to you later."

"Bye, Aaron."

I hang up and take a deep breath before calling Luke, adding petals to my flower doodle.

It rings several times before going to his voicemail. His smooth voice triggers a feeling in my core that's difficult to ignore.

"Hi, Luke, it's Jessica. Aaron let me know about your dad. I'm so sorry. Please give me a call back when you have a minute."

I hang up and type out a text, too.

So sorry to hear about your dad. Please let me know if there is anything I can do.

I return to the journal entry I was working on but am interrupted a minute later by an incoming text.

Thanks

His one word response makes me feel like my text was inadequate.

I can't even imagine what you're going through. I can come down there this afternoon if you want some company.

I tap my fingertips on my desk and stare at the screen, waiting for a reply.

I appreciate the offer, but I'm okay.

I hate that word, okay. People toss it around whether they are or not. It's such a throwaway word. I can't imagine he's really doing well, but I'm not going to force myself on him.

I'm always here if you want to talk.

His simple replies don't give much away about his mood, but he didn't want me to come down there, hell, he didn't even want to pick up his phone to talk to me. It hurts a little, but I know our relationship isn't what it used to be. I remind myself this isn't about me and I'm not the only person he has to talk to. I try to get on with my day, but thoughts of Luke permeate the rest of the afternoon, making attempts to get work done only moderately successful.

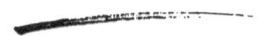

After dinner and a round of miniature golf, Amelia came home and went straight to bed, exhausted from her week.

The latest cliché rom-com and a pint of rocky road have turned the remainder of my Friday night into the escape I needed after an emotionally draining day spent worrying about Luke.

As the credits roll, I head into the kitchen to dispose of the now empty container. I'm refilling my water glass when the sudden chime of the doorbell almost causes me to drop the now full glass. I glance at the microwave clock, it's well past midnight. My mind races with scenarios of who could be at my door at this hour, and none of them are pleasant.

I slowly creep toward the front door, careful not to make noise that would alert whoever is standing on the other side of it that I'm near it. I peer through the peep hole, but don't see anyone, so I peek through the blinds of the big window facing the street. There's a white sedan sitting in front of my house. The driver is still in the car with the engine running.

The doorbell rings again and I jump. I look through the peep hole again, but still don't see anyone.

I'm debating what I should do when a familiar voice startles yet relieves me at the same time. "Jessica, it's Luke."

I open the door to find him leaning against the wall adjacent to the door.

"You're home!" He smiles widely and pushes himself off the wall. He walks past me into the house before I get any words out.

I turn to follow him in but am stopped by another man's voice.

"Mrs. Taylor?" The driver of the white sedan is walking up my driveway.

"Um, no, I'm not Mrs. Taylor."

"Oh, sorry. He said he wanted to go home to his wife." The young man blushes realizing his mistake and the implication that if I'm not Mrs. Taylor I may not be happy to hear of her. "He gave me this address," he quickly adds.

"No, I mean there is no Mrs. Taylor, but I'm…a friend," I try to explain, without making the young man endure too much complicated backstory.

"Okay." The young man blushes again and I realize I've implied something very different than I intended.

I bite my tongue and resist the urge to clarify anything else about my relationship with Luke.

"Mr. Taylor overpaid me. He gave me three hundred dollars."

I look back into the house. I can't see him at first, but then he stumbles into view while trying to remove one of his shoes with the opposite foot. He nearly falls over but catches himself on the side table. Thankfully he has chosen to sit down on the couch before he continues.

"Keep it."

"Are you sure?"

"Yeah, I'm sure he was a pain in the ass." I laugh.

The young man, finally convinced that his patron isn't in trouble with me or "Mrs. Taylor", visibly relaxes. "He was fine. He actually gave me some really good advice about starting my own business."

I nod and smile at the young man. "Thank you for getting him here safely."

"Have a good night, ma'am. And thank your friend for me in the morning, will ya?"

"I will. Good night." I shut the door and walk to the living room.

Luke has removed his shoes and jacket and is laying face-up, eyes closed on the couch. I go upstairs and grab a pillow and blanket from the linen closet. I plan on covering Luke up and heading back upstairs to my own bed, but when I return he's sitting up watching the television through unfocused eyes.

"What're you watching?" he asks, shaking his head. The movement causes him to sway to one side.

"Currently I'm watching a very drunk man trying to sit on a couch." He squints at the television. There's something boyish in his study of it and it makes me smile.

He turns his attention toward me. "I forgot how much I like tequila." He pats the couch and I take a seat next to him, handing him the pillow.

"I have a feeling you'll forget again by tomorrow morning."

Luke laughs and lets his eyes gaze down. He reaches up and touches the bow in the center of the neckline of my pajamas. "I like your jammies," he says with a smirk.

I slap his hand away from the Hello Kitty pajamas Amelia got me for my birthday. She earned money helping my mom with yard work and was so proud of the fact she paid for them with her own money. "Amelia got them for me."

"Is she here?" Luke jumps up from the couch. I quickly grab his leg and then his arm and pull him back down. "You're not waking her up."

"Okay." Luke frowns at me, like a little kid. "I miss her."

"She misses you, too." I try to think of the right words, even though I suspect there aren't any. "Luke, I'm really sorry about your dad. Do you want to talk about it?"

"Not really." Luke takes a deep breath and leans back with a thud against the back of the couch. "I realized something tonight."

"What's that?" I curl my legs up underneath me.

"I'm an orphan now." He stares up at the ceiling.

"Luke…" I stop when I realize I don't know what to say.

"I am, both of my parents are gone." He squeezes his eyes shut like he may be able to rid his head of the pain if he pushes hard enough.

I quietly scoot to the other end of the couch in an effort to give him a little space, but not leave him alone. We sit in silence for several minutes. His efforts must have worked for now because his pained expression transforms into a small smile. He opens his eyes and although the sadness is still there, there is also a hint of playfulness and his smirk is back. "It's awful, people are going to start calling me little orphan Lukey."

His search for some light in the dark is heartbreaking and encouraging at the same time. "No one is going to call you that. Besides I think you have more in common with Daddy Warbucks than you ever will with Annie."

Luke cocks his head to one side. "It's not usually my thing, but you can call me daddy if you want."

I shake my head and toss a couch pillow at him. The alcohol has dulled his responses and it hits him in the face. I can't help but laugh. "I'm never calling you daddy."

He laughs and then yawns.

"You need some sleep." As I walk to the kitchen, I hear rustling fabric and assume Luke is taking off his jeans. I busy myself getting him a glass of water and ibuprofen from my purse.

When I return to the family room, he's already laying down underneath the blanket. I see Luke's pants and t-shirt have joined his jacket on the arm of the couch. I stand in front of him and he opens his eyes.

"You should take these and drink some water."

"Thanks," he says as he sits up. The blanket falls to his waist revealing his bare, muscular chest.

I watch him swallow the pills and then lick his lips to wipe away any excess water. Even in his drunken state, he notices me watching him. I expect him to smirk or say something laced with sexual connotations, but he doesn't. He simply smiles and lays down, covering himself with the blanket.

He closes his eyes and I take that as my cue. I'm about to switch off the light when his voice, raspy from too much tequila, stops me.

"Remember when you used to love me?"

His words strangle my heart and my voice catches in my throat. I turn around and look to the couch, where he's laying with his eyes closed. He appears to be passed out, so I switch off the light.

As I leave the room, his voice fills the darkness. "I used to be a very lucky man."

I hear faint noise coming from downstairs. I pull on my robe, clean my teeth and run a brush through my messy hair.

When I come in to the family room, Luke is already dressed and folding the blanket.

"Good morning," I say softly, not wanting to startle him, not to mention I'm sure his head is in no condition for loud noises this morning.

"It's definitely morning, the good part is debatable." Luke looks surprisingly well considering.

"Coffee?" I offer, already pulling mugs from the cabinet.

"That would be great."

I busy myself making coffee while Luke disappears into the powder room. He emerges as I'm placing a mug on the counter for him.

"Thanks." He nods and raises his mug to me. "For this and for letting me stay here last night."

"Not a problem."

"Last night was a shit show. I thought grabbing a drink would take the edge off, dull things a little. I don't remember a lot past a certain point, but I do remember buying more than one bottle of tequila and pouring shots for everyone at the bar." Luke scrubs a hand across his stubble.

"Very generous of you."

"Very stupid of me. I hope I wasn't too much trouble last night."

"You were fine. I don't know that I've ever seen you that drunk."

"And you never will again." He drains his cup and sets it down.

"How's your head? Want more ibuprofen?"

"Please."

"Do you need a ride back to San Diego?" I ask, grabbing the pill container from my purse and tossing it to him.

"You don't have to do that, you've done enough."

"Oh, I wasn't going to take you. I was asking if you needed one." I wink at him.

Luke narrows his eyes at me, but his mouth curls up. "Enjoy it, Adams. You've caught me in a weak moment. Next time you see me you won't be able to outwit me so easily." His use of my maiden name became something of a term of endearment between us and it warms something in my chest.

"I believe it." I smile. "Seriously, I can drive you back if you want."

"I already called an Uber. I wanted to be sure to be out of here before Amelia woke up. As much as I'd love to see her again, it's probably not a good idea."

The moment has passed, and we settle back into our complicated reality. I nod and press my lips together.

Luke walks back to the family room and grabs his keys and wallet from the end table. "Thanks again, Jess. Yesterday was a rough day and…"

"You don't need to explain. I'm happy I could help in a small way." I lean back against the counter. "If you ever want to talk, I'm happy to listen."

"Thanks." He looks like he wants to say more, but instead looks down at his phone. "My ride is here."

I push off from the counter and follow him to the door.

"I'll see you on Monday," he says as he steps onto the porch.

"I thought you were traveling this week?" Luke mentioned a few weeks ago needing to be away from the winery this coming week, that he needed to travel with Christina to introduce her to more key players in the investments she'll be taking over.

"Not anymore." He looks down briefly.

"Right, sorry." I said it without thinking. He'll be busy with funeral arrangements this week.

He turns to head out to the waiting car but stops and turns back to me again. "You don't have to, but if you want to come to the funeral…I mean, you're one of the only people left in my life that knew my dad."

I hide my surprise and answer quickly. "I'll be there."

Luke stands still for a moment, cocking his head to one side. "It's odd how a death can bring people together. I haven't seen my aunt in years, not since she had a falling out with my dad. She called yesterday, and we talked for over an hour."

"That's good." Luke doesn't talk about his family often and I want him to continue. "Death has a way of forcing people to reexamine things and to let go of things that don't ultimately matter."

Luke nods. "Right. It also reminds people of what they have and what they should be thankful for. It reminds people what's worth fighting for."

I see something in Luke's eyes, almost a determination. I wait for him to elaborate, but he doesn't. Instead he turns and heads out to the waiting car, leaving me to wrestle with my complicated feelings.

Chapter 18

*I*t's the first official day of fall, but you'd never guess it by the weather. The heatwave engulfing southern California makes me thankful the funeral is taking place closer to the coast, where the onshore breeze is a welcome relief from the triple digit temperatures of Temecula.

The ceremony is simple and tasteful. Luke's dad was a well-respected executive at a large corporation headquartered in downtown San Diego, so the lawn is filled with men in expensive suits and women in heels not suitable for the grass we're standing on. Even though I feel slightly underdressed, I'm thankful I decided to go with a simple black tank dress and flat sandals. I may not be as fancy as some of the other mourners in attendance, but I'm definitely more comfortable.

I stand in the back and search for Luke. He let me know Claire and Finn weren't going to be at the ceremony today. It was a nice gesture on his part, but unnecessary. Meeting Claire made me realize she's not the enemy I had drawn her to be in my head.

He's sitting up front with what's left of his family. I recognize his aunt and cousins from the times I met them in high school. Luke previously mentioned his uncle passed away while he was in college, after we broke up.

The pastor speaks, followed by several of Mr. Taylor's business colleagues. They all talk about how dedicated he was to his career, but also his family. It's interesting to hear how much outsiders thought he adored his wife and son, knowing Luke doesn't remember things the same way.

I bow my head during the closing prayer and say my own version which includes a request for peace for Luke.

"Amen," the pastor says, and the crowd begins to disperse. Luke is approached by various people. He shakes their hands and offers slight smiles to everyone.

After several of these polite encounters, he scans the crowd. He finds me and excuses himself from the man who just handed him a business card.

"Hey." Luke walks toward me, hands in pockets.

"Hi." I resist the urge to pull him in for a hug.

"You came."

"Of course. How're you doing?"

"It sucks." He runs a hand through his hair. "I'm looking forward to this day being over."

"I can only imagine."

"It's like we finally figured out how to have some sort of normal relationship and now he's gone." Luke shakes his head.

"I'm so sorry, Luke. It's not fair."

"It's not, but I'm glad he got to meet Finn, and that I have a picture of them together. He lit up when he met him, said he reminded him of me." Luke stares distantly at the crowd. "Some of these people knew him better than I did."

I realize Luke needs to hear something. "Luke, your dad loved you, even if it wasn't in the way you wanted."

Luke shrugs. "Yeah, but I'm going to make sure Finn gets what he needs from me."

"I know you will." I place a hand on his arm and he looks down at it.

"He quit drinking and was trying to reconnect with me for months before I agreed to meet up with him. I had low expectations going in, but he held Finn for a long time. Told him he was lucky to have such a great dad, and grandpa, of course." Luke smiles remembering the moment. The thought of the three generations of Taylors together makes me smile, too.

I don't resist when the urge strikes again. I wrap my arms around him and lean my forehead against his chest as it rises and falls with Luke's heavy breaths. He wraps his arms around me, too, and holds on until we're interrupted.

"Hey, Luke." I look up to see a familiar face. "My mom asked if you could pick up ice on your way over."

Luke looks at his cousin. "Yeah, sure. Hey, Noah, you remember Jessica from when we were teenagers."

"I thought that was you." Noah gives me a hug.

"It's been a long time. How are you?" I say as he lets go. Noah is a few years younger than Luke and used to practically idolize him. He would follow him around family events and tag along on some of our weekend trips to the beach. Luke would pretend to be mildly annoyed by his presence, but I always suspected he actually enjoyed it. Noah was like the brother he didn't have.

I take a good look at Noah. He looks like an older, bigger version of the kid I once knew. Despite being related, Noah doesn't look much like Luke. His father had darker features, mimicked in Noah's olive skin, dark hair and warm brown eyes. As enamored with Luke as I was back then, I still recognized that Noah was a good-looking kid. The girls flocked to him as much for his good looks, as his easy-going attitude and great sense of humor. Seeing Noah today, I'm assuming not much has changed.

"I'm doing okay. How about you? Married? Kids?"

"Divorced, one daughter." I will let Luke tell Noah about our complicated second attempt at a relationship later. "What about you?"

Noah hesitates before answering. "Married, no kids."

"Where is Kendall?" Luke asks.

"She couldn't make it. She sends her condolences." Noah looks back at the crowd. I could be mistaken, but he looks uncomfortable.

Luke smirks. "Noah here, definitely married up. Kendall is everyone's favorite Alves." Luke has always given Noah a hard time about everything, but especially about girls. I remember him teasing him relentlessly before his first date. Poor Noah was so nervous, he didn't eat all day and almost fainted walking in the restaurant.

"Better not let my mom and sister hear you say that," he smiles back at Luke, but I sense he's bothered, either by the joke or something else. Maybe it's simply because the two of them haven't seen each other in quite some time, but I feel like there's more to his reaction.

"It was nice to see you again, Jessica. You heading over to my mom's?" Noah changes the subject.

"My aunt is hosting a lunch at her house. You're welcome to come," Luke clarifies.

"Thanks for the invite, but I have to get back to the winery." My comment causes Noah to throw his hands in front of him.

"Wait a minute, you work at the winery you own?" Noah points at me and then Luke.

"Well, I actually worked there before Luke owned it, but yes."

Noah's eyes grow wide and he laughs as he slaps Luke on the shoulder. "You really are something else, Luke. What did you do? Track her down and buy the place?"

Luke clears his throat. "Something like that." More details he will undoubtedly fill Noah in on another time.

"After all these years you really never gave up, did you?" Noah shakes his head and steps up and hugs me again. "I'm guessing I'll be seeing you again soon."

"Oh...I don't know." I don't want Noah to get the wrong idea about Luke and I, but even if now were the appropriate time, I'm not sure I'd be able to define our current relationship.

"All right, little cousin, if you're done making things awkward, I'm going to walk Jessica to her car."

Noah smirks and gives one last wave goodbye.

Luke mutters as he watches him walk away, but the curl of his lip gives away he's happy to have his cousin back in his life. "You sure you don't want to come to my Aunt's?"

"I have to get back to work," I say, as he walks beside me toward the parking lot. "I have deadlines to meet, my boss is very strict with his deadlines."

"Your boss sounds like a real jerk," he says a smile playing on his lips.

"He's not that bad." I wink at him. "But seriously, I need to get things ready for Sebastian's first day tomorrow."

"Obviously, I didn't plan on not being there for his first day," Luke says, turning serious. "Thank you for offering to be there with him."

"It's not a problem. What time is the will reading?"

"I need to be downtown by nine. I'll come to the winery after, but I have no idea how long it will take."

"Don't worry. Sebastian will spend most of the morning with Mindy filling out paperwork and then I'll go over all the things we discussed the other day and make sure he receives an extensive tour of the winery. I'll have more than enough to fill his first day."

"Thanks, Jess. That place would fall apart without you." He clearly says the words without thinking, causing us both to pause uncomfortably. "I didn't mean...I was simply trying to say thank you."

"No, I get it." I stop at the edge of the parking lot and give him another quick hug. "Take care of your family and yourself. I can handle Sebastian and the winery."

"I know you can." Luke gives me a small squeeze before letting go.

"Good morning, Sebastian." I walk across the floor of the tasting room to greet our newest employee.

"Good morning, nice to see you again." Sebastian's handshake is strong and his smile warm, reminding me what I liked about him the first time we met.

"I'm going to walk you over to meet with Mindy in human resources. After you're done there, we'll get you a tour, have lunch and get you acquainted with some of the logistics of the business. Luke may or may not be in this afternoon."

"Sorry to hear about his father. Were they close?"

I think about how much I should share. I decide to answer how I think Luke would.

"They hadn't been for several years, but they were working on it."

Sebastian nods in understanding. "Say no more, I have a difficult relationship with my own dad, so I totally understand."

I nod sympathetically, thinking how difficult relationships with our fathers seems to be a common theme between the three of us. "Yes, well everyone is really excited to have you here." As I say the words, Nicolette walks in the room. Her expression is definitely not one of excitement.

"I need to talk to you later, Jessica," she says sternly.

I'm taken aback by her tone and her disrespect. I've seen her be manipulative, but never downright rude. "Good morning, Nicolette." She looks annoyed by my simple response. She opens her mouth, but I cut her off. "I'd like you to meet Sebastian."

Forced to finally acknowledge him, Nicolette only offers a tight smile. "Good morning, Sebastian. Welcome."

"Good morning, Nicolette," he replies politely offering her his hand. She takes it and releases it after a quick shake.

Nicolette turns back to me with a huff. "I have meetings with the sales staff all morning, but I'll be by your office this afternoon."

I would tell her that would be fine, if she hadn't already stormed off.

Mindy calls at ten to let me know Sebastian is ready for me. We walk the winery. I introduce him to everyone, but avoid Nicolette's office and another potential icy interaction with her.

"And finally, this is the finance office." I punch in my code and open the door. "This is Linda. She handles all the payables, along with other accounting related duties. Linda, this is Sebastian. He's going to be helping Luke on the operations side."

"Nice to meet you, Sebastian." Linda stands and shakes his hand. "Welcome to our little, dysfunctional family."

"You'll have to answer to Luke if you scare him off on his first day," I warn.

"Luke doesn't scare me." Linda smiles. "Good luck, Sebastian."

"Thank you." Sebastian follows me into my office and I shut the door.

I sit down across from him. "Luke asked me to give you a set of the financials from last month, along with some additional reports we've been preparing for Nicolette each month. They should give you some indication of what we've got going on. I also included a reference sheet with the names and positions of your direct reports."

Sebastian presses his lips together as he looks over the list. He sets it down on the desk. "Can I ask you something?"

"Sure."

"I'm a big believer in being direct, so I'm just going to ask. How are things going with Nicolette?"

"Fine." My voice is way higher than normal.

"That good, huh?" Sebastian scoffs.

"No, everything is fine. We have different work styles, that's all. From what I know she's been doing a good job so far." I learned my lesson from Nicolette to be careful what I say to anyone before I understand their motives.

"I respect that you don't want to say anything to me, but based on her interaction with you this morning and what I know about her, I would assume you're her current target?"

I don't say anything, but my face gives me away.

"Listen, I'm familiar with her tactics. I hate to be a gossip, but I like you and think I can trust you."

"You can," I assure him. I have no intention of repeating anything he may share with me, not even with Luke. I told him I would stay out of the Nicolette situation and I plan on keeping my word.

"Besides it's not a secret, everyone in the valley knew about Nicolette and how she operates."

I nod indicating he should continue.

"Nicolette plays dirty. She has a history of coming into places, undermining those she works with, usually getting a few people fired and then getting promoted. It's her normal course of business."

"How many wineries has she done this at?"

"Three in Napa."

"I'm not sure you can fault her for getting someone fired. If they were doing something worth being let go for, you can't place all the blame on her." I don't like Nicolette and this information isn't exactly surprising, but I can still look at Sebastian's claims neutrally.

"Sure, but when you have someone like her it's difficult. She leverages her knowledge of others against them and twists it a little where she needs to, not enough to be called a liar but enough to where the other person is misrepresented. I personally know two people she's done it to and I've heard stories of others."

I must make a face because Sebastian leans back in the chair, a satisfied look on his face. "Ah, I can tell you've already been "nicked"."

"Nicked?"

"Sorry, the term we used when Nicolette went after someone. She goes around leaving little nicks, in people's psyche, their reputations, their trust. Nobody realizes what she's done until all the nicks add up and the place is a bloody mess."

I scrunch up my face. "That's a very gruesome description."

"Yes, but not inaccurate." Sebastian leans forward in his chair. "It's not surprising if she's chosen you as her first target. You're a high-ranking female in the company with a close connection to the owner. You're a threat to her achieving the status she wants here."

Nicolette sounds more calculating than I even gave her credit for, but I don't know Sebastian well enough to accept every word he says as absolute truth yet. "You're clearly not a fan of hers. Why did you accept the offer to come here?"

"I trust my instincts and could tell in Napa you were the type of people I wanted to work with. Look, I don't know Nicolette personally, only what I've heard. I'll give her an honest shot and I hope she proves the rumors wrong, but I'm going to be cautious with her."

"Fair enough." I look at the time. "We better get to lunch. We have a reservation in our restaurant at noon."

Sebastian says nothing else about Nicolette during lunch. He shares stories about the De Luca's, including one about the time Mr. De Luca had too much to drink at a work Christmas party and got a little too handsy with Mrs. De Luca for everyone's comfort.

After lunch I walk Sebastian over to Ryan's office. He'll spend the next couple of hours with him getting acquainted with the tank yard and wine making facilities.

"Sebastian seems nice," Linda comments when I return to my office.

"He is. I think he'll be a great addition. I'm going to try to get caught up on emails. Do you have time to meet tomorrow to help me plan out the budget reviews for next month? I want to be able to provide some additional schedules to Luke, Nicolette and Sebastian."

"Sure. Tomorrow morning?"

"Perfect."

I retreat to my office and get to work. I'm filling out a credit line request for a new vendor when I hear the office door open.

"Hi, Nicolette," Linda says loudly as a tip off. Seconds later Nicolette storms into my office.

"Hi, Nicolette," I echo. Nicolette shuts my office door forcefully and sits across from me.

"Why is Sebastian here?" Her nostrils flare as she stares me down.

I'm always a little startled by her directness, but this is on a whole new level. "I'm not sure I know what you mean?"

"Don't play innocent with me, Jessica. I'm sure Luke has shared his thoughts on bringing Sebastian onboard."

"I really don't know, Nicolette. Luke doesn't share those types of decisions with me."

Nicolette lets out a sour laugh. "Please don't insult my intelligence."

"Listen, I'm not sure why you think I know anything. I found out about Sebastian's hiring last week, along with everyone else. I was told he's taking over the high-level operations, while you were going to remain in charge of the day-to-day operations."

Nicolette studies me a moment. "You know, I almost believe you're telling the truth."

I move my hands to my lap and clinch my fists. "I don't really care what you think, Nicolette."

"Of course you don't." Nicolette glares at me with such venom, I bite back even though I know I shouldn't.

"What the hell is that supposed to mean?"

Nicolette's cold stare is unflinching. "It's easy to be confident when you're fucking the boss."

My eyes widen. "Excuse me?"

"It's very clear you two have an inappropriate relationship." Nicolette points one of her manicured fingers at me. "Don't think I don't see it."

I regain my sense and realize it would be pointless to defend myself from Nicolette's assumptions. "It's none of your business what kind of relationship I have with Luke."

"It is when he plays favorites."

"Luke does not play favorites. He does what he thinks is right regardless of who made the suggestion or who he sides with. Do you not remember getting your way with your budget?"

"Yes, and then I got in trouble for inviting his son and girlfriend to the photo shoot. They should've been here. We're a family winery and our owner should have pictures with his family."

Luke hasn't been secretive about his co-parenting situation with Claire. I think Nicolette is just trying to get me riled up. "You don't get to blame that on me. It's your fault for not asking him. Luke doesn't like to be surprised."

"The only reason he didn't want them here is because of you." Nicolette's eyes shoot daggers at me from across the desk. "Can't you see how unhappy he is? You lead him on just a little bit to keep him from moving on."

Suddenly the door to the office opens and I stare wide eyed at Luke. He remains calm, but his clenched fists give away how angry he really is.

Nicolette quickly replaces her look of shock with a fake smile "Hi, Luke," she says brightly. "We were discussing Sebastian and how you see his role working with mine."

"That's not what I heard." The hard lines on Luke's face partnered with his eerie calmness make him look downright scary. For once I'm glad I'm not the one he's staring at.

Nicolette startles. "I'm not comfortable discussing this in front of her." Nicolette shoots me a look of disgust. "Can we discuss this in your office?"

"No. Meet me in Mindy's office in five minutes." Luke continues to stare at Nicolette. She takes the cue that it's time for her to leave. He waits until she's gone before turning back to me. "What time are you here until today?" His eyes are still blazing, but he's unclenched his fists.

I look at the time. It's already three o'clock. I need to pick Amelia up by six, but I could always call my mom or Grant if I need to. "What time do you need me here until?"

"Can you wait for me?" Luke's stiff shoulders and steady scowl tell me he needs to talk after his showdown with Nicolette.

"Sure."

"I'll be back soon."

Linda leaves at four thirty. I sit at my desk waiting for Luke's return. An hour later, the wait is over.

I answer my phone. "Hi, Luke."

"Can you come up to my office?"

"I'll be right there." I turn everything off, grab my stuff and lock up, planning to leave straight from Luke's office.

The sky has taken on a bright orange hue as the sun heads for the horizon. Similarly, activity at the winery flares up right before closing, the last few guests booming laughter echoes from the patio. I catch Sebastian coming out the big double doors of the tasting room.

"Good night, Jessica."

"Good night, Sebastian. Hope your first day went well."

"It did, thanks to you. See you tomorrow."

It's quiet above the tasting room where Luke's office is located. Monica's office is dark, she's clearly gone for the day. Nicolette's is vacant as well. Luke's door is shut so I knock to let him know I've arrived.

"Come in," he calls.

I walk in and I'm startled by Luke's appearance. He has dark circles under his eyes and is sitting slumped in his chair.

"You look awful," I say and immediately wish I had chosen better words.

Luke gives a half-smile. Even in this state, there is something about his smile that instantly makes me more comfortable. "Rough day."

"How was the will reading?" I sit across the desk from him.

"Fine." Luke runs a hand through his hair. "That's not true. It was hard." Luke shakes his head as if he's trying to come back to the present moment. "I fired Nicolette."

"You did?" I try to sound surprised, but after what I witnessed, and the information Sebastian shared with me, I'm nothing but relieved.

"I hoped she would take my advice and change her approach at work, but she didn't. I don't want to work with someone like that." Luke shrugs. "She made my decision easy when she tried to implicate Monica in something that wasn't her fault."

"I'm sorry you had to come back to that. You didn't need that today."

"No, but it seemed inevitable. I'll have to deal with her later, but for the time being I can focus on getting Sebastian up to speed."

"What do you mean you'll have to deal with her later?"

Luke leans back. "A woman like that isn't going to appreciate being dismissed. I'm planning on having to deal with her through lawyers at some point."

"You think she's going to try to sue you?"

"Maybe." Luke toggles his head from side to side. "Probably."

"What a mess." I had a bad feeling about Nicolette from the beginning, but I didn't expect this much drama from her. I had expected some mean girl behavior, not firings and lawsuits.

"It'll be fine. I have Mindy as a witness and I already gave my lawyer a head's up regarding potential fallout. I'm not going to waste energy worrying about it."

I nod and fiddle with the hem of my skirt.

"You know it's not true, right?"

I don't even consider playing dumb, he knows me too well. "I know Nicolette was trying to get a reaction out of me, but—"

"No buts, that's exactly what she was trying to do." Luke frowns at me. "I'm not unhappy and I'll move on when I'm ready."

My chest constricts, and I wince at the sudden pain.

"You feeling okay?" Luke sits up.

"Yeah." I look at the clock on the wall. "I'm sorry, but I have to go pick up Amelia. You should get home and get some rest." I stand and walk toward the door, and Luke's slow footsteps follow.

I grab the door knob and start to turn it, but Luke places his large hand over mine. "Wait, I need to tell you one more thing. I have to confess to one more lie I told you."

I squeeze my eyes shut, as if doing so will block his unwanted words. "We don't need to do this, Luke."

"Look at me," Luke commands, but I remain frozen with my hand on the doorknob. Luke grabs my shoulder and gently turns me around to him. "It's not what you think. Look at me."

I open my eyes and brace myself for the remorse I expect to see on Luke's face in reaction to whatever lie he's told this time. The regret isn't there. Instead he's wearing a soft expression, a hint of a smile trying to camouflage the sadness still visible underneath.

"There was a time when I said you weren't the same person anymore and I was done. That was a lie on both accounts. You are the same amazing woman you've always been and I'm still the impatient man trying to be deserving of you."

I open my mouth to speak, but Luke continues. "Nicolette was wrong about a lot of things, but my feelings for you wasn't one of them." Luke stares straight at me, hope flickering in his eyes.

The intensity causes me to look down at my shoes as I remind myself to breath and take in as much air as my lungs will accept. Part of me wants him to grab me and kiss me and make me forget all the pain of the last year. But I'm not ready to give him all of me and Luke Taylor is not the type of man you only give a piece of yourself to. I squeeze my eyes shut. "I have to go."

I open them in time to see his smile fall.

Luke takes a step back and runs a hand through his hair. "I want you to be happy and if leaving the winery will accomplish that then I won't make it any more difficult for you. But I believe in us and if you decide you want to give this another shot, a chance to finally get it right, all you have to do is say the word and I'm yours."

I place my hand on his cheek and give him the most honest answer I can. "I'm not ready," I whisper, and leave.

Chapter 19

"Thank you, gentlemen. That was a very productive budget meeting."

"Thank you, Jessica. I'm still wrapping my head around a lot of the details here, this helped a lot." Sebastian slides the papers in front of him into a neat stack.

"It's only been a month. I have no doubt by next month you'll understand the operations more thoroughly than I do." Luke turns to me. "Thank you for putting this all together."

"Thank you for agreeing to stick to most of the budget."

Luke nods. "I'll try to stick to the operating budget as closely as possible, but I would like to revisit the expansion budget."

"I'm not sure I like the sound of that, but let me know when." I give him a sideways look.

Luke gives a light laugh. "It can wait until after Thanksgiving."

"Well, thank you again to both of you. Sorry to rush off, but I have a meeting with Monica." Sebastian quickly exits the conference room.

Luke and I are alone, something I've avoided for the past month.

I finally decided last week that I'm not ready to leave this place. It may have been the lunch I had with Linda where we spent as much time laughing as we did eating, or the meeting I had with Monica to discuss some new events she would like to present to Luke. I can't remember the exact moment I decided, but once I did, I felt a sense of relief. I'm not sure why I haven't come up with a way to tell Luke yet. Maybe because I know he'll be looking for more answers than I'll be able to give him. Maybe because I'm still unsure what this means for us and how we move forward from here.

To his credit, Luke hasn't pushed or pressured me in anyway, he hasn't even asked about us or my scheduled departure. Despite his recognition of being an impatient man, I've seen mostly the opposite from him lately.

He's been different at work, too. His willingness to compromise with not only me, but the rest of the staff hasn't gone unnoticed and he's been able to repair most of the damaged relationships with the managers. Luis, our chef, is still skeptical of him, but that's simply his nature.

"Jessica." He says my name like it's not the first time he's said it trying to get my attention.

"Sorry, did you say something?"

He tilts his head at me. "Lost in thought?"

"I guess so."

"I asked if you're free after lunch."

"Linda and I are going out, but then, yes, I'm free after that."

"Can you come by my office? I have your letter of recommendation ready." He looks at his phone and keeps his eyes there as he continues to talk. "I figured you would want to start looking for something new before the holidays. It's going to take Mindy some time to round up candidates, too, so she'd like to get an ad out next week."

"Of course. That's a good idea," I say, instead of what I really need to say to him.

"I have to run to a meeting myself, but we can discuss this more after lunch."

"Sure."

Luke leaves me alone in the conference room, his absence creating a hollow feeling in my chest.

"Linda, I want to thank you for all your help and support. I would say over these last few months, but you've been a great friend a lot longer than that." I sip my iced tea.

"Anytime. Thank you for being such a great boss."

"When is your flight?" Linda is taking next week off to spend the holiday with her daughter and new son-in-law in Mill Valley.

"Not until tomorrow morning. Did you decide to take some time off next week?"

"I was thinking about it, but with Luke off I want to be there to help Sebastian. I'll just take Thursday and Friday off. Amelia will be with Grant most of next week anyway."

"I know you'll miss her, but he's really stepped up as a father, hasn't he?"

"I hate to say it, but I think he became a better dad since the divorce." I still have moments of guilt stemming from my failed marriage, but most of the time I admit that we're all handling it pretty well. "It was his year to have her for

Thanksgiving, so when he asked to add a couple of extra days to his time, I agreed. My mom and I decided neither of us really wanted to cook, so we're going to dinner at Temecula Creek Inn."

"I love that place. I'm sure your dinner will be better than mine. Chloe can't cook but is insisting on not needing any help. Richard loves Thanksgiving, so I promised him I'd make a full dinner after we get home from our trip."

I laugh. "You're a good wife, Linda." My mood switches to a more serious one "They're placing an ad for my replacement next week." I haven't shared my decision to stay with anyone at work yet.

"And you don't sound too happy about it. Does this mean I've been successful in my attempts to convince you to stay? Or maybe a certain handsome boss with sparkling blue eyes has?"

"They don't sparkle." I roll my eyes and raise my water to my mouth, trying to cover the little lie I've just told.

Linda smiles. "Are you really thinking of staying?"

"I am. Things have been good. I have a lot of faith in Sebastian and his ability to lead the operations."

Linda clasps her hands together. "This is the best news. What about Luke? You seem to be getting along well."

"He's been great, asking more questions, listening more. I think he's going to be really good for this place. He's got some really exciting ideas about how to grow the business."

"You may not think his eyes sparkle, but yours sure do when you talk about him." Linda grins widely at me.

"They do not." I roll my eyes, not wanting to admit she may be right. "He wrote me a letter of recommendation. I'm meeting with him after lunch to get it."

"Well, he'll be happy to hear that it was a wasted effort."

"I wish this was a margarita." I point to my tea.

"I don't think you have any reason to be nervous. And you just gave me one more thing to be thankful for this year."

Luke's door is open when I arrive at his office. When I'm a few steps away I hear his voice.

"I see it now, it's time for her to move on. She'll be happier elsewhere, somewhere she can really shine."

I freeze. It's apparent from the pause that Luke is on the phone. I shouldn't be eavesdropping. I take another step, pausing when I hear his voice again.

"I know. I thought we could make it work for her, but sometimes things just aren't a good fit, no matter how badly we want them to be."

Who is he talking to? Mrs. Bianchi? Mindy? This is ridiculous. I take another step.

"She's a professional, she'll have no trouble finding something else and it's ultimately what she wants, maybe a little sooner than we originally planned."

I freeze again.

"Her feelings may be hurt at first, but she'll understand that moving forward with finding her replacement is best for everyone. Like I said, it's just not the right fit anymore."

My stomach sinks. I try to digest what I've overheard. I wanted Luke to listen to me and he finally has. I told him it would be easier for both of us if I left and it appears that

I've finally got him to agree. Right in time for me to second guess my decision.

"She can't be mad at me for saying good things behind her back." He laughs. "You're right, she's going to be pissed. I need to be the one to tell her, I have a meeting with her this afternoon."

Another pause. "Don't worry. I'll make sure she feels good about the decision when I talk to her."

I take a deep breath and step in front of Luke's open office door. I mouth, "Is now a good time?"

He holds up one finger. "I have to go, but thanks for the feedback."

He puts down the phone receiver and grabs an envelope off his desk. "Come in. I have your recommendation letter. It dawned on me that you'll want to take your time finding a new position, so I wanted to get this to you as early as possible."

"Thank you."

"I admit I haven't written too many of these. Luckily, this is probably the easiest one I'll ever have to write." He gives me a genuine smile while holding out the envelope to me.

"Thanks?" I take it from him.

"I meant it was easy to think of great things to say about you." Luke tilts his head at me. "Our loss is definitely somewhere else's gain. By the way, I was talking to Adrian Phelps and they're looking to hire a second controller, since their current one will be focusing primarily on their new winery. I know you know him already, but if you're interested, I'm happy to put in a good word, as well."

"Thanks." It seems to be the only word I can say.

Luke's phone rings and he pauses to look at it. "I'm sorry, I need to take this."

"No problem." I stand slowly, my hesitation evident. "Thank you again for this." I raise the white rectangle with a wave.

"Jessica." Luke catches me before I walk through the door. I turn to see him answer the phone. "Give me one minute, Ashley." He looks back up at me. "You're making the right decision. You're going to be a great addition to a lucky company."

"Right."

I hesitated in talking to him and now Luke has come to the conclusion my departure is a good thing. I can't blame him for finally believing what I've been trying to convince him of even if he picked the absolute worst time to start listening to me.

"Hi, Jessica." Vince, the owner of 'It's a Grind' greets me. I've been meeting Emily and Vivien here for years, enough for Vince to anticipate my order and pull out a large cup.

"Hi, Vince. Let's see, too late for a chai, so I'll take a—"

"Chamomile tea with room for milk." Vince finishes my order and smiles.

"I'm not sure if that's a testament to your great customer service skills or my predictability."

"Maybe both? Are you meeting Miss Emily and Miss Vivien tonight?"

"I am." Vivien called after my meeting with Luke this afternoon and asked if I could meet for coffee tonight. I could've used something a little stronger, but Vivien said she wasn't in the mood for alcohol tonight.

"Hello, pretty lady." Vivien looks more tired than normal. She gives me a quick hug.

"Is everything okay?"

Vivien yawns. "Yeah, I'm just really tired. Before I forget, I wanted you to know I talked to Luke today." Vivien called me a couple of days ago and asked if it would be all right if she contacted Luke about making a donation to the private school where she works.

"How did it go?"

"Good. I hate to even ask, but he made it very easy and made a generous donation."

"I figured he would, he cares about kids."

"I know he's busy, so I appreciated that he didn't make me feel like I was bothering him."

"I'm sure he didn't mind at all, probably made his day actually." I think back to the phone call I overheard.

"What's wrong?"

"He gave me a recommendation letter today."

"That must have been hard for both of you." Vivien stares at me, reading my expression. "Wait, are you having second thoughts about leaving?"

"Yeah. I've been trying to think of how to tell him, then he handed me that letter and I completely blanked on what to say."

"Hello, ladies, sorry I'm late." Emily bursts though the coffee shop door.

"You're not, it's a quarter past seven." Vivien smiles.

"Weren't we supposed to meet at seven?" Emily calls over her shoulder from the counter.

"Yes, but that's seven fifteen on Emily time."

"Very funny." Emily pays for her drink and joins us on the comfy, overstuffed chairs. "You better not have gotten into anything juicy without me."

"Nah, just work stuff." Vivien waves her hand.

"I sent my resume out this week to a couple of places, so fingers crossed I find something soon. If I have to spend too much more time fetching acai bowls for these hipsters, I may end up strangling one of them with their stupid bow tie."

"Emily!" Vivien reprimands with a smile on her face and Emily takes genuine delight in seeing Vivien riled up. This is their friendship in a nutshell.

"Good luck. I hope you find the perfect job this time." I smile at her.

"Thanks, love." Emily winks at me then turns to Vivien. "Why the emergency meeting?"

"So, I have news." I suddenly notice Vivien is practically beaming. She's wearing a wide grin as she sets her cup on the table. "I'm pregnant."

"Vivien! That's amazing! How far along?" Emily asks as we both look at Vivien's perfectly flat belly.

"Almost three months." Vivien can't stop smiling.

"Congratulations, Viv. I can't believe you kept this from us for three months." I think back over the last few months, trying to remember any signs I may have missed. When we had dinner together last month, Vivien passed on a glass of wine saying she had a headache.

Vivien's smile fades. "We didn't want to say anything too soon...in case..."

I stand up and walk over to her. I lean down and wrap my arms around her. "I'm so happy for you. And don't worry, enjoy it. You and this baby are both going to be healthy and perfect."

We spend the next hour discussing Vivien's pregnancy. At first, I can't help but remember my loss, but within minutes I'm only thinking of Vivien's happiness. I do admit I'm jealous of her lack of morning sickness. Emily says she's jealous of her increased breast size.

"How did Mama Fisher react to the news?" Emily asks about Ed's mom after Vivien tells us they're waiting to tell her family in person at Thanksgiving dinner in New York.

"She's been really weird." Vivien shakes her head. "All of a sudden she's acting like we're best friends. She wants to take me shopping when we get back from our trip. Says I'll need some stylish maternity clothes to show off my baby bump."

"That's not weird, that's nice," I say, but I understand why Vivien gets a weird vibe from her mother-in-law's sudden change of tune.

"She also told me she thinks I'm going to be an excellent mother." Vivien raises both eyebrows.

"Wow. Who knew getting knocked up was the way to get on her good side?" Emily smirks.

Vivien nods. "Right? She called me earlier to ask about my favorite foods. She wants to start bringing over dinner at least three nights a week."

"I'm so jealous. I want someone to feed me and take me shopping. Maybe I need to get pregnant." Emily laughs.

Vivien and I pause and look at each other.

"What?" Emily frowns. "I'm not allowed to have kids?"

"Of course you are, you've just never expressed any interest." I take a sip of my drink.

"I believe the exact words were 'I'll give up sleep for sex and sometimes even sex for sleep, but I'm not giving them both up.'" Vivien points at Emily.

"I'm allowed to change my mind." Emily shrugs her shoulders and dismissively waves a hand in the air.

"Have you?" I cock my head to one side.

"Have I what? Changed my mind about kids?" Emily shrugs again. "Maybe. I mean with the right person, yeah."

I grin at her. "And is Rob the right person?"

"He could be." Emily tries to hide her smile behind her cup, but we both see it.

"I can't believe it!" Vivien tosses her head back in laughter. "Is our perpetually carefree friend finally ready to settle down?"

"Slow down. I'm ready to entertain the idea, not go wedding dress shopping." Emily raises a hand indicating her reluctance to go too far down the happily ever after trail.

"First babies, now wedding dresses…you're going to give Vivien a heart attack." I see Vivien's wide smile and know how relieved she is. We've had conversations where she's expressed concern over Emily ending up alone. I haven't worried because Emily has always seemed happy.

"Maybe one day I'll elope and show up for dinner with a ring and a husband." Emily laughs.

"That's not funny." Vivien frowns at her. "I fully expect for you to pick out some hideous bridesmaid dresses for us to wear because you think it'll be funny."

Emily laughs. "You know me too well. Fine, no eloping, but I need to figure out my job situation before anything else."

"Speaking of jobs, when are you going to tell Luke you've changed your mind?" Vivien looks concerned.

"You're staying at the winery?" Emily's eyes widen.

"I was thinking about it, but now I don't know."

"Jessica…" Vivien drags my name out.

"What did I miss?" Emily looks back and forth between us.

"Jessica decided she wants to stay but didn't tell Luke so he wrote her a letter of recommendation and is starting to look for her replacement," Vivien summarizes.

"So?" Emily looks confused. "He wants her to stay, he'll be happy."

"Exactly." Vivien looks pleased that Emily is agreeing with her.

"Maybe I haven't been able to find the words to tell him because deep down I think it would be a mistake to stay?"

"Or maybe you're worried that by staying you'll be forced to figure out your relationship with him." Vivien looks at me pointedly and Emily nods in agreement.

"You're right." I admit. We sit in silence for a moment while I think. These women will reject any half-hearted answer I spit out too quickly. "Something's different about him. He seems, I don't know, more mature maybe?" I take a sip of tea. "Or maybe I'm different? While I know the miscarriage will stay with me forever, it doesn't feel as overwhelming, as suffocating as it did in the beginning."

"What about his son and Claire? Do you think you could be a part of that?" Emily asks cautiously.

"Not so long ago, I couldn't even picture a scenario where that would work."

"And now?" Vivien asks.

"I don't know, maybe?" I shake my head.

Both women give me a look and I instantly know what they are suggesting. I need to stop avoiding the conversation with Luke that needs to happen.

I walk into the dark, quiet house. I don't think I will ever get used to how still this place feels without Amelia in it.

I set my purse on the counter and pull out the envelope containing my letter of recommendation. I take a deep breath and open it.

To Whom It May Concern:

> *It is with great pleasure that I recommend Jessica Rogers. As an integral member of the management team at Bianchi-Taylor Winery, she has proven herself to be a tremendous asset. Her skill and professionalism has aided in the smooth transition during the sale of the business by the long-time owner. As an investor in the company for the past year and a half, and now the new owner, I can testify that her insight and guidance have been instrumental in ensuring the continued success of the operations.*
>
> *As a controller, Jessica has a firm grasp on all financial areas of the business, but moreover she possesses the instinct to make sound decisions. Her excellent people skills further enable her to successfully inspire and execute plans throughout the company.*
>
> *Jessica has been a pleasure to work with and will be greatly missed by myself and the organization. She will*

thrive most in an environment where she is challenged and respected, a place where her thoughts and ideas will be heard. Any company would be lucky to have this strong, valuable professional on their team.

Luke Taylor
Owner, Bianchi-Taylor Winery

I feel a sticky note attached to the back of the letter, so I flip it over.

Jessica,

I'll forever regret that we couldn't make this work. I wish you nothing but the best because that's what you deserve. You'll be missed more than you will ever understand.

Luke

Chapter 20

I stare at Luke's name on my phone. I type out a few words, then delete them and set my phone down.

"This is ridiculous," I mumble to myself, and pick it back up.

I push the button and listen. By the third ring I'm tapping the fingers of my free hand rapidly against the countertop.

"Hello?" Luke's voice is low and gravely. I look at the clock to double check the time. It's only nine.

"I'm sorry were you sleeping?"

"No." Luke keeps his voice a loud whisper. I hear a door shut. "I'm glad you called."

I can't help but smile.

"I was hoping you could conduct a second interview for me next Tuesday. It's a candidate for my assistant and if you like her, I'd like to hire her before someone else does."

My smile drops. "Sure."

"Thanks." Luke pauses. "You must have called for your own reasons, though?"

"I did." My stomach swirls and I pace the kitchen trying to release some nervous energy. "I want to talk to you about something, but I think it would be better in person. Would it be okay if I came down there to talk?"

"Umm…" Luke's hesitation has me instantly regretting I asked.

"Never mind. It's late, we can talk when you get back from your break." I'm speaking too quickly, so I take a deep breath.

"No, we can talk. It's just…Finn's here tonight. He's asleep, but if you want to come over that works for me."

I worry about how I'm going to feel once I'm there, but I fight through those feelings. "Are you sure?"

"Yeah." He sounds a little surprised, but not like he doesn't want me to come.

"Okay, then I'll see you in about an hour?"

"See you then."

A little more than an hour later I'm pulling up to Luke's house. It's a nice, California style single story. It's so different than his modern San Francisco apartment, but this feels more like the Luke I know.

I check my reflection in my car mirror and run a hand through my chestnut waves. I take one last deep breath and kill the ignition.

My thoughts race as I make my way up the lengthy path to the front door. The multiple steps make me thankful they are lined by lights. I've been trying to decide what exactly I want to say the whole drive here with little success. At some point I decided to just wing it, so I ring the doorbell without any further hesitation.

Luke answers and a surge of warmth overtakes me. His pajama bottoms and t-shirt match his relaxed demeanor. "Glad you found it okay." He steps aside, and I enter.

I take a few steps into the entry and look back over my shoulder. "This is nice, Luke."

"Thanks. It's a rental. I'm still deciding if it's easier to be closer to Finn or closer to work." Luke passes me, and I follow him. "What can I get you? A cup of tea?"

"Sure, but only if it's decaf."

"I have chamomile." Luke knows this is my go-to nighttime drink. He turns around and sees my smirk. "What…a guy's not allowed to enjoy a cup of tea from time to time?"

"I've never seen you drink a cup of tea, that's all."

"Well, I do." Luke calls from the kitchen. "From a very manly mug."

I snicker. "I believe it."

Luke prepares my tea the way I like it and grabs a bottle of water for himself. I follow him to the living room and sit at one end of the oversized sofa.

"What did you want to talk about?" Luke casually unscrews the cap and takes a big drink of water.

I think about setting down my tea, but decide I'd rather keep it to occupy my hands. "I read your recommendation letter. It was lovely, thank you."

"It was easy to say great things about working with you. The only hard part was making sure it didn't sound too personal."

I take a sip of tea. When I look back at Luke, he's patiently waiting.

We sit for several seconds, me trying to think of the best place to start. "Why is it the moments you have the most to say are the hardest to actually speak?"

Luke nods and looks at his lap. "I think I know where your head's at, but I don't want to put words in your mouth."

I readjust one of my legs underneath me. "I didn't expect to enjoy working with you."

"I think maybe there was a compliment somewhere in there?" Luke smirks.

I crack a smile. "You know what I meant."

"Sorry, so you were saying I'm your favorite person you've ever worked with." Luke motions for me to continue.

"I don't think that's exactly what I said."

"Are you sure? Because you're my favorite." Luke's smoldering stare distracts me from what I was going to say.

"Could you stop being charming for a few minutes? It's distracting."

"You think I'm charming?" Luke cocks his head to one side, a confident grin spreads across his lips.

I roll my eyes. "I didn't come here to flirt. I came here to ask to stay on as the winery's controller."

Luke leans back. "So, you drove down here to talk about your job? I already told you you're welcome to stay as long as you want."

I take a steadying inhale. "I know, but I heard you on the phone today, talking to someone about it being a good idea for me to move on. It's not fair for me to change my mind as soon as you've accepted the idea. I understand if the offer has expired, but I can't leave without at least letting you know how I feel."

Luke runs a hand through his hair. "The conversation you overheard wasn't about you. I was discussing Ashley, my assistant in San Francisco, with Aaron. At first, we thought she could stay on and be Christina's assistant, but it's not the right fit. I had to tell her today that she should start looking for something else."

We're interrupted by sweet, infant cries and my heart clenches.

"Give me a minute." Luke jumps up from the couch.

I wait for a couple of minutes, then decide to go find him. I stand at the beginning of the hallway and listen. I don't have to wait long before I hear Luke's soothing voice coming from one of the rooms near the other end. I follow his voice until I catch sight of him. He's standing in the dimly lit room, rocking and talking to his son. The sight of the small baby cradled in Luke's strong arms takes my breath away for a moment.

"That's a good look on you." I lean on the doorframe.

Luke startles, but gives me a warm smile when our eyes meet. "I changed his diaper, but I think he's hungry."

"Here, I'll hold him while you get his bottle." I walk toward Luke with outstretched arms.

Luke knows I wouldn't offer if I wasn't ready, so he nods and hands Finn to me. I cradle him in my arms so I can get a good look at him. He looks so much like Luke, but he has his mom's nose and smile.

I spend several minutes staring at him. It reminds me of nights with baby Amelia, nights I was content to simply watch her sleep.

I sense his presence and look to see Luke standing in the doorway. He smiles briefly before reaching out to retrieve the now sleeping baby. He stops when he spots his closed eyelids.

"I guess he wasn't hungry after all."

"I'll set him back in his crib." I place the sleeping baby down in his bed and Luke and I carefully exit the room. I wait as Luke slowly shuts the bedroom door, trying not to make a sound. "He's amazing, Luke."

"Thanks. I don't have any comparison, but I've been told he's an easy baby."

We begin down the hallway. I reach the other end and realize Luke has stopped and is leaning against the wall.

"I need to be honest with you. I want you to stay at the winery, but it's hard. It feels unnatural when I try to treat you how I would any other employee. You'll never be just another employee to me."

"I know."

"But I know that place means as much to you as it does to me and I won't take that away from you."

"I don't want to make this difficult for you." I take a step toward him.

"This is bearable. I may regret it later, but for now we're good."

"I don't want you to regret keeping me."

Luke shakes his head. "I only meant I may regret working with you when I have to witness you moving on. It's impossible to prepare to watch the love of your life get over you."

My chest aches and I reach out to touch his arm.

He stares down at his hands. "It's all right. I've been thinking a lot lately. I know I was meant to love you, but I have to accept I wasn't meant to have you." His words are thick. They sound like they almost got stuck in his throat. "Jess, I'm sorry for a million little things, for not being patient enough, for not being forthcoming with information, but mostly for thinking I could solve everything on my own. My actions hurt you and I apologize. You deserved better from me."

I'm literally speechless as Luke stands before me. I sense an openness from him that's been missing for far too long.

I squeeze my eyes shut. "Thank you."

"You're welcome." His voice is low.

I open my eyes and look into his glossy ones. "You said more in the last two minutes than you have in months."

Luke leans his head back again the wall behind him. "My therapist calls it 'evolving into an emotionally mature male', I call it getting my shit together."

"You're seeing a therapist?" I can't hide my surprise.

Luke only nods.

"Since your dad died?" It would make sense that a tragic event would propel Luke to seek out some help, although I'm still stunned to hear he's taken that step.

Luke clears his throat and shifts his weight to his other foot. "Before that, actually. Right after your mom's surgery."

I think back over the last several months. Luke's been different at work, more patient, a better listener. His confidence, while still intact, has been muted slightly. He admits when he's wrong quicker and seeks out advice more readily. All the little changes I've seen haven't been my imagination. Luke, while still wholly himself, has been slowly growing. "I think that's great."

Luke pushes away from the wall. "I don't know if it's great or not, but I didn't like what I was seeing in myself. I saw too much of my dad in me and knew something had to change."

Now seems like the right time to open up to him. I lean against the wall opposite him and stare up at the ceiling, not wanting to look at him while I get some things out. "I was broken after the miscarriage and when you said you were going to move forward and become a dad despite my failures. Even though it wasn't planned, it felt like a betrayal. I was drowning and was so angry you were going to survive without me." Shame courses through every vein.

"I would never have left you behind," Luke says, but I keep my eyes focused on the plain white ceiling.

"I panicked. I convinced myself that you needed to be with your new family and I couldn't be a part of it. I pushed you away trying to save both of us." A tear escapes my eye. "And ultimately it worked, you settled into being a good father for that little boy in there, and I healed."

Luke steps in front of me and wipes the tear from my cheek, his fingertips trail my still outstretched neck. "Letting you go when I knew how much pain you were in was the hardest thing I've ever had to do."

I lower my face to meet his. "I don't trust men easily and I trusted you. I know you think you did it for good reason, but it was devastating to me when you didn't tell me what was going on. I can't be in a relationship where I have too many questions." I try to focus him, but the tears are making everything blurry.

"I was trying so hard to answer everything I didn't even realize I was creating more questions. I won't make that mistake again." Luke looks at me intently but waits for me to make the next move.

"I'm sorry I didn't forgive you sooner, but I do now. No matter where we go from here, I want you to know that."

Luke reaches up to brush my hair away from my face, his fingertips grazing my cheek. "Where do you want us to go from here?"

I take a deep breath and let the shaky words exit my mouth. "I don't want to be hurt again."

Luke grabs my hands and rubs his thumbs across my knuckles as I stare at them. "Jessica, I can't change what's happened, but I promise I would never do anything to knowingly hurt you. I'm a better man than I was yesterday, and I'll be an even better one tomorrow."

The doorbell rings and Luke slowly releases my hands. "That'll be Claire to pick up Finn. It's her night, but she asked if I could watch him while she went on a date."

Luke walks to the front door and unsure of what to do I head into the kitchen to get a bottle of water and dry my eyes.

A moment later they walk in the family room together.

"Hi, Jessica. Nice to see you again." She's kind enough to ignore my red eyes and trembling hands.

"Nice to see you, too." I manage to say in an almost normal voice.

She follows Luke down the hallway and a few minutes later they reappear, Claire carrying Finn in his infant seat with one arm, and the diaper bag in the other. "Thanks again for tonight."

"Anytime." Luke grabs a blanket draped over the back of the couch. "Don't forget this."

"Thanks. Goodnight, Jessica."

"Goodnight, Claire."

Luke walks them out and I take a seat on the couch.

I drain the entire contents of the water bottle before he returns and sits next to me.

"Not too awkward?" He places a hand on my knee.

"Not at all. Finn is perfect, and I think Claire and I will get along just fine." I angle my body toward his and he takes the cue.

Luke reaches up and gently threads his hands through my hair, placing one on each side of my head. He pulls my face toward his as he leans in. When he places his tentative lips against mine, I sigh.

He pulls back, his deep sapphire eyes fixed on mine. "I've loved you for half my life, ever since you entered it. Sometimes I've had to do it from a distance, but I always have, and I always will."

I kiss him once and pull back far enough to look in his eyes again. "Let's figure out a way where you never have to do it from a distance."

Chapter 21

"Another successful negotiation." Luke beams from across his desk.

"I can't believe I agreed to your new expansion budget," I mumble as I gather my things.

I register out of the corner of my eye that Luke has left his chair and is walking behind me. "You did and there will be no renegotiating at dinner tonight."

"Don't worry, I remember the rules." After a discussion turned battle of the wills during dinner one night a few weeks ago, we agreed to make every attempt to keep our work life and personal life as separate as possible. Work is going well, but our personal life is going even better.

Everyone has adjusted to Luke's return quickly and enthusiastically. The first night Luke came over to the house Amelia insisted they pick up where they left off in their backgammon lessons. Apparently, he was teaching her how to play when they were spending time together after the miscarriage. My mom looked slightly nervous when I told her over coffee that we were getting back together. Her reaction lightened considerably when I also told her we decided to see a couple's counselor to help us work through our remaining issues.

Luke brushes my hair away from my neck, his fingertips causing a tingling sensation to travel through my body. "Luke…" I warn with a smile, knowing it's already too late.

He places a gentle kiss on the side of my neck and I close my eyes. "Do you really want me to stop?" he whispers against my skin.

"No, but you're breaking our other rule." I tilt my head giving him even more access to the length of my neck.

"I break all of my rules for you, you know that," Luke says with a raspy voice, before placing his mouth back again my skin. He sucks gently, and a moan escapes my throat.

"We're at work, Luke." At this point I don't really want him to stop, so I only half-heartedly attempt to remind him that we've tried to remain professional at all times at the winery.

"It's late, everyone's gone by now. Besides, I've shown a lot of restraint." He moves his lips to my ear where I feel his warm breath tickle across it. "I haven't taken you in my office once." He pulls my earlobe in between his teeth and my breath hitches.

He releases it and spins my chair around until I'm facing him. He steadies himself against the hand rests and leans down. I raise my mouth slightly toward him and he accepts the invitation. His tongue pushes at my lips and I gladly let him in. Our tongues swirl around each other and our mouths grow greedier. I don't protest when his hands leave their spot on the armrests and land on the buttons on my blouse. He makes quick work of the top two, then stops.

"We're going to break every rule we can think of." Luke's mouth claims mine again leaving no room for the last feeble attempt at resisting I was planning to make.

Luke pulls me up from the chair and leads me to the couch on the other side of the room. "I didn't think I needed this couch in here until this moment," Luke says as he finishes unbuttoning my blouse. He slides it off my arms and watches me remove my skirt.

"Leave them," he says in a low voice when I reach for my shoes.

I stop and smirk at him.

"God, I'm a lucky man," he says, watching as I remove the little remaining clothing I'm wearing.

With my clothes completely removed, I make quick work of his belt and zipper. His dress pants pool at his feet and he laughs. "I'm going to have to take my shoes off first."

I shoot him a seductive grin and slowly bend down, taking his underwear with me as I go. When I take him in my mouth, he gasps and steadies his feet, trying not to fall over.

I slide my mouth up and down, while massaging him with my hand at the same time. His moans and occasional profanity laden mumblings clear indicators he's enjoying himself. I pick up my pace and grab his ass, holding him in the exact location I want him. This prompts a deep groan and an "Oh, fuck," from him.

I have every intention of finishing him off in this fashion, but my plans are thwarted when he grabs me by the arms and lifts me up. I open my mouth to protest, but his words beat mine.

"On the couch," he says with authority, as he kicks off his shoes and violently shrugs his pants from his ankles. "I'm too worked up to take care of you properly, so I'm going to fuck you hard now and later…"

I lay back on the couch as he quickly undoes his tie and strips his work shirt off. I watch as he walks naked across the room to his desk and retrieves a condom from his wallet. His muscles take turns tightening and relaxing as he does, and I enjoy the view. "And later?" I ask, a playful smile on my lips.

"And later, I'm going to enjoy finding out how many orgasms you're capable of having in one night." Luke looks at me through hooded eyes as he rolls the condom down his length. "Sound like a plan?"

I nod and Luke smiles. He lays on top of me and kisses me deeply, one hand tangles in my hair, the other reaches down between us. It doesn't take long before I'm wet enough for him to slide in.

He pushes into me quickly and forcefully, causing me to gasp and fight for a full breath of air.

"You are perfect," he says as he pushes into me again.

"Luke…" I breathe out as he pounds into me. "You feel so good."

This seems to encourage him even more and he picks up the pace. Luke takes both my wrists and lifts my arms above my head as he thrusts into me relentlessly. "You are so beautiful." His eyes move from my chest up to my face and he leans down and gives me a quick but passionate kiss.

He rises up and grips my hips, slamming our bodies together at an increasingly rapid rate. He stares at me as I start to unravel and grins wickedly.

"Luke." I cry out his name and watch as his handsome face contorts, giving away how I affect him. With a series of powerful thrusts he finds his climax, riding it out until he slumps on top of me.

He stays that way, breathing heavily for a few minutes. "Can we skip dinner?" he asks against my shoulder.

"No." I chuckle. "We don't get to see Aaron and Andi very often."

"Fine, but nobody better order dessert." Luke stays laying against me. "I want to get you home early."

"I can't believe you're going to Mexico for two weeks. I'm so jealous." I take a sip of my wine.

"We've both been working too much, we need a break before we burn out." Andi glances at Aaron before continuing. "I told him it was either this or spend a week back east with my family. Needless to say, Mexico won."

"Nothing against your family, but two weeks in the sun sounded more appealing than a week being snowed in and playing cards with Uncle Tony."

Andi laughs and grips Aaron's forearm. "That was one time."

"And I still haven't recovered." Aaron shakes his head.

"My family can be a little competitive when it comes to cards," Andi explains to Luke and me.

"A little?" Aaron raises an eyebrow.

"So, it runs in the family?" Luke cocks his head at Andi. Luke has always been competitive, but I've heard stories about him meeting his match with her.

"You're one to talk." Andi points at him and smiles. "You let me know when you're ready for that Monopoly rematch."

"Nope." Aaron interjects. "You two are never allowed to play that game again. Trust me, Jessica, that's not something you ever want to witness."

"Fine, we'll think of another way to have a rematch." Andi sips her wine. "What are you two doing for the holidays? I imagine the winery's busy during this time of year."

"We're spending Christmas Eve with my mom, then both kids will spend Christmas Day with their other parent. I assume we'll spend a quiet day at home?" I look at Luke. Once we figured out our schedule with the kids, we didn't talk much about what we would do after they left.

"Actually, I was going to see if you want to get away for a couple of days. Noah and Kendall were supposed to be using the cabin the week after Christmas but had to cancel. We could head up on Christmas and relax for a few days." Luke's dad left his cabin in Lake Tahoe to Luke and his aunt. He included instructions that the property must remain in the family and if sold all proceeds must be donated to charity. Luke said it was his dad's attempt to fix the broken family dynamic he created and even though the stipulation probably wasn't legally enforceable he planned on honoring it.

"I don't know. There's a lot going on at the winery right now." I grab a piece of bread from the basket.

"And there always will be. We have to find time to get away." Luke places his hand on my leg under the table.

"True." I'll probably come back to a pile of work, but I could use a break. Plus, the thought of spending some quiet time with Luke is something I don't take for granted. "Let's do it."

"I'm not sure my mom's going to let us leave with him." I wrap my arms around Luke as he reaches for another cookie on the counter. My mom has been holding Finn while she watches Amelia open her gifts.

Luke places his hand on mine and squeezes. "Thank you for including us today."

The last few weeks with Luke have felt surprisingly easy. So comfortable, I almost feel silly for thinking it would be any different. Amelia isn't Luke's daughter and Finn isn't my son, but when we're all together it does feel like we're a family.

"Thank you, Luke!" Amelia bounces over to kitchen holding up a chess set.

"Thought you may be interested in learning how to play?" Luke smiles at her and she throws her arms around him.

"I am. Thank you."

Luke squeezes her. "Great. We'll start when you get back from skiing."

"I wish you guys were going, too." Amelia looks at me when she says it, but she's still hugging Luke.

"It's good to have a special thing to do with your dad. He's probably a much better skier than your mom and me."

Amelia releases him and nods. "He's really good."

I smile at my amazing little girl. "That's the cool thing about our situation, Amelia, you have lots of adults who love you who are all good at different things. Dad can teach you how to ski, Luke can teach you chess, Grandma can teach you how to bake…"

"And you can teach me how to be the best mom."

"Yes, she can," Luke answers, before I have the chance to disagree. Amelia runs back to her remaining pile of presents and Luke pulls me to him. "You're the best mom I know."

Luke is singing along with the radio as I look out the window admiring the mountain landscape we're speeding by.

"You're quiet," he says in between songs.

"Just tired. That six o'clock wake up from Amelia was a little early. You must be exhausted." Luke had to drive Finn back to Claire's before coming back to my house after leaving my mom's house last night. I peered at the clock when he climbed into bed after midnight.

"I'm fine." Luke's smiling. "I enjoyed her excitement."

"Was it hard not having Finn there?"

"I don't know." Luke scrunches his eyebrows together. "I guess I don't know any different. I'll always have to share the holidays with Claire, so it's not like something's changed, this will always be our normal."

"He seemed to really like his new toys last night." We sat and watched Amelia introduce Finn to his new playthings last night. They were really cute together, she explained things to him as he gazed up as her smiling.

"He did." Luke removes one of his hands from the steering wheel and places it on my thigh.

Luke falls silent again, so I resume admiring the scenery.

"My mom was a fragile woman," Luke says out of nowhere.

"How so?" I turn to look at him. He stares straight ahead, focusing.

"She battled depression for years." He takes a deep breath and lets it out slowly. "She tried to kill herself when I was twelve."

"What?" Even though I know I heard him correctly, I'm having a hard time absorbing this new information.

"I've never told anyone. My dad told me we shouldn't talk about it." Luke grips the steering wheel a little tighter.

"It's okay to talk about it, Luke." I hold my breath. I don't know what hurts more, thinking of Luke going through that with his mom or not being able to talk about it all these years.

"I'm the one that found her." Luke still won't look at me. The fact that he seems embarrassed makes my heart ache for him.

"What happened?" I ask softly.

"I was supposed to be heading out of town with my best friend and his family, but I forgot my lucky hat so I rode my bike back home. She didn't answer the door when I rang the bell, so I went around back and climbed through the dog door. I grabbed my hat and was headed back downstairs, but something in me made me stop…I don't know what." Luke glances as me briefly. "I went to her room and found her passed out. At first, I thought she was sleeping, but I wanted to say goodbye again. I couldn't wake her up, so I called 911. I found out later she had taken a whole bottle of pills."

"Luke, that's awful." I try to imagine a twelve-year-old Luke having to make that phone call.

"When I visited her in the hospital she cried and told me how sorry she was. She told me I was the best thing in her life and that I saved her." Luke takes another deep breath. "I just went home to get my hat."

Luke won't want sympathy, so I try not to say too much. I don't want him to bottle it up again. "It wasn't your job to save her, but I'm sure you were both glad you forgot that hat."

Luke nods, but keeps his attention on the road. "After that, I was afraid to leave her alone for a long time. When my dad found out I skipped a couple days of school and baseball practice, they got in a huge fight. He told her if she went off her medication again, he would divorce her and take me with him."

I conceal my gasp. "Luke, that's a very scary experience for a kid."

He nods again but doesn't say anything else.

We spend the rest of the drive holding hands, letting the simple contact work to heal the invisible wounds, wounds I now know he's been afraid to tend to for years.

This is not what I pictured when Luke used to tell me they were going to his family cabin for vacation. From the gourmet kitchen to the high beamed ceilings, this place isn't the rustic little place I had imagined. In fact, it's larger than my house and includes breathtaking views of the lake from almost every room.

"I had maintenance and cleaning people come in and do a refresh, new linens, new dishes and kitchenware, but otherwise it's exactly like it was the last time I was here," Luke says as his eyes roam the space. I follow him upstairs, where he sets our bags in what I would assume is the master bedroom, not merely because of its size, but also because it has a luxurious bathroom attached. My eyes go back and forth between the large windows offering more views of the lake and pines and the two-sided fireplace separating the bedroom and the large claw-foot tub in the bathroom.

"I may never leave."

Luke smiles. "It's nice here, quiet. We can bring the kids to the snow in the winter and boating in the summer. I can teach Finn to snow ski and both kids to water ski."

"You told Amelia you don't snow ski." I narrow my amused eyes at him.

"I never said I don't ski." Luke corrects. "I don't want to infringe on his thing with her."

"So, you don't think Grant's a better skier than you?" I tease.

"Not a chance." Luke looks at me like I'm crazy before heading out to grab the rest of our bags.

I tour the remaining upstairs rooms on my own. I was right, this is the master, but the other three bedrooms are amazing as well. They all have lake views and their own bathrooms, although not quite as fancy as the master bathroom.

"I figured restaurants might not be open tonight, so I had the kitchen stocked. What do you want for dinner?" Luke finds me in one of the other bedrooms admiring the view. "This was my room." He says as he wraps his arms around me from behind.

"I remember you coming up here with your family. I was a little jealous that your family had a lake house." I place my hands on top of his.

"You know, I spent many nights in here thinking about you."

I turn around. "Thinking about me, huh?"

Luke smirks. "Maybe more than just thinking. I was a teenage boy after all."

I slap his arms playfully, and Luke kisses my forehead. "I asked my parents if you could come with us once and they looked at me like I was crazy. My mom politely said she didn't think it was a good idea, but my dad said something about not needing his teenage son to become a dad."

I bury my head in Luke's chest. "So embarrassing. I'm really glad you never told me this back then."

Luke laughs and lifts my head. "It was apparent to everyone how in love we were. You don't get over something like that."

"I love when you say things like that to me. You've really become quite the romantic." I smile up at him and I'm rewarded with a kiss.

"I'm not trying to be. I say what I feel in the moment." Luke looks around the room. "I never thought we'd be here, not in this cabin, not in this room."

I catch his eye and waggle my eyebrows at him. "About to make some teenage boy fantasy come true?"

Luke winks at me. "I love when we're on the same page."

After Luke properly showed me his childhood bedroom, we spent the evening by the fire, eating a simple dinner of cheeses, meats and fruits.

We went to bed early after deciding to spend today driving around the lake. I fell asleep quickly wrapped in Luke's arms, like I have many times before, but this time felt different. I'm not sure exactly what's shifted, but I'm experiencing a level of comfort with him that I'm not sure was ever there before.

It seems like opening up about his mom on the drive here was just the beginning. So far during our drive around the lake, I've learned several more things about Luke. First, he's more stressed out about the winery then he lets on. He's mentioned several times that he needs to stop answering every email while he's on vacation, but every time he thinks I'm not looking he's on his phone. I assure him that I understand his obligations as the owner, but it's clear he's going to struggle to maintain a work life balance in his new role. Considering he bought the winery with the intention of allowing for more time for family, I want to help him find that balance.

The second thing I learned is that Luke is afraid of owls. Apparently, he had a traumatic experience as a kid when he tried to help an injured one he found at the cabin. During one of the times we pulled off the road to take a little hike one flew through the trees and Luke actually jumped. I couldn't help but laugh. I've never seen Luke act afraid of anything and it was sort of endearing.

The third and most important thing I learned was how guarded Luke really is. There was a point when I brought up his mom and how she must have loved this place. His whole body language changed in an instant and he grew instantly quiet. My guess is he's still feeling vulnerable from the information he shared with me yesterday. It must have been really hard to keep that to himself all these years. It had to have been extremely uncomfortable for him to share that with me and I remind myself I'll have to be patient with him.

We talk about the kids and envision what their futures may look like. Luke admits that he'd love to see Finn take an interest in baseball. It makes me happy that he's retained his love of the game when he could have easily grown to resent it.

"How's your soup?" Luke asks, shaking me from my ponderings about our day.

"It's really good. Do you want a taste?" I motion toward my bowl of homemade split pea soup. We stopped at this cute little place not far from the cabin for lunch. The Fire Sign Café makes several of their menu offerings from scratch including the creamy, salty soup.

"Sure," Luke says, and I feed him a spoonful. "That's good."

"How's your benedict?" Luke commented when reading the menu that it's what his mom used to order here.

"Good." Luke takes a sip of his coffee. "I know we're not supposed to be talking about work, but can I run something by you?"

"Always." I smile.

"I've been thinking about adding onto the property." Luke tests the waters.

"Okay, how much?" I squint at him over my tea.

"Space or money?" Luke asks.

"Both." I eye him suspiciously.

"A lot." He flashes me one of his disarming smiles.

I sigh and set down my cup.

"We should build a hotel," he says, before taking another bite of his eggs.

"Seriously? We don't know anything about running a hotel."

"Lack of experience hasn't stopped me before." Luke laughs. "We can bring in talent with hotel experience and we have Sebastian. He knows a lot already."

"That's true." I tap my feet on the ground. "If that's what you want to do, let's make it happen."

"Really?" Luke's eyes widen over his cup of coffee.

"Yeah, I mean I think it's crazy, but let's do it. I'm sure you'll do your homework and find the right people to help along the way. I trust you."

Luke sets down his fork and looks at me thoughtfully. "Just when I thought I couldn't possibly love you anymore."

I smile sweetly at him. "I love you, too."

Chapter 22

There was no way to prepare for this day, so I didn't. I buried it, tried to focus on all the bright, wonderful things I have in my life. Despite my best intentions, the darkness invades moments after I open my eyes.

I lay in bed, completely still. I don't want to wake Luke. I need some time to deal with my feelings before I'm ready to deal with his, too. He won't understand and I don't have the energy to try to explain it to him again. Besides, I don't want to ruin what we have right now.

I'm focusing on my breathing, reminding myself that I'll get through this when Luke wraps his arm around me. He doesn't say anything. He doesn't ask me what I want to do today or try to drag me out of bed for a run. I wasn't sure if he would, at least not right away, but he remembers what today is. He doesn't ask if I'm okay because he knows I'm not.

We lay like this for a long time, still and speechless. Finally, Luke kisses the back of my head. "Do you want to talk about it?"

"No," I whisper, and hold back a sob. I won't be able to hold it back much longer. I won't need to hide in bed all day like I needed to a year ago, but I need to release the pain.

Everyday isn't hard anymore, but this gruesome anniversary date is. "I'll be right back."

I climb out of bed without looking back at Luke. Once I'm hidden behind the bathroom door, I turn on the water and let the tears spill.

My eyes are squeezed shut when I hear the bathroom door quietly being pushed open. "I need a minute." I attempt to disguise my voice, but it cracks, giving me away.

Luke slowly steps in the room and pulls me against his warm, broad chest. "You don't have to hide from me."

He doesn't say anything else as I cry softly, dampening his skin with my tears. When my body starts to relax, and my breathing begins to return to normal he quietly leads me back to bed. Once I'm back underneath the fluffy comforter, Luke walks around to the other side and joins me, again wrapping his strong arms around me.

"Are you sure you don't want to talk about it?" He gently strokes my arm.

I shake my head and focus on the feel of his warm, solid chest rising and falling against my back. After several minutes my inhales sync up to his and we stay like this, his body leading mine so I don't forget to breathe.

"Do you mind if I talk about it?" His hoarse voice is tentative.

"Go ahead." He's never wanted to talk much about the miscarriage before. As painful as it is, I'm glad he's ready now, even if I am a little nervous about what he might say.

"I didn't know I even wanted to be a father until you came back in my life. It wasn't until you told me you were pregnant that I could even really picture it. I never had the need to have a piece of me in this world, but the idea of having a piece of me and a piece of you together…well, that was intoxicating."

Luke shifts his body even closer to mine and holds me tighter. "Neither of us were prepared for that dream to come to such an abrupt end. I thought if you knew how saddened I was by the loss, it would only make you feel worse."

I keep my back to him, but I don't want him to take all the blame for this. "I was in a bad place, Luke. Looking back, I don't think it's fair that I expected you to react a certain way. I wish I had been more understanding of what you were going through. At the time I remember feeling so alone, but I don't know that doing things differently would've changed that much. I think miscarriage is a lonely thing no matter who you're with."

Luke places a soft kiss on my shoulder. "Losing the baby was awful, but when I thought I may lose you, too…I didn't know what to do. I thought my job was to make things better, to find the solution."

I roll over and face him. "You didn't fail, Luke. I promised not to leave, and I did. When our version of happily ever after changed, I panicked. I let the changes and the struggles cloud all the good. I promise I'll never lose sight of who we are again."

Luke smiles softly before wrapping his arms around me. We stay like this, silent and connected, for a long time.

At some point, I doze off again and when I wake up, Luke is gone from the bed. I run a bath and turn on the gas fireplace, something I've been thinking about since we got here. I'm about to step in the hot water when I hear a light knock.

"Yeah?"

"Can I get you a cup of tea? A glass of wine?" Luke says through the closed door.

My instinct is to tell him I don't need anything, but then I remember what our therapist said about learning to lean on him.

"I'll take a cup of tea."

"Sure." I hear the lift in his voice and I know I've made the right decision.

About ten minutes later Luke comes in with a tray containing a large mug of tea, small containers of milk and honey and a plentiful assortment of fruit on a plate.

"Well, you certainly have the room service part of the hotel business down. This looks great. Thank you."

"Let me know if you need anything else." Luke kisses the top of my head and leaves.

An hour later, I climb out of the lukewarm water and wrap myself in a robe. I find Luke in the kitchen, signing along to a Maroon 5 song and making lunch. He smiles brightly when he turns around to see me watching him.

"Hey, there. Want a sandwich?"

"Sure."

"Look outside." He nods toward the large glass slider.

"It's snowing?" I can't contain the excitement in my voice as I walk over to get a closer look.

"It probably won't be enough to stick."

"It's so pretty, though." I see Luke's reflection as he approaches me from behind. I turn my head over my shoulder to him. "I see why your family loved it here."

"I'm glad you like it. You seem happy here."

I tilt my head to one side and look at him. "This place is amazing, but I'd be happy anywhere with you." I wrap one of my arms through his as we continue to watch the small flakes fall and melt on the deck. "Thank you for today."

Luke stares at me for a minute. I'm a little disappointed when he doesn't lean in for a kiss. "I'll be right back."

I watch Luke take the stairs two at a time.

He has a small object in his hand when he returns, but I can't make out what it is. "I have something of yours I need to give back."

I meet Luke at the couch where I sit cross-legged, and Luke turns his body toward me.

I don't understand Luke's sudden nervousness until he holds out the box. "I originally gave this to you when I thought I was ready for a wife, and that was my mistake." Luke opens it and my ring sparkles. "I should've waited until I was ready for a partner. I promise to love you, support you and include you in my life. We've had to battle for it, but are you ready to finally get our happy ending?"

"I am." I watch as Luke slides the ring back on my finger. After, he places his warm hands on either side of my face and kisses me deeply. I break the kiss for a moment to look in his beautiful, adoring eyes. "To wind up with you, the battles have all been worth it."

Acknowledgments

I am forever thankful for the support of the many people that have made this little dream of mine come true.

To my beta-readers, Kathi and Vanessa, thank you for continuing on this journey with me and for continuing to cheer for me. I appreciate every second you've spent reading and having conversations with me. From times I couldn't get a plot point just right to times I needed to make sure my characters were being true to themselves to times I was too excited about a direction the book was headed. Thank you for everything. This book wouldn't be what it is without you.

To my wonderful editor, Nikki, thank you for all your guidance and wisdom. Most don't understand how hard it is to turn your work over to someone. To turn over what feels like a piece of yourself to someone and invite in criticism. You made the process less scary and more importantly, you made the book better.

To Fiona Jayde, thank you for once again designing an amazing cover that captured the essence of my story. Your patience and beautiful talent are such a joy to work with.

To Tamara Cribley, thank you for your work in making the inside of this book look professional and streamlined. It's your final touches that make me tear up when every I open one of my books.

An abundance of thanks to my fellow writers. Only another writer knows what this feels like and I am inspired by all of you. I am inspired because we sit and we doubt and we cry and we laugh and we hope and we dream, but no matter what we keep writing. I believe it's an absolute truth that we only regret the things we never attempt and I will never regret something that has brought me more enjoyment and fulfillment than I ever imagined. Writers don't write to live up to others' expectations, we write because without it our words would suffocate us.

My dear readers. I am humbled every time someone tells me they liked my stories or asks when the next one is coming out. There are thousands of books to be read and I am truly honored you took the time to read mine.

Thank you to all my family and friends whose continued support is cherished and not taken for granted. I am lucky to have you all in my life.

About the Author

Jennifer K. Thomas grew up being told she could accomplish anything she wanted to, but it took her some time to realize she wanted to be a writer. After spending many years exhausting the left side of her brain in the world of corporate finance, the right side of her brain was screaming for more action. After toying with ideas and characters for years, she finally worked up the courage to write her first book, *Crushed*, in 2018.

Jennifer lives in beautiful Temecula, California with her husband, daughter and their two adorable high-maintenance dogs.

Visit Jennifer at jenniferkthomas.com or and Facebook at www.facebook.com/authorjenniferkthomas.

www.ingramcontent.com/pod-product-compliance
Lightning Source LLC
Chambersburg PA
CBHW030554180626
46816CB00005B/1537